# THE ATLANTIS COVENANT

THE ATLANTIS COVENANT is a work of fiction. All names, characters, places and occurrences are entirely fictional products of the author's imagination or are used fictitiously. Any resemblance to current events or locales, or to persons living or dead, is entirely coincidental.



ISBN: 9781672476331

# THE ATLANTIS COVENANT

THE HUNTER FILES

№ 1

ROB JONES

*For my children,*
*Never let go of your dreams –*
*Or they'll fly away without you.*

# CHAPTER ONE

To ascend into heaven, you must first work your way through the seven levels of purgatory. Pride, envy, wrath, sloth, avarice, gluttony and lust. Each one a single but essential step on the long and arduous journey up the mountain into paradise.

Max Hunter slammed his back up against the wall of the ancient Iraqi tomb and wondered which level he was on right now. He closed his eyes for a second and hoped to hell the soldiers hadn't seen him. He was wrong. One of them shouted orders in Arabic and they advanced down the long tunnel toward him. Peering around the burial chamber's stone door casing, he counted twelve of them. They wore ballistic helmets and combat vests and gripped Cold War Zastava assault rifles in their hands.

Envy, he decided. That was the level of purgatory he was on, and the situation was getting out of hand. Yesterday, he had enjoyed a lunch of slow-cooked lamb with roasted nuts and raisins alongside his old friend Adil al-Amiri, the head of Mosul's Antiquities Authority. The professor had assured him he had permission to enter the tunnels beneath the Tomb of Jonah and excavate the Statue of the Winged Guardian. Now, he had that artifact clutched to his chest and a dozen armed men were hunting him through a labyrinth deep beneath the Gates of Nineveh.

Hunter knew danger better than most. Sometimes he even went looking for it, but he also knew there was a line. When he heard a familiar voice shouting at him from the other end of the tunnel beyond the antechamber, he knew he had crossed that line.

"There's nowhere to run, Max."

Brodie McCabe.

That good-for-nothing, cheating, low-down son of a bitch, relic-thieving scumbag. Just hearing his voice after all these years gave him chills. He kept his cool and called back down along the tunnel.

"Is that really you, Brodie?"

"In the flesh."

"Fancy meeting you here. I thought you'd joined a convent."

McCabe laughed without humor. "Hand over the statue and I'll let you live."

In the darkness of the tomb, Hunter shook his head and let out a cynical laugh. The soldiers' boots crunched on the gravel, louder with every step. "That's unusually generous of you. It's just a shame everything you ever say is a lie."

"Don't make me chase you into the tunnels. These soldiers are hungry and tired and not in a very good mood."

"Some soldiers," Hunter shouted cynically. "How much did you pay them?"

"That is not your concern, but needless to say they are fully in my employ. If you don't come out and give me the statue, I will order them to come in there after you and kill you."

He scanned the tomb once again for another way out. Nothing but a giant statue of Nergal, the Assyrian God of the Underworld standing at the end of the tomb in a bricked-up stone portico. The marble deity stood below a marble pediment and looked serenely back at him as if it knew the answer to all his questions.

"Maybe I'll let them know what you did to the last men you employed back in Angkor Wat. The Cambodian authorities still have an arrest warrant out on you for their murders."

"But sadly, none of these soldiers speak English, Max." He laughed again. "And if I recall correctly, you cannot speak Arabic."

*Damn it.* Hunter scratched his jaw and cursed to himself in the silent tomb. "No, I never got around to it."

"That's too bad. These men believe you are an antiquities smuggler who intends on selling the statue to ISIL and they're not very happy about it. It seems no amount of schmoozing the old Antiquities Director over plates of quzi is a substitute for good, old-fashioned bribery."

How the hell did he know about his lunch with al-Amiri? Hunter stared down at the ancient statue in his filthy hands and took in the neat inverted ziggurat in the base and a faint inscription running around inside it. He already knew it dated back at least to the days of the early Assyrian Empire, but the carved letters would take some serious deciphering if he wanted to know the secret they had held for so many centuries. Whatever happened today, he couldn't let it fall into McCabe's hands.

He had to stall for time.

"You want to pay for it?"

The laughter grew colder. "You're playing for time, Max. I'm sending the soldiers in."

"Shit."

The soldiers stormed toward him, forced to run in single file because of the ancient passageway's narrow width. When the first man burst into the tomb, he raised his rifle and aimed it at Hunter. Another three from the squad came inside the dark, clammy chamber seconds later. They were young men, mostly in their twenties and dressed in the standard desert camouflage uniform Hunter knew so well. Sweat formed a film on their angry, hate-filled faces.

"I don't suppose I could pay you guys to turn your guns on McCabe instead?"

The lead man screamed in Arabic and lifted the muzzle of his weapon until it was pointing directly in his face.

"I guess that's a no, but is it a firm, final no?"

Another scream and another pace forward. Cornered, Hunter had no choice. He was no fool and he knew the odds, but if he wanted to get out of this tomb alive he had to take on all four of the soldiers at once. As for those outside the chamber, he'd cross that bridge when he got to it.

The men moved deeper inside the tiny manmade chamber with their guns fixed firmly on the target: Max Hunter. One of them shone a flashlight down at the strange metallic figurine in his hands and then up in his face.

After speaking to him in Arabic, Hunter replied. "And I guess *that* means you want me to hand it over?"

The soldiers moved forward again. They were brave, but they didn't seem to realize that in such a small space, the rifles worked against them.

Sliding the statue inside his canvas bag, he lunged at the closest man, ripping the gun from his hands. He brought the stock of the weapon up into his face, smashing his nose into a bloody pulp. A pained scream filled the chamber, followed by the other soldiers taking a step back and shouting in Arabic as they aimed their guns at him.

Hunter moved fast, striking the wounded man hard in the side of the head and knocking him out. Another soldier fired at him; the roar of the old Soviet assault rifle deafeningly loud in the enclosed tomb. The bullet missed and buried itself in the sandstone wall beside him and he returned fire with a warning shot and dived behind the altar.

The soldier who had fired made a move for him. He ran toward his hiding place repeatedly firing on him as he advanced. Hunter tucked his head down to protect his face from the chunks of altar stone being blasted into the air by the soldier's bullets. Back in the tunnel he heard McCabe demanding to know what was going on.

When the soldier reached the space behind the altar, Hunter threw a handful of grit in his eyes and scraped his boot through the dirt in a small arc, hooking the man's legs out from under him. He fell back and cracked the back of his skull on the chamber's south wall. It was a lucky result, but Hunter usually found winging it was the best way to get what he wanted.

Usually.

He scrambled to his knees and brought the rifle up into a firing position, but the next soldier was faster. As the young Iraqi leapt over the altar and landed beside him, he fired his gun. The bullet smacked into the dirt an inch from Hunter's boot and kicked up a small cloud of dust.

"Shit!"

The soldier landed with a crunch and swung the gun back around to him, preparing to fire again, but when Hunter heard the dry-click both men knew the gun had jammed.

"Got to love fifty year-old Soviet rifles."

More soldiers now ran across the tomb to the altar, but Hunter moved fast. Clambering to his knees, he lunged at the man with the jammed gun and tackled him to the floor. He grabbed the gun and twisted it from his hands before piling the stock into his face and knocking him out cold.

The former guards officer tried to unjam the semi-automatic rifle but it was no dice. *No surprise there*, he thought. Rifle jams could take minutes to clear. Another soldier rushed him, this time around the closer end of the altar. Hunter spun around and swung the jammed rifle up, just clipping the soldier's chin in the arc and knocking him off his balance.

He struck the teetering soldier a second time with the stock and knocked him out. This man's weapon wasn't jammed, so he disarmed him and swung the gun around at the rest of the approaching soldiers. He fired on them and forced all but one into a retreat back in the tunnel with McCabe. Spinning around and scanning through the darkness and gun smoke in the tomb for another way out, he saw a soldier. The man had split from his squad and was aiming his gun at him.

When the two men fired at each other, the report of the semi-automatic rounds was once again almost impossibly loud in the confines of the ancient tomb. The bullets tore chunks out of faded murals painted on the walls and blasted clouds of dust over their heads, but neither hit the other man.

McCabe's enraged voice screamed outside in the passageway, and Hunter heard the other soldiers making their way toward the tomb entrance again. The thirty-round detachable box magazine fixed to the belly of the Zastava wasn't going to keep him out of trouble for long, especially at a rate of fire of six hundred rounds per minute.

Once again, he searched the tomb with desperate eyes.

Nothing.

He exchanged fire with the rogue soldier once again, knowing he was almost out of lead. He turned and fired on the entrance, raking the stone archway with bullets and exploding clouds of stone fragments and dust down on the heads of the approaching squad. It drove them back, but for the last time.

He was out of bullets.

So was the soldier already inside the tomb, because now he rushed him, keen to bring the scalp back to McCabe. He drew a combat knife and raised it in the air, ready to slash down and plant it in Hunter's neck.

Hunter had no choice but to charge into the fight. He crashed into him, grabbing his hand and rotating it until the wrist bones shattered. The man screamed and dropped the blade. It clattered on the dusty stone floor and the soldier struggled free and tried to reach down and grab it.

Hunter brought his knee up and rammed it into the man's face, smashing his nose to pulp and spreading it all over his face. He grunted in pain and jerked backwards giving the Londoner enough time to piledrive a savage uppercut into his chin. The direct strike was hard and fast and his filthy fist slipped off the soldier's face, slick with sweat.

The back of the man's skull smashed into the outstretched arm of the Nergal statue and forced it back until the finger was now pointing at the bricked-up wall behind him. Clouds of dust tumbled from the top of the archway and a deep grinding noise filled the tomb. Hunter watched in amazement as the dust cloud cleared to reveal a door slowly opening inside the center of the archway.

"A secret passage," he muttered, running toward it. Glancing at the dead soldier, he gave him a mock salute. "Thanks. Talk about using your head to get out of a problem."

McCabe was ranting in the tunnel beyond the antechamber and the rest of the army squad were charging forward, guns blazing. Hunter checked the winged statue was in his bag, and under a hail of automatic gun fire, he ran into the unknown darkness on a wing and a prayer.

# CHAPTER TWO

Hunter fumbled for his flashlight and switched it on, all the time sprinting along the narrow hidden passageway, only seconds ahead of his own death. It was cramped, filthy, thick with cobwebs and there was debris and rubble all over the floor. Behind him, a squad of Iraqi soldiers wanted to blow his head off. *If you say anything about my job*, he thought, *say never a dull day.*

Then there was light.

The artificial light of McCabe's soldiers as they jogged into the tunnel in pursuit of him. The beams threw his shadow out in front of him along the ancient tunnel. This time, there was no shouting, just a rifle shot. He felt the bullet trace over his head and ricochet off the curved vaulted ceiling of the stone passageway.

"Damn it!" he cried out. "That nearly hit me, guys! Be more careful, would you?"

He ducked his head down and ran faster, his boots scuffing in the dirt as he jogged toward a bend in the tunnel up ahead. When he rounded the corner, he saw a flight of stone stairs leading into a wall of large granite blocks inside another archway. It was the mother of all dead ends.

"That's not helpful at all."

Running up the steps, he traced his hands over the wall and searched for some kind of a hidden lever. There had to be something; why build the steps? Then something caught his eye on the façade above the blocks. He blew a thick layer of dust away from the surface to reveal a line of hieroglyphics.

"Getting slightly more helpful."

His flashlight died.

"Much less helpful."

His trembling hands rummaged around in search of his lighter. The sounds of the soldiers' boots trampling over the debris in the passageway behind him grew louder as he scanned the line of tiny symbols. Similar to early Assyrian. Interesting. He remembered his Rawlinson – the names of metals, animals, tribes, cities, men and gods, and the points of the compass have a special sign attached to them, either a suffix or…"

The bullets drilled into the curving wall of the passageway's bend fifty feet farther back, shattering the brickwork. Hunter almost jumped out of his skin when they exploded behind him and ricocheted into the darkness.

Focus, Max.

He focused on the bas-relief glyphs in the dim glow of his lighter. The special sign was either a suffix or a prefix, and that meant things were getting a little clearer. He recognized the symbols for mankind and at the apex of the archway, those of the heavens and Nergal and Anshar, the Assyrian sky god. Each of the symbols had a corresponding one below on the granite stones blocking his way.

"It's a code," he muttered. "Follow Anshar to ascend into the heavens. Anshar, Anshar…"

He hurriedly wiped more dust and cobwebs from the stone blocks inside the archway until he found a picture of Anshar. The god was carved onto a small brick at the base of the wall.

"Oh, what the hell…"

He kicked the brick and pushed it inside a cavity. To his astonishment, the wall slid back in increments until it formed the rest of the staircase. He ran up the steps with bullets clanging off the granite steps under his feet. If he could just reach the top and get outside the tomb complex at least he stood a chance of getting away from McCabe for long enough to get the statue to safety.

The steps now went all the way to the tunnel ceiling, and at the top, he pulled the sleeve of his leather jacket up over his fist to form a sort of glove and punched into the packed dirt. Two, three, four strikes later he broke through and daylight streamed down into the stairwell. He breathed a sigh of relief, but he was still in trouble; he could hear the sound of the soldiers breathing as they pounded along the tunnel below him.

He worked fast. The fading Iraqi desert light was bright enough to light up the dust motes floating in a thin cloud in front of his face as he punched a bigger hole in the ceiling. It got big enough to climb through, just in time. The soldiers turned the corner and reached the bottom of the steps just as he was throwing his canvas bag up through the hole in the ceiling. He reached his arms up either side of the hole and grabbed hold of more solid ground. Then he pulled himself up out of the stairwell and into the hot, dry desert air.

"Hello, Dr Hunter."

The exhausted archaeologist stared up and saw the silhouette of Brodie McCabe standing above him, legs spread wide and arms crossed casually over his chest. Behind him, a Jeep Wrangler was parked up beside a canvas-top truck sprayed with the insignia of the Iraqi Army.

"We have to stop meeting like this, Brodie."

McCabe laughed as Hunter crawled up out of the hole and slid his bag back over his shoulder in a desperate bid to hold onto the treasure inside. "It's over, Max. I guess your little trip to the Gates of Nineveh didn't work out quite how you planned?"

"You got that right! I'm going to absolutely smash this place on Trip Advisor."

McCabe signaled to one of the soldiers who raised the stock of his rifle and clubbed Hunter between the shoulder blades. He tumbled down into the hot, dry gravel as more rifle stocks pounded down into his back. The palms of his hands pushed down in the grit as he tried to raise his body off the ground, but another blow to the back of his head thrust his face back into the gravel. He struggled not to pass out when he saw McCabe's expensive Oxford loafers move a step closer.

"Give up, Max."

"I won't let you beat me, Brodie."

"I think that ship has already sailed. Despite your best efforts back in the tomb, you are surrounded by many armed soldiers who all want to see you hanged for stealing their country's precious relics."

Hunter huffed out a sour laugh. "That's a joke."

"I'll have you arrested and thrown in jail for years. I'll testify. So will these men. Do you have any idea what life is like inside an Iraqi prison?"

"Actually, yes, but that's another story."

"And yet this is still a joke to you. I have the power in my hands to crush your life, Max."

Hunter shrugged. "Smoke 'em if you got 'em, right?"

McCabe spoke in Arabic and one of the soldiers pulled a combat knife from his belt. Hunter flinched when he saw it, but the soldier used it hack the strap of his canvas bag. When it was severed, he handed the bag over to McCabe.

He opened it and grinned. Reaching inside and pulling out the winged statue, he held it up into the dying light of the setting sun and gasped. "We have it at last."

As the soldiers whooped and cheered, Hunter twisted his head up to McCabe. When he spoke, it was through split, bloody lips encrusted with sand and flies. "Enjoy it while you can, because this time you're going to prison."

McCabe struggled to contain his laughter. "Please, Max, enough already. You know, it's scum like you, coming into these countries and looting their ancient treasures, who really bring archaeology in disrepute."

"You're the scum."

McCabe kicked him hard, burying his shoe in his ribs. Hunter clenched his jaw and muffled a cry of agony. Bolts of pain coursed through his ribcage like electricity and he heard McCabe giving the soldiers more orders. They grabbed him and hauled him roughly to his feet until he was face to face with his old enemy.

"I keep telling you to give up but you just won't listen."

Hunter winced as one of the soldiers bound his wrists behind his back with a nylon cable zip tie. He blew out short, sharp breaths to alleviate the pain of the injuries he had sustained in the beating. "If you think I'm the kind of guy who gives up, then you obviously don't know me very well."

McCabe stuffed the statue back inside the canvas bag. "I know you well enough, Max."

More orders in Arabic, and then the men dragged him away to the army truck behind McCabe's dusty Wrangler.

"Where are you taking me?"

"Back to my camp." McCabe walked back over to the Jeep. "We're holding you there until the Iraqi Police arrive and arrest you for the theft and attempted smuggling of various precious artifacts I recently excavated there."

Hunter was confused. "So what happens to the winged statue?"

McCabe turned and held the bag up in the air. "This? This is going back to where it belongs – to where it has belonged for thousands of years."

"I think the desert sun has given you heatstroke, Brodie. What the hell are you talking about? The last person to own that statue died at least a thousand years before Christ."

"As I have told you before many times, you don't know as much as you think you do."

"You're insane."

"I'll pass on your thoughts to the rightful owners of this statue, Max. I'm sure they will care even less about them than I do." He opened the door of the Wrangler and dropped the bag onto the seat. "And please, try to escape on the way back to the camp. My men have orders to shoot you on sight if you attempt to flee their custody. It will save me having to fill out a witness statement."

The soldiers bundled him up onto the back of the truck and sat opposite him with rifles in their hands. He considered jumping out and making a break for it, but with his hands tied and McCabe's last words echoing in his mind, he decided to keep his powder dry and wait for a better opportunity.

The growl of a diesel engine and its vibration on the bench seat knocked him from his thoughts. A loose resonator rattled under the chassis and then a puff of exhaust fumes billowed out into the air behind them. Hunter guessed he was in for a long ride, and when he gave the soldiers a big, bright smile, they ignored him. One of them made a joke in Arabic and they all laughed. Hunter turned and looked out of the back of the truck.

They had left the track now and were driving out into the desert to the west of Mosul. It was isolated and bleak, and yet the stark inviting beauty of most deserts was there, enriched further by the reds and deep ambers of the fat sun setting slowly just out of sight ahead of the truck. At this time of day, the sands sometimes looked as soft as velvet, and as the temperature dropped for another cool night, the stars above the desolation grew sharper.

The truck rumbled on, lost in the column of dust kicked up by McCabe's Jeep when the wind occasionally shifted. Behind them, in their own dust trail, Hunter watched the awesome sight of the moon rising over the desert to the east. Even the soldiers stopped their jokes to watch it. When the sun finally slipped below the horizon, the moon's ghostly light swept over the sands like liquid silver. For a moment, Hunter almost lost himself in the beauty of the moment.

And then the truck pulled to a stop and the engine spluttered into silence. The Iraqi men around him burst to life, flicking their cigarettes over the tailgate and kicking him with their boots. Unshaven, tired and with a sheen of sweat on his face, he jumped down onto the sand and took in McCabe's camp.

*So this is where he was looking for it...* he thought smugly.

Centerd around a large excavation site in the middle of nowhere, it was more like a small ramshackle town. Mesh tarps flapped in the breeze and the smell of roast lamb drifted over to him on a cloud of smoke from a crackling campfire. He absorbed the atmosphere until McCabe stepped out of the Wrangler and ordered the men to bring him into camp.

One of the soldiers prodded him in the back with his rifle stock.

"All right, I get the hint."

He made his way down a gentle slope, carefully navigating the gasoline lanterns and guy ropes as he went. His face was bashed up enough without adding to the damage, and with his hands tied behind his back he couldn't break a fall.

They were nearing the center of the camp when he saw a team of German archaeologists talking as they ate their evening meal. They looked up but ignored him, turning away and continuing their quiet conversation as they ate bowls of steaming stew and drank from stainless steel canteens. As he reached the fire in the middle of the site, the moon was lighting the highlands to the south of Mosul and a desert lark scrounged for titbits in the twilight.

"You wait here," McCabe said, and issued more orders to the soldiers. "I have business."

"Don't be long, Brodie. You know how I miss you."

McCabe ignored the jibe and wandered over to a big military surplus tent a few yards behind the campfire. He was holding Hunter's canvas bag in his hand and glanced at his watch as he approached a man outside the tent.

"Is he in?"

"Yes."

An amber glow lit the tent but there was no sign of anyone inside. When the man called out for someone, Hunter saw a tall man's shadow fall on the front wall of the tent. Only his silhouette was visible, but whoever he was, he was a big, well-built man and as lean as a butcher's dog.

When he saw the shadow, McCabe took a step back and started to fiddle with his free hand. "Gaius?"

"Come in, McCabe, and pray you bring me the good news I have been waiting for."

# CHAPTER THREE

Amy Fox drove to work faster than normal, overtaking cars on the Whitehurst Freeway like it was going out of fashion. The sun flashed on the surface of the Potomac River and she put on a pair of sunglasses, settling back in her seat. Cruising past Georgetown Park and Foggy Bottom, she tried to make sense of the voicemail that had summoned her into work so urgently.

The traffic was getting heavier, but up ahead she saw her exit. Pulling right and joining Constitution Avenue, she drove east past the Ellipse before turning left onto Pennsylvania Avenue. Traffic was heavier again, but she soon reached her destination and swept up to the security barriers outside FBI headquarters. She showed her ID to the guard and he raised the boom gate and waved her through.

She pulled down into the underground parking lot, killed the engine and stepped out of her neat BMW coupé. She locked the car, and paused to check her hair in the reflection of the driver's door. She wore a crisp, white shirt under a smart, black suit. The understated pearl stud earrings sparkled in the artificial strip lighting, and her sunflower blonde hair was down. She decided against this, and tied it up into a neat bun before walking to the main building.

Entering the lobby, she passed more security and took the elevator up to her office. The Office of Antiquities had been her home for over three years now, but she still had a buzz of excitement at the start of every day. Even more when the director called her in halfway through her day off.

As expected, both her office and that of her boss, James Gates, were empty; the team was already in Briefing Room A, waiting for her to arrive. She hurried down a carpeted corridor and felt a wave of pride. The walls were decorated with pictures of the various ancient artifacts the team had rescued from the dark world of international smuggling and crime, and she had played an integral role in each one of them.

She pushed the door open with confidence and found the team assembled around a large fourteen-seater conference desk. Director Gates was at the head of the table and Jodie Priest and Quinn Mosley were sitting opposite one another either side of him. Sal Blanco and Ben Lewis were at the other end of the table. They all turned as she stepped into the room.

"Amy, thanks for coming in so soon," Gates said. "I'm glad I got hold of you."

"Your voicemail was kind of urgent." She set her bag on the table and turned suspicious eyes to her boss. Repeating his message back to him in a question, she said, "Come into work immediately, this is the big one?"

Gates gave her that long, crooked smile of his. "Why do you think I ordered everyone in on their day off?"

"Not the quality of the coffee, that's for sure," Quinn said.

"Not the coffee," said Gates, gesturing to one of the seats. "Please, take a seat and we can get started."

"You get any tickets for the ride in?" Lewis said.

Amy looked at her grinning colleague. "I'm sorry?"

"I know where you live, Amy, and you got here *fast*."

"Speedfreak," Jodie said.

"Reckless breaker of the law," said Quinn, making Blanco chuckle.

"What did you guys expect," she said, "with a voicemail message like that?"

Quiet laughter as she sat down, and then Gates walked over to a large whiteboard on the wall at the far end of the briefing table.

Amy got comfortable in her chair. "So what is this about, Jim?"

"Operation Ratline. As you are all aware," he began, "thanks to a lot of hard work and intel gathering we recently retrieved a large haul of stolen artifacts following a lengthy operation into a ring of relic smugglers headquartered in New York. They were bringing stolen antiquities into the United States and Europe from all over Mexico and South America, and we ended that."

"Well aware?" Quinn said. "I worked until about two a.m. most nights."

Gates looked at the young goth. As usual, her face was obscured behind thick layers of black and white makeup. "And your country loves you for it."

"Really?" she said, pulling her hoodie up over her head and disappearing inside its shadows. "Because that's not what my paycheck says."

Amy gave the young woman a disapproving look and then turned back to Gates. "You were talking about the stolen relics."

"Right," he said. "We inventoried the stolen artifacts so we could begin to return them to their rightful owners. Some belonged to museums, others to art galleries and some were in private collections. During the cataloguing, our agents found some anomalous objects."

Lewis and Jodie responded to the description with suspicion, but Amy went straight in for the kill. "Anomalous objects? What the hell does that mean?"

"It means they found something not corresponding to anything we have ever seen before."

"You mean nothing on our records, at all?" Amy asked.

"Not just our records," Gates said. "When I say *we*, I mean humanity."

Jodie thought he was joking. "Wait, you're trying to say something not from this world?"

"Right now, I don't know what I'm saying."

"So what are we talking about?" Blanco asked flatly.

"We're talking about some rings and other jewellery, plus some ceremonial daggers and a raft of black and white photographs, including a very intriguing one of a winged statue. The daggers are highly unusual and have the same winged figurines as we see in the picture carved into their handles, so they're clearly linked. We have never seen anything like these things before, from any culture, at any time."

"That's as freaky as it gets," Jodie said.

Gates looked at her with something approaching sympathy. "You'd think."

"What does that mean?" Amy asked.

"The Nazis knew about them, too."

Amy was shocked. "How do we know that?"

"The photographs had Nazi stamps on them, and we've dated them to the early nineteen-forties."

"Getting more intriguing," Quinn said, raising an eyebrow.

Amy felt oddly numb as she took in the words. Gates was as solid as a rock, and twice as reliable. To say he gave conspiracy theories short thrift was an understatement, and yet the look in his eyes right now worried her. "And this stuff was definitely found on the latest operation?"

He nodded. "That's right, in the haul we bagged coming into Miami. Judging from the condition of the photographs, especially the one of the statue, I'd say they've been circulating around the world on the black market for a long time. I suspect the whole lot came out of Buenos Aires before the raid two years ago."

A round of serious nods. Everyone knew about the raid on Cavallo's place.

"And where is all of this stuff right now?" Lewis asked.

"What do you think is in that box you're all looking at, cigars?"

"Whoa," Jodie said. "Way to freak me out, boss."

Quinn jokingly rolled her eyes. "They're not radioactive." Turning to Gates, she raised her eyebrows. "Right?"

"They're not radioactive, and yes, that was one of the many tests I ordered to be done on them."

Amy leaned forward and pulled the box toward her. Clicking open the locks and lifting the lid, she saw the black and white picture on top. The winged statue in the image was as Gates had described, but being a pragmatic former US Navy officer he had left out how beautiful the ancient object was.

She was looking at a tiny figurine with the face of an angel, an arched back and outstretched arms beckoning her to come forward. The creature's wings spread out from its back in gentle, shallow curves almost like a cupped hand. "This is incredible," she muttered.

"Wait till you see the daggers."

Jodie snatched the picture from Amy's hands but the older woman never even noticed. Looking down into the box, she was instantly struck by the daggers' beauty. The blades themselves were in carved sheathes, and the handles reflected the light streaming in through the window, each of them some kind of smooth, polished stone.

"Pretty, aren't they?" Gates said.

"I see what you mean, boss," Lewis said. "I have never in my life seen anything like these before. What about you, Quinn?"

She shook her head, eyes fixed on the daggers. "Nu-huh."

"Amy?"

"Not really, but they look similar to some of the ancient Egyptian daggers we've retrieved."

"I agree," Gates said. "But right now, we're more interested in the missing statue in the Nazi photograph. There's very little information on the daggers, but we think there's an inscription running around the base of the statue that might tell us more about where all these artifacts come from."

"So where do we go from here?" Lewis said.

"In the raid, we also found a shipping manifest that detailed the names of various high-profile antiquities collectors, some clean, others not so clean. We can't tell who got the winged statue, but from some of the information on the manifest we believe Oskar Rorschach is very interested in buying it."

A new, fresh silence fell over the room. They all new about Rorschach, too.

"How do we know this?" Blanco asked.

"Because Rorschach is an insane collector of antiquities and would sell his own mother if it meant getting a rare piece?" Lewis said.

Gates smirked. "Better than that. We found a laptop in the raid and went through the emails. Rorschach is dealing with a third party anonymous dealer who was also buying from Cavallo. We found data going to Rorschach saying that the winged statue is in the possession of another collector and Rorschach wants to buy it."

"Which is more than we've been able to get on Rorschach after months of surveillance," Amy said. "Damn it! I should have been able to get hold of this information by now. It's not like it's a small operation – he has a staff of dozens, including several Americans. I should have gotten hold of this. I feel like I've let everyone down."

Gates gave her a reassuring smile. "Take it easy, Amy. This is tricky stuff. As we all know, someone is trying to buy up and control the entire antiquities market, and it looks like Rorschach is either a serious part of the operation or maybe even running it. He's going to play his cards close to his chest."

Amy shuddered. "And we all know who you mean when you say *someone*."

"Let's not get into conspiracy theories just yet," Gates said. "Jodie, you look worried."

"It's just what you said earlier about Nazis and nothing like the statue existing anywhere on earth. Now you're talking about *them* being behind this. It's making me nervous."

"That freaked me out, too," Lewis said. "Just being honest."

Quinn turned her mouth into a mock-pout. "A rough tough marine like you?"

"Hey," Lewis said sarcastically. "I'm a very emotional person."

Amy fixed her eyes on Gates. "Presuming we can locate the statue and intercept Rorschach's purchase of it, I'm guessing we're getting an expert in to authenticate all this stuff?"

"We're looking into it, but it's going to have to be someone with an encyclopaedic knowledge of archaeology and with top secret military clearance."

"They must be a dime a dozen," Quinn said. "I'll call 1936 and get Indiana Jones to come over."

A low laugh filled the room, but the tense atmosphere soon returned. Amy turned away from the daggers and looked at her boss. "You can't be thinking about sending this material off site?"

Gates gave a low, nervous chuckle. "Hell no. I doubt these things will ever leave the FBI's dark and dingy vaults for the rest of eternity."

"So, what then?" Lewis asked.

"It means getting someone to come in, doofus," Quinn said. "Right?"

Gates nodded. "Right."

Any felt a twinge of anxiety. Already, she was starting to get a bad feeling about all of this. "You have someone in mind?"

"Sure."

"Who?"

"Just a guy."

"Just a guy?"

"Sure."

"A Yale guy?"

Gates shook his head.

"A Harvard guy?"

Another shake, this time accompanied by a smile. "Oxford. His name is Dr Max Hunter and he's at the top of the pile. He's the lead field archaeologist at UNESCO and a former military man."

"Wait – Oxford, as in England," Lewis said. "As in what the hell happened to Top Secret classified stuff being seen by American eyes only?"

Gates raised an eyebrow. "Not really. More as in, the world's leading authority on ancient ceremonial weapons and religious statues. We need to get to him first because if Rorschach is after the winged statue he's also going to be trying to get hold of Hunter."

"But what about the Top Secret classified stuff being seen by American eyes only?" Lewis repeated.

"He already has the necessary clearance to look at the daggers, Ben, so you can climb back into your crib and calm down."

"And don't forget the pacifier," Quinn said.

More laughter took some of the tension out of the room, and as her initial fears began to mellow, Amy suddenly felt a flash of excitement. "How quickly can we organize this?"

"Usually pretty fast, but not this time."

"So what's the problem?"

"We're not one hundred percent on this, but we think Hunter just got kidnapped in Iraq."

Lewis shook his head and sighed. "Holy crap, by ISIS?"

"We don't know. I spoke with Adil al-Amari. As some of you know, he is the head of the Heritage Department at Nineveh Antiquities, which is part of Iraq's State Board of Antiquities and Heritage. He's had a ton to deal with over the last couple of years, including ISIS and ISIL attacks on heritage sites and even looters digging tunnels beneath Jonah's Tomb in an attempt to steal various artifacts thought to be buried there. He thinks maybe looters snatched Hunter."

"I'm not liking the sound of this," Blanco said. "Do we know what Hunter was doing out there in the first place?"

"Yeah," Quinn said. "What was he looking for?"

"We don't know that either. Al-Amari wasn't giving anything away."

Jodie pulled a cigarette out of her pack and rolled it in her fingers. "Sounds like we don't know anything."

"Not true," Gates said. "We know we need to locate this winged statue and we also know we have to get to Hunter before Rorschach. This means Amy has some serious work to do."

Amy smiled grimly. "You can say that again."

"So what are you waiting for?" Gates said.

"Leave it with me."

# CHAPTER FOUR

With moonlight streaking across the northern Iraqi desert, Hunter watched Brodie McCabe waft the fly sheet aside and step inside the big, military tent. Behind him, some sap inside a piece of wood on the campfire exploded. One of the archaeologists gasped and fell back off his portable folding chair. Another made a hearty joke in German and the rest of the small group fell about laughing as their friend dusted himself down and set his chair back up.

Time slowed, and Hunter started counting stars. The soldiers around him never lowered their rifles and kept a safe distance from him. After how he had fought in the tomb, they knew what was good for them. There was some small talk in Arabic, and then they passed a cigarette around. When McCabe came out of the tent, one of them threw it to the ground and crushed it with the heel of his army boot. Hunter saw McCabe was holding the canvas bag, but there was something much smaller in it now.

"What now?" Hunter said. "We wait here all night for the police?"

McCabe seemed distracted. "The police aren't coming out here anymore."

"What?"

"My employer has modified the plan."

"What are you going on about, Brodie? Your employer seems to have had quite an effect on you. You've gone white."

"You are to be executed tonight. Immediately, in fact." He barked some orders at the soldiers and they grabbed him roughly by the shoulders. "I'm sorry to say, you were caught by these soldiers in the act of stealing a glorious winged bull dating from the neo-Assyrian period."

He opened the bag up and showed the winged bull to Max. "I know you'll appreciate such a wonderful piece. We found it not far from here while we were looking for the much more precious winged statue you found to the east. Unfortunately, when the soldiers ordered you to stop, you ignored them and they were forced to fire on you."

"You can't be serious, Brodie. I know you're an arsehole, but this has to be a new low even for you. You're talking about cold-blooded murder."

"And defamation of character, Max. Just imagine what UNESCO will make of it all when they read about how naughty you've been, not to mention your old college in Oxford. The world-famous Max Hunter caught giving into temptation and selling stolen artifacts to ISIL."

"You're having a laugh."

"No, I am not." McCabe put the canvas bag over Max's shoulder. He spoke in Arabic and dismissed the soldiers.

"Removing the witnesses?" Hunter said.

"Don't make this any harder than it has to be, Max. One quick shot and it's over. Painless. Now turn around."

Hunter raised his chin and stared McCabe in the eye, not looking away or blinking once. When he spoke, his voice was steady and hard with defiance. "If you want to shoot me, then you can look me in the eye when you do it."

"Very well, as you wish!"

McCabe reached down for his pistol and fumbled with the leather holster flap. It was the only break Hunter needed. He bent his knees and sprang forward into McCabe's body, burying his shoulder in his enemy's chest and bowling him over.

McCabe crashed onto the sand with a soft thud and brought his arms up to push Hunter away. The London archaeologist had one chance left, and that was the heavy-duty headbutt he now drove into McCabe's nose, smacking his head into the ground. He cried out in pain, his smashed nose producing a thin, nasal, squealing sound.

Hunter eyed the knife on McCabe's belt and now rolled to the side so his back was facing the other man's body. Pulling the knife out, he manoeuvred it around until the blade was pointing upwards and then used the serrated edge to slash through the zip tie and free his hands.

McCabe was on his feet now, blood streaming down his pulped nose and rage in his bulging eyes. He scooped a thick river of blood coursing over his lips and chin and flicked it on the sand at his shoes. "You bastard, Hunter. I'm going to enjoy this."

He moved his arm down to his holster, he flicked open the flap and reached for the gun, but it wasn't there.

"Looking for this?" Hunter said.

McCabe stared open-mouthed at his old nemesis. "How the hell did you get that?"

"When I took the knife. I keep telling you, Brodie, I really am a very disarming sort of guy. Now, raise your hands to the heavens and pray for mercy."

"You wouldn't dare shoot me."

"Why not?"

"Because every armed man in this camp will be over here in seconds."

"That's my problem," Hunter said. "Yours is that when I'm finding a solution to it you'll be lying on the sand with a bullet through your head."

"Go ahead," McCabe said. "Because thirty seconds later you'll be lying next to me with a hundred bullets in you, not one."

"You might be a lying, thieving, snivelling toerag, Brodie, but you do make a good point."

Hunter didn't wait for a reply, but spun on his heel with the gun in his hand and made a break for the tents. McCabe screamed for the soldiers to come back just as Hunter slipped out of sight and disappeared behind one of the tents. He was away, but he didn't have long. He had to get back to Gaius's tent, retrieve the statue and try and find a way out of the camp.

He sprinted back to the military tent, diving to the ground and rolling up to the base of the canvas. Soldiers yelled and flashlight beams criss-crossed over the campsite. Spitting out a mouthful of sand, he darted his arm out and lifted the side of the canvas a few inches. There, on the table in the middle of the tent, the winged statue sat serenely in a shaft of moonlight coming in through a slit in the front flap.

"Come to daddy." Hunter felt like laughing, but the sound of the soldiers shouting as they searched the camp for him, closer now, wiped the smile from his face. He slid beneath the side of the tent and crawled closer to the table. It was tight, with the rim of the canvas scraping against his shoulders as he went through.

He heard footsteps and quickly crawled back to the gap in the tent. Rolling back outside, he cursed how close he had come, but then his mind was concentrated further by the sight of Gaius. He was in the darkness to the side of the table, on his knees and mumbling some sort of mantra, hands clasped before his chest in sombre prayer.

"What the hell?"

Hunter was shocked, but not deterred. He could take Gaius if he had to, and now moved to crawl under the canvas to retrieve the statue. He slipped his right arm under the tent wall and began to crawl back inside when the desperate, terrified screams of a woman stopped him in his tracks.

# CHAPTER FIVE

He continued crawling inside the tent when a second bloodcurdling scream froze him to the spot once again, but this time Gaius snapped out of his meditation and sprang to his feet.

"Bollocks," Hunter said. "What now?"

Gaius called out for McCabe who now ran into the tent.

"What's going on?"

"Another looter, sir," McCabe said, nervously wringing his hat in his hands.

"Another one?"

"I've ordered her immediate execution."

"A good precaution."

Hunter felt his blood to turn ice in his veins.

"What about Hunter?"

"He's still on the loose, but we have soldiers combing every inch of the camp. There's no way he can get out into the desert without someone on the perimeter seeing him and alerting us."

"Kill the looter and bring Hunter to me."

"As you wish, sir."

Hunter watched McCabe slap his hat back on and leave the tent. Gaius turned away and walked across to the statue.

He picked it up and held it in the moonlight. "Not long now."

Hunter knew this was his only chance. When McCabe had executed the woman, he would be next. If he was going to grab the statue and make a break for it, that time was now, while Gaius was alone. Now or never.

The woman screamed again, closer this time. Hunter turned and looked through the guy ropes to see two soldiers dragging her away from the camp. She was wearing male clothing and her head was covered in a man's *keffiyeh* headdress. In her hands was a bag filled with whatever she had stolen from the camp.

McCabe ordered the soldiers in Arabic and they ripped the bag from her hands and emptied it out onto the ground. Two or three small figurines and some clay pots tumbled out and fell over the moonlit sand. He barked more orders and the soldiers dragged her screaming away from an army truck and up to the top of a dune. When they marched back down to the bottom and pulled their rifles from their shoulders, he knew what happened next.

He turned his head back and looked under the canvas at the statue. The ornate form of the strange peachy silver color, the outstretched arms, the angelic curved wings and the serene, passive face. It stared back at him in the silver light of the moon and he was only dimly aware of Gaius dropping to his knees and once again praying to it.

Now or never.

He reached toward it, but the looter's screams stopped him in his tracks again.

*Now or never, Max.*

He moved toward the statue once again, silently crawling under the canvas until his hand was only inches away from the table. Then he heard the woman sobbing as the soldiers took up position and slid cartridges into the chambers of their bolt-action rifles.

Damn it.

He slipped back out of the tent, sprang to his feet and ran down the gap between the two tents until he had a clear shot of the soldiers and McCabe. There was no time to take out McCabe because the soldiers were the ones about to kill the woman. He knew when he fired on them, McCabe would be gone and so would his chances of the getting the statue, but he had to do it to save the looter's life.

He aimed his gun at one of the soldiers and fired, killing him swiftly with one professionally aimed bullet to the head. The other soldier spun around but he had anticipated the move and now fired on him, too. His body slumped to the floor a second after the first man's and McCabe sprang out of sight like a gazelle, taking cover behind a tent and yelling for more soldiers.

The woman didn't wait for another chance. She turned and fled down behind the dune and was out of sight a second later. Hunter figured if anyone knew which way to get out of here then it was her. He sprinted up after her but the soldiers opened fire on him.

He dropped to his belly and crawled under the chassis of the truck. It was cramped and hot; his shoulder blades rubbed against the exhaust as he wormed his way further beneath the military vehicle. Crawling out of the other side, he made a break for it. When he reached the brink of the dune, he stopped and scanned the area north of it where she had gone.

He found her easily in the moonlight and could hear her footfall as she ran into the night. He dived down the dune's slipface and followed her. Looking behind at the top of the dune, he saw the silhouettes of McCabe and at least half a dozen more soldiers, plus some of the archaeologists as they scanned the bottom of the dune for the fleeing thieves.

"There!" McCabe yelled. "They're over there!"

Hunter caught up with the woman, and the two of them ran side by side as the soldiers made their way down the sandy slope. One slipped and cartwheeled down the leeward slope all the way to the bottom and another opened fire on them in the moonlight.

They ran along a flat interdune stretch between two more enormous dunes before the woman darted to her right. He turned around the base of the dune in pursuit of her and saw a motorbike. "Better than nothing," he said. "I'm Max by the way."

"Zahra."

They both heard the soldiers yelling, and then the roar of an engine. Moments later, the nose of McCabe's Jeep crested the top of one of the dunes. In the rear, one of the soldiers was holding a submachine gun.

"Not a good development."

Zahra climbed on the bike and pushed down on the kick-start lever. The engine spluttered for a few seconds and then died. She did it a second time, and McCabe's Jeep drew closer. Hunter heard another engine and realized one of the Iraqi army trucks had driven around to the north and was trying to cut off their escape route.

"Looks like we're surrounded," Zahra said, kicking the lever a third time and still getting no response from the two-stroke engine.

"We're in trouble."

Both of them jumped with a start when a rocket-propelled grenade streaked out of the sky and roared over their heads at the front of a twisting column of white exhaust smoke. To their surprise and relief, it was going toward the Iraqi army truck, which it struck in a direct hit to the cab. The massive fireball exploded in the night and lit both their faces in a warm orange glow.

"What the hell?" Hunter said.

Zahra's face was etched in confusion and fear. "I hear a helicopter."

The chopper was on them in seconds, flying low and fast over the ancient sands before zooming up over a dune and then pitching down abruptly just ahead of them. It spun around ninety-degrees until it was side-on and the door slid open.

"Looks like my ride is here," Hunter said.

"I'm glad you have such good friends."

McCabe's Jeep was navigating the bottom of the dune and turning in their direction. The soldier in the back raised his submachine gun and fired on the helicopter. Most of the rounds missed, but the end of the arc struck the tail boom and clanged off the metal.

Hunter and Zahra scrambled through the sandy dust created by the downdraft until they reached the bullet-pocked chopper. The door opened wider now, and Hunter pushed Zahra inside before climbing halfway in after her. The chopper instantly spun around and headed away from McCabe, leaving him out on the dunes beside the burning army truck.

Hunter breathed a sigh of relief and felt his heart slowing down to something resembling normality. Then, he heard the familiar, welcoming and slightly smug voice of a woman he knew almost better than anyone.

"Perhaps I can be of assistance to you this evening?"

He stared up at her and grinned. As the chopper raced away, his legs were still hanging out of the door. He crawled inside the cabin and closed the door as Zahra clambered up into a seat opposite the woman. In the front, beside the pilot, a man was disassembling a small RPG launcher.

"I think maybe you can," he said.

The mysterious woman smiled sweetly at him, and the aircraft raced away, vanishing seconds later deep in the night's sable craw.

# CHAPTER SIX

Juliette Bonnaire's long red hair was tied up in a neat, professional bun and she wore a plain black suit. Even here in the back of an emergency rescue helicopter, every inch of her was typically crisp, clean and elegant. She looked down through her polished horn-rimmed glasses at the dirty, dusty heap of a man in the cabin footwell and gave him a weary smile.

"Bonsoir, Max."

He crawled up off the floor and sat beside her in a cloud of dust. "Howdy."

"Who's the woman?" she asked. "Your latest conquest?"

"Hardly, we just met tonight," Hunter said.

"So give it another hour or so?"

"She was looting. They were going to kill her."

Zahra spoke up. "I am not ashamed. These men come to our country and steal our artifacts. When I take them, at least I don't pass them onto ISIS or international smugglers."

"Then what do you do with them?"

"I say I found them in the desert and sell them to the museums."

Hunter laughed. "It's a living."

"And thank you for saving my life."

Hunter smiled. "Think nothing of it."

Juliette sniffed. "It only cost us two years' work."

"Hey, I got us both out alive," Hunter said.

"And I think maybe now," Juliette said in her rich French accent, "that you can thank me for making you wear the little GPS tracker."

"It makes me feel like a dog, Juliette." Hunter gently rubbed his fingers over his old army dog tags around his neck. The latest addition was a micro GPS tracker supplied by UNESCO at Juliette's request. "You know that."

"But how many times has it helped me to save your life this year, mon chiot?"

"Who's counting?" he said.

She held up three fingers and gave him a stern look. "Trois."

His smile was fading. "You're counting. That's who."

"I'm counting because I'm also the one paying for everything. It costs a lot of money to mount an operation like this and the budget is not unlimited. Planes, helicopters, cars, local knowledge, protection and when you're really firing on all six cylinders, bribing law enforcement officials and diplomats."

"You couldn't do this without me, Juliette, and I'm not your puppy."

"I love you Max, but you do realize you are paid by UNESCO to retrieve the artifacts *without* causing international crises wherever you go?"

"Please, you're making me blush."

Zahra looked on, a faint smile of amusement dancing on her lips.

Juliette sighed. "This is no joke. You are an Oxford PhD-holding archaeologist who represents the United Nations' agency for cultural and natural heritage. Your days galivanting around the world as a British Army officer are over. Getting shot at by Iraqi soldiers as you scramble out of a tomb is not good optics. It's already on the BBC, CNN and all three of France 24's language service websites."

"They'd been bribed."

"Sorry?"

"The soldiers."

"Now I've heard it all."

Zahra spoke up. "Where are we going?"

"Back to Mosul," Juliette said. "Is that all right with you, or can I divert the aircraft somewhere? It only costs three hundred dollars per hour to keep it in the air."

"Mosul is fine."

"How considerate."

A tense silence fell over the small cabin and the chopper cruised through the night, low over the desert sands. They made the trip back to Mosul in less than half an hour, and then Hunter and Juliette watched Zahra walking away from the helipad toward her brother's old car. As the blades whirred to a stop, he turned to his boss and looked at her, regret etched on his dirty, lined face.

"It was McCabe," he said darkly.

"What?"

"The man who bribed the soldiers."

Juliette looked at him in shock. "Brodie McCabe was here in Mosul?"

Hunter nodded. "Right there in the labyrinth under the Gates of Nineveh, Juliette. He lied to the soldiers and told them I was a smuggler. They flushed me out of the labyrinth and then drove me out to their camp. I'm sorry, but McCabe got the statue."

"That bastard got the winged statue?"

He gave a slow, reluctant shake of his head and rubbed his bruised, aching back. "He gave it to someone named Gaius. You heard of him?"

"Never."

"But still, I saw it, Juliette. With my own eyes."

She took a deep breath. "Was it as we expected?"

He nodded slowly, dragging his moment of glory out for as long as possible. "Exactly as we thought. The inscriptions around the base left no doubt."

"So we were right," she said. "Atlantis was real."

"I think so, but I need to see it again to be sure, I need to spend time making a proper translation of the inscription. Working while McCabe's soldiers were shooting at me wasn't exactly the easiest thing I've ever done."

"Get real, Max. If McCabe has the statue we both know we'll never see it again. It's probably already on the black market."

"Yeah, I know. But it means the text in the missing Plato dialogue I found in Athens was accurate." His voice trailed away. "It means there are two more out there somewhere. The three Winged Guardians of Atlantis… and I let one of them slip through my hands like water."

"At least you're alive."

He took a deep breath and patted his stomach. "Sure. All I need is a few days in Oxford and I'll be back to my normal self again."

"You're not going back to England."

"Eh? Why not?"

"Because I have a little surprise for you."

A cool breeze blew off the desert beyond the airport. He ran his hands through his sandy, sweat-soaked hair. "I hate surprises, Julie. Especially your surprises."

She gave a wicked laugh. "I think this one you will like."

"What makes you say that?"

"Because you have been invited to the home of Oskar Rorschach."

He turned and gawped at her. "As in the world's greatest collector of antiquities?"

"The very same."

"What does he want?"

"He wants you to authenticate some pieces he is thinking of buying."

Hunter felt his heart quicken. "What sort of pieces?"

Juliette brought out her phone and showed him a scanned photo of an old black and white photograph. The picture was of a set of daggers unlike anything he had ever seen before, and in the corner was a small smudged stamp.

"My God, look at the pommels on these blades! These tiny carved statues are identical to the one McCabe just stole from me."

"Are you sure?"

"Yes, and what the hell is that stamp in the corner, the emblem of the Ahnenerbe?"

"Indeed."

Hunter stared in disbelief at the stamp on the photo. It was a downward-pointing sword in an oval with the words DEUTSCHES AHNENERBE written around the outside of it. The reference to the Nazi ancestral heritage think tank chilled his blood. As a subdivision of the notorious SS, the Ahnenerbe was run directly by Heinrich Himmler and was dedicated to proving Nazi racial doctrines. He felt he might be slowly wading out of his depth.

"This is massive," Juliette. "We know the Nazis were looking for Atlantis but I had no idea they found anything relating to the place. If these carved statues really are the same as the one McCabe just stole from me, then they must be linked. Where are they now?"

"That is what you are going to Switzerland to find out."

"When?"

Juliette pointed to a Cessna Citation parked up on the opposite apron. "Right now. That over there is Mr Rorschach's private jet, and waiting on board is his personal assistant. By all accounts, she cannot wait to meet you."

"Can't blame her for that, Julie. She's only human."

"Max."

"Sorry – is there somewhere I can clean up first?"

She pulled a small black and silver key-card out of her pocket. "There's a modest transit hotel in the airport. I booked you a room with a shower and organized some fresh clothes."

The moonlight shone on the card when he took it from her. He leaned over and kissed her on the cheek. "You're a dream, Julie. I'm forgetting about McCabe already."

"Play it cool, Max. There's a good chance we're about to run into some serious trouble. Maybe McCabe – maybe someone even worse. A lot of powerful people are going to want a piece of this. Watch your back."

"Relax, I'll just be myself."

"That's what I'm worried about."

# CHAPTER SEVEN

The Apostle studied Gaius's mild and calm face for any signs of deception. The head disciple was unflappable, but also inscrutable. He was talking to him on a wall-sized plasma screen fitted in his office, sitting in the darkness and listening carefully to everything he was telling him.

"I want to see it," he asked.

Gaius obeyed instantly and lifted the small statue off the table in the middle of his opulent tent. Holding it up in the moonlight, the disciple chanced an appreciative smile.

The Apostle stared, unblinking. "It's bigger than I imagined it."

"It's heavy, too, Teacher."

"And is it made from pure orichalcum?"

"It appears to be an alloy of gold, copper and the very purest orichalcum. I have already had Crixus run his tests on it. The orichalcum element is five nines fine."

The Apostle gasped. The purity of precious metals was rated on a system called millesimal fineness, with five nines fine describing the very purest of 99.999%. "You have done well."

"My most humble thanks, Teacher."

The Apostle rested his elbows on his desk and steepled his fingers, smiling in satisfaction. Silver had the highest thermal conductivity of any element, and the purer the silver, the higher it went. This metal, according to their Holy Scriptures, had even greater conductivity, and their test proved it.

"You look perturbed by something, Gaius."

"Dr Hunter escaped from the camp tonight. He ran out into the desert with some filthy vermin of a looter and flew away in a helicopter. I'm worried he might be a problem going forward with our plans."

"How long did he have alone with the statue?"

"Not long, Teacher. He had only been inside the tomb a few minutes when McCabe tracked him down and sent the soldiers in after him."

The Apostle considered the matter. Hunter had come up on his radar before and was well-respected as an archaeologist. His military background meant he was happier to go into many of the more dangerous areas of cultural interest and excavate, as had happened this time. Iraq was not the safest environment for academics to work in, especially not out in the northern deserts, and yet Hunter had gone there, in pursuit of his insane dreams.

How much had he gleaned from the statue before McCabe took it from him? This was the million dollar question. Was it long enough to learn anything of significance, or was he still fumbling around in the dark?

"We have the statue," he said at last. "That is all that matters. I wish to see it immediately. You are to bring it to our headquarters at once."

"Yes, Teacher."

"You are also to send McCabe and some disciples to destroy Hunter."

"I will do so with great relish."

"I'm sure the Magus will be pleased when I report this news, and you are a good disciple, Gaius. You are a fine example to your men."

Gaius bowed his head. "I am humbled by the compliment, Teacher."

"Go to your work, Gaius – our long journey is almost over. We will meet in our headquarters."

The Apostle pushed a small button on his desk and the plasma screen went dark. The original oil painting, *The Course of Empire* by Thomas Cole, slowly descended from a slit in the ceiling and covered the plasma screen. The British National Gallery thought they had the original, he mulled with amusement. But they did not.

He looked at the chaos in the painting and smiled. Terrified people ran for their lives, smoke billowed up from burning buildings. Soon all of this would be brought to the world once again, only so much worse. He felt no guilt; it was a fate this miserable world richly deserved, and then a new world order would rise from its smoldering ashes.

His master would consolidate power over the world and rule it totally, but only if Atlantis was found. The ancient kingdom harbored powers so terrifying it almost scared him to think about them. No one alive had ever seen anything like the devastating might the cradle of humanity hid under its secret veil.

But could this power be harnessed?

Yes, but only if the ancient teachings were followed.

His spine tingled with fear when he considered the long line of Apostles tracing all the way back to the very origins of mankind. His skin prickled when he thought about how he was a part of all this, alongside the world's most powerful men and women. They were all working together to make this work, to find Atlantis and harness its ancient powers.

He was just one cog in the machine, but an important cog. He knew that Hunter had to be stopped, and so did James Gates and his FBI Office of Antiquities. They were asking too many questions and prying into too much that didn't concern them. Gaius and the rest of the disciples would kill them all, long before they ever got close to the truth.

He leaned back in his chair and sipped single malt whisky from a cut glass tumbler. The Dalmore 62 was a steal at one quarter of a million dollars per bottle, but money meant nothing to him. He was the Apostle, and he answered only to one higher rank, the Magus. No one else in this world could touch him.

He took another sip, which was at least a thousand dollars' worth of the whisky, and closed his eyes once again.

After years of slow progress, the most lethal hunt on earth was gathering speed at last.

# CHAPTER EIGHT

Hunter tightened his seatbelt for the third time as the Cessna Citation banked around another snow-capped mountaintop. The pilot had just extended full flaps and lowered the gear, and Klara Steiner was now stepping through the cockpit door. She flashed a pleasant smile with her scarlet lips and wandered down the aisle toward him.

The Swiss woman was tall and blonde and lithe, and had worn a smart charcoal pencil suit when she met him at Mosul International Airport. As Oskar Rorschach's personal assistant, he had sent her out to meet him and join him on the flight back to their Swiss headquarters.

"Welcome to my homeland," she said, sitting beside him and buckling up her seatbelt.

"It's very beautiful." The plane ran through some turbulence and jolted them up and down for a few seconds. Outside his window, he saw they were now descending past the snowline.

"It certainly is," she laughed. "You look nervous."

"These mountains seem kind of close. If you don't mind my saying, I hope your pilot knows what he's doing."

"He's been with us for over twenty years, Dr Hunter, and the Rorschach Foundation hires only the best. You, for example."

"I accept the compliment," he said. "But I'll wait till we're on the ground before I extend the same to the man flying this plane."

"There's really no need to worry. I thought you were a pilot once?"

He nodded. "After I left the Guards I flew Apache helicopters in the Army Air Corps, but that was a long time ago in a previous lifetime far, far away."

His expression raised an inquisitive smile on her face. "I see, yet you're a nervous flyer?"

"Helicopters are different. If you don't know where you're going you can hover in the same place until you work out where to go. These things have to go at a dangerously fast speed just to stay airborne."

"If you have more faith in rotary aircraft, you can talk to our pilot when we land. He has thousands of hours of experience in those too."

"Really? That's unusual. It seems like Mr Rorschach really does hire only the best."

"As I say, only the best. And remember, when we land we have another flight up to the main Rorschach Foundation corporate headquarters complex. You will be delighted to hear the trip can only be made by helicopter."

"Sounds like the fun's only just beginning, but then I'm just a biased old rotorhead."

"A biased old rotorhead with an archaeology doctorate from the best college in the world."

"If I didn't know you guys wanted something from me, I'd say you were trying to flatter me."

She laughed once again. It was a light, subtle laugh, full of good humor. "Please, we're nearly there. Just sit back and enjoy the flight."

"I'll try and do just that, thanks."

They descended further, and he caught a glimpse of a snow-packed neve tucked away in the mountains off the port wing. Beyond it, he saw the tell-tale signs of a tributary glacier sliding down into another snowy moraine. Below it, the first roads and then the warm lights of a few hundred homes scattered on the outskirts of a snow-dusted Samedan. Then, seconds later, they were over the western end of the small airport with the spoilers flicking up and the jet engines in full reverse thrust.

"What do you know?" Klara said with a smile. "We made it safe and sound after all."

They moved quickly through a small, almost empty customs room, and then walked back out across the apron to a smart blue and grey Eurocopter sporting the Rorschach Foundation logo on its door. The rotor blades were already whirring by the time he and Klara reached the chopper, and when they buckled up their seatbelts once again, they were airborne.

*

Deep in Rorschach's corporate HQ building high in the Swiss Alps, a slightly nervous Hunter buttoned up his suit jacket and  followed Klara Steiner along a polished concrete corridor. The long space was decorated with elegant marble statues of gods and goddesses from across the ages, and keeping up with her wasn't easy. She walked fast, and her smart heels clipped crisply on the hard floor causing a tinny echo behind them.

They reached a stainless steel door and Klara pushed a series of tiny metal buttons on a keypad. There was a short buzz and the door slid open to reveal an office and a woman sitting on a leather couch. She wore large fashionable tortoiseshell glasses perched on a slim nose and when she rose from her chair he saw she was tall and dressed in a well-tailored charcoal-grey suit.

She walked over to him with an easy confidence and they shook hands. For all that, there was an anxious look in her eyes when she turned to face their new guest. "And you must be Dr Max Hunter."

"Guilty as charged."

"You look different from the picture on the UNESCO website."

"More handsome, I hope."

"Older."

He laughed. "Maybe the picture needs updating. I'll talk to my boss."

"Hello Dr Anderson," Klara said, stepping in. "I hope you haven't been waiting long?"

"Not at all."

Klara looked at Hunter. "Let me introduce Dr Kirsten Anderson," she said with a generous wave of her hand. "She works here at the Foundation, specifically in the antiquities acquisition department."

"Pleased to meet you, Dr Anderson," Hunter said.

"Likewise, Dr Hunter."

"What's your field?" he asked.

"I have a PhD in cartography."

"A PhD in maps," he said. "I bet you'd be lost without that."

The women's smiles faded. "Sorry to disappoint, but I've heard them all before, Dr Hunter."

"Please, it's Max."

"Shall we meet Mr Rorschach?" Klara said. "I know he's very keen to move this along as fast as possible." She buzzed the intercom. "Dr Hunter and Dr Anderson are here, sir."

"Wonderful." The voice was low and gruff. "Please send them in."

Hunter followed Klara and Kirsten along another short corridor behind her desk and into a large open-plan office with a tremendous view of the Alps from a dual aspect window wall. Sitting behind a large mahogany desk, an old man with white hair heard them and looked up. He slammed his laptop down, pushed his chair back and rose to greet them.

"Thank you, Klara. That will be all."

She left them, swishing the heavy doors closed behind her as she went. Rorschach smiled at Kirsten and then over to Hunter. "Dr Hunter, how good to meet you at last."

"Likewise, I'm sure."

Rorschach shook his hand vigorously until Hunter thought it might fall off.

"I have read all of your articles and follow your career with interest. It's a privilege to have you here at our headquarters."

"I'm sure the privilege to be here is all mine. I was excited when I saw the photograph you sent to Professor Bonnaire."

"As was I when I first saw it."

"And you have some other relics possibly related to it?"

"Yes, indeed. They were all sent to me together by a man keen to sell them."

"May I see them?"

Rorschach smiled thinly. "That's why you're here." He pushed a button and a butler walked into the room holding a polished wooden box. He set it down on the desk, bowed and left the room in silence.

"The daggers are in this box," Rorschach announced proudly as he clicked open the small golden clasps and opened the lid. "Please, indulge yourself."

Hunter was instantly spellbound in wonder when he took in the sight of the ancient blades. Behind him, Kirsten was staring at them with eyes full of surprise and wonder.

"These are very unique knives. May I?" Hunter asked.

"Of course."

He took one from the box and turned it over in his hands. "They're certainly older than Early Assyrian. The carved handles are exquisite, and the miniature winged statues on the pommel are intriguing to say the least."

Kirsten's eyes widened. "I never knew these were in the collection," she said. "When did we purchase them?"

Rorschach gave her a warm, fatherly smile. "I don't have to run everything by you, Dr Anderson. This was a private transaction, not official Foundation business."

"Have you run any tests on them?" Hunter asked.

"Yes, and the results will shock you."

Hunter gave the dagger one final look and then returned it to the case. "Tell me about these results."

Rorschach spoke bluntly. "The blades of these daggers are a highly unusual alloy of gold and copper and…"

Hunter's eyes darted over to Rorschach's wide grin. "And what?"

"Great minds think alike, Dr Hunter." Rorschach saw the expectant look on his face and laughed.

"What's going on?" Kirsten asked.

Rorschach said, "Some think Plato was talking about a gold-copper alloy when he talked about a metal he called orichalcum. In fact, I now believe the metal he described was an alloy of three metals – gold, copper and the mysterious orichalcum."

"I've never heard of that before." Kirsten said. "But then, I'm a cartographer not a metallurgist or an archaeologist. What's the significance of it?"

Rorschach looked at Hunter and the two shared a moment of excitement. "Please, Dr Hunter, the floor is yours."

Hunter paused. "When Plato was describing the metal he called orichalcum, he was talking about a building material used in the Kingdom of Atlantis."

The sound of the carriage clock on Rorschach's desk seemed to grow louder.

Kirsten said, "I'm sorry, Atlantis – as in the mythical civilization?"

"Not everyone agrees it's a myth."

"But is there anything to substantiate it?" she asked, clearly shocked.

Hunter shrugged. "Hard to say. Plato wrote about it in his *Critias*, one of his later dialogues. It's not a long document, and there's not very much in it. Until recently it was all we had, but then I discovered a second dialogue called the *Diocles* in Athens. That changed everything."

"How so?"

"In it, Plato described the existence of what he called three Winged Guardians. These were statues made from a strange metal that he believed had supernatural properties. Thanks to his writings, I was able to locate one of the statues in Iraq. After that I knew my instinct all these years had been right. Atlantis was real."

"But you could still be wrong," Kirsten said. "The statues themselves don't prove Atlantis. It could still be a myth, right?"

Hunter pointed to the daggers on the table. "Are they myths?"

"Well..."

"And the statue was no myth, either."

Rorschach chuckled. Clearly enjoying the conversation.

Kirsten saw the carvings on the sheaths once again. "I guess not. I have to say, I'm shocked by this."

Hunter nodded. "Most people are, but it's not so crazy. Plenty of civilizations have crumbled away and faded into the mists of time. Ours will too, in time."

"This is a lot to take in," she said. "If Atlantis was real, what exactly was it?"

"There are some theories claiming Atlantis was the Scandinavian Olympus, and that Odin was a king there, but it's not a favorite of mine. I believe Odin was a mythological deity, and the evidence backs that up. The Nazis thought Atlantis was the cradle of their own depraved mythologies. As for me, I just think it was an ancient civilization with a lot to teach us."

"All sounds nuts to me," she said. "I'll stick to old maps."

Hunter smiled politely. "Tell me, Mr Rorschach, how did you come by these items?"

"It is a long and mysterious story, Dr Hunter."

"And how does it begin?"

"Like all the best mysteries, it begins with betrayal and deception," Rorschach said, pausing for just long enough to call the butler back into the room. "But first, I think we should share our stories over a fine dinner. Tell me, Dr Hunter, do you like blue lobster? My personal chef used to work at Le Gabriel."

Hunter paused. "Er…"

"Perhaps something else?"

The no-nonsense Londoner shrugged innocently. "A burger would do me just fine, to be honest."

Rorschach eyed the former soldier with suspicion. "This can be arranged. Phillipe, make it so."

The butler bowed and left room in silence.

# CHAPTER NINE

Taking a large bite out of the best burger he had ever eaten in his life, Hunter sat back in his seat and watched Rorschach whisper in the ear of his butler. When he left the room, Rorschach said, "On your flight over here, Professor Bonnaire told me you found a labyrinth beneath the Tomb of Jonah."

"Guilty as charged."

The Swiss antiquities collector set down his heavy silver cutlery and stared at him in disbelief. "I have searched for that labyrinth for half of my life, Dr Hunter. Words cannot express how envious I am. You are a very accomplished man."

"Sounds like you've done your research."

"Dr Anderson is the researcher. Not only is she my maps expert, but she also helped Klara look into your background before we invited you here. I imagine she knows more about you, than you do yourself."

Hunter turned to Kirsten. "Oh yeah?"

"Try me."

He set down his burger and linked his fingers, resting his hands on his stomach as he leaned back on the soft leather seat. A smug smile appeared on his face. "The stage is yours."

"Born in west London and travelled the world because of your father's job as a top-ranking diplomat. When you hit eighteen you joined the British Army and rose to the rank of captain in the Grenadier Guards. On promotion to major, you transferred to the Army Air Corps for a few years before leaving in your mid-thirties to study archaeology at the University of Oxford."

"That's all on my CV, or *resumé* as you might say. All public."

"After less than one year working at Carmarthen College you were poached by Juliette Bonnaire at UNESCO."

"I prefer talent-spotted, or at a push, head-hunted."

"Tell me, Dr Hunter," Rorschach interrupted. "Deep down in that Iraqi tomb, you weren't searching for a winged statue by any chance?"

Hunter stopped eating and stared over at him. "I'm sorry?"

"A winged statue, Dr Hunter. A larger version of the tiny carvings on the pommels of these daggers?"

Hunter fought hard not to look surprised, but stopping body language leaks was almost impossible. From Rorschach's grin, he knew he had failed. "As a matter of fact, I was – and I found it, too. I held it in my own two hands until it was stolen from me by a relic-thieving bastard called Brodie McCabe. Now I doubt I'll ever see it again."

"I wouldn't be so sure if I were you," he said. "Did it happen to look anything like this?"

Rorschach clicked a button on the table and a projection screen slid down on the wall beside them. When a giant image of a winged statue exactly as he had seen in Mosul appeared on it, Hunter stared at it and blew out a deep breath. "One of the three Winged Guardians of Atlantis Plato referred to in his *Diocles*. Where did you get this picture?"

"This is a photograph of what I call the Acassuso Idol."

"Why Acassuso?"

"It's the name of the suburb in Buenos Aires where it was recently discovered."

"Buenos Aires? What the hell was it doing down there?"

"We have no evidence yet, but our working hypothesis is that the statue was taken down to Argentina on the Nazi ratlines during the end of the second world war. We certainly know it was in the possession of the Reich from 1942 until the fall of Berlin and then smuggled out of the country."

"This is unbelievable."

"The statue then went missing for a very long time. Recently I received a gift of these daggers and the photos from an acquaintance of mine in Cuba. He wants to sell me this statue."

"And where did this acquaintance get it from?"

Rorschach paused. "Not long ago, the Buenos Aires police raided the home of an antiquities collector by the name of Eduardo Cavallo, following allegations he was trafficking stolen artifacts from the Middle East."

"Did you know about any of this?" Hunter asked Kirsten.

She shook her head. "No, I did not. I thought the Foundation dealt only with proper, official sources when making its purchases."

Rorschach gave her a patronizing look, then continued. "The police got a shock when they searched his warehouse and found a hidden basement with over two hundred relics from the Nazi regime, including original swastika flags, a bronze Nazi eagle sculpture and several busts of Adolf Hitler. I suspect the winged statue, not to mention many other artifacts including the daggers, were among the hoard, but Cavallo unloaded them before the raid."

"So let me get this straight," Hunter said. "A man in Cuba claimed he got the daggers and the statue from an unknown source in Argentina?"

"In Buenos Aires." Rorschach repeated casually as he picked up an olive wood lobster mallet and began smashing open one of the claws. "And he sent me the daggers as a taster."

"I should have been told about this," Kirsten said.

"You are my maps expert, not my statues expert and I already explained this was a personal transaction."

Hunter decide to break the tension. "The Nazis must have found them in the Middle East. Or on their North Africa campaign, and smuggled it out of Europe at the end of the war to keep it out of the Allies' hands. Tell me, who is this mysterious Cuban acquaintance who wants to sell you the winged statue? Is he a *bona fide* collector or black market?"

The Swiss man chuckled. "He got a Nazi stash from an artifact thief who was raided by the Argentine Police, Dr Hunter. What do you think?"

Hunter grinned. "And here I was thinking Oskar Rorschach was always on the level."

"Me too," Kirsten said with disappointment.

Rorschach shrugged and sipped more wine.

"Who is this Cuban?" Hunter asked.

Rorschach hid behind his wine glass. "I trust the hamburger is to your liking?"

Hunter took another bite of it. "It's excellent."

Rorschach nodded enthusiastically. "I knew it would be. Chef Marcel is a genius. Wagyu beef, seared *foie gras* and black truffle shavings. All enjoyed with this outstanding 1995 Chateau Petrus, Bordeaux's finest."

"You're spoiling me, Oskar, but I'd still like to know the identity of the Cuban dealer trying to flog you the winged statue."

The Swiss billionaire took a long swig from his glass of Merlot and let the silence stretch into minutes.

"Who's the seller, Rorschach?" Hunter asked impatiently.

Kirsten started to speak, but Rorschach stopped her with a polite wave of his hand. "The statue in the Nazi photograph is in the possession of a man named Raul Vazquez. He is a Cuban collector who has a reputation for employing any means necessary to acquire new pieces, and he doesn't part with them easily."

"So what make you think he wants to sell it to you?" Hunter asked.

Rorschach smiled. "On a recent visit to Mexico, Klara found out that Mr Vazquez has run into some big problems regarding a major fraud trial. The nature of his business means cash flow is sometimes an issue and right now he needs money."

"He needs money?" Hunter asked.

"Lots of it, and fast," Rorschach said. "The competition between Raul and I when it comes to collecting antiquities is no secret among those who know us both, but this time I think he will roll over and sell me the statue. The problem is, he's not above having a fake one manufactured and selling it to me instead of the original you see in this picture."

"Which is where I come in," Hunter said. "I'm beginning to join the dots."

"But you must be careful," Rorschach said. "Raul is a criminal. He's one of the biggest collectors of antiquities and relics in the world and most of his collection was acquired illegally. Bribery, blackmail, theft – even murder – are all part of his arsenal. Ironically, we think this is one of the rare times our Cuban friend actually paid fairly for a piece. He claims he paid the smuggler over a million dollars for it."

Hunter whistled. "That's a lot of cigars."

"He wants three million for it," Rorschach said casually. "That's even more cigars."

"That's a lot of money."

Rorschach sipped his wine. "Yes, but it's the only way we can get that winged statue out of his possession. He claims there is a map, too, hence Dr Anderson's participation in this evening's banquet."

"A map?" Kirsten asked.

"A Nazi map, but he would say no more. I don't yet know the significance of the map, but he paid another half million for it, so I'm guessing it's going to lead to even more valuable artifacts. We need to move fast. We surely can't be the only ones who know about this. Half of the black market is going to want to get hold of that statue, and I'm certain the American FBI may be involved."

"The FBI?" Hunter said. "I don't like the sound of this."

Rorschach nodded, mouth full of lobster. "I believe a separate shipment going to another dealer was recently intercept by the FBI in Miami, so they're out there all right. If this is true, then we're talking about a race, Dr Hunter. A race between the Rorschach Foundation and the FBI. They will hide the treasures away forever, but it is my intention to put them into public view by handing them over to UNESCO."

Hunter gave him a double-take. "That's very generous."

"I would own them, of course."

"Naturally. But wait, I thought this Vazquez was bankrupt or something? If so, how did he buy the daggers from Cavallo?"

Rorschach laughed. "You are very perceptive. These daggers were sold to us months ago, long before the Cuban Government froze Raul's assets."

"Got it."

Rorschach pushed away his plate and looked at Hunter and an increasingly uncomfortable-looking Kirsten Anderson. "I think with the existence of these statues and their inscriptions, we can make a prima facie case for a total rethink on the subject of antediluvian civilizations, and more specifically Atlantis."

"Which is still a major shock to me," Kirsten said.

Hunter pushed his napkin away. "So when do I leave?"

"You leave immediately," said Rorschach. "You and Dr Anderson, of course."

"Oh, no," he said. "I travel and work alone."

"Not this time," Rorschach said. "You will verify the statue as authentic, but Dr Anderson is required to authenticate the map. Not only that, but only she is authorized to purchase them from Vazquez. She must be there with you or the deal is off."

Hunter thought about telling him where to get off, but this was bigger than any of that. Rorschach was offering him the chance to solve the greatest mystery in human history. Atlantis.

"Seems fair enough," he conceded at last. "Where in Cuba?"

"Old Havana," Rorschach said.

Kirsten looked at him over the top of her glasses. "Don't tell me, you know it?"

"It's a UNESCO world heritage site, Dr Anderson. So yes."

Rorschach caught them scowling at one another and laughed. "I think this could be the start of a beautiful relationship! Now, go take my private jet to Cuba."

# CHAPTER TEN

Hunter woke up and stretched his long legs. Turned out, getting shot at by rogue Iraqi soldiers wasn't as easy as it looked. He had bruises all over his legs and hip, not to mention two or three cuts and grazes on his arms and elbows and chin. He was just contemplating going straight back sleep when Kirsten appeared in the aisle.

"I thought you might like a cup of coffee."

"Thanks," he said.

"Drink up, we're almost there. You slept nearly the entire flight."

"I guess I needed it."

She crashed down in the seat opposite him and put her coffee down on the table. "We didn't get a chance to talk properly back there. Oskar can be a little serious."

"I'm sure he's the life and soul of the party."

She rested her chin on the back of her hand. "He's not so bad when you get to know him."

"You were upset that he kept you in the dark over the statue?"

She nodded. "You could say that. It's unlike him."

"Tell me," Hunter said. "How long have you worked at the Rorschach Foundation?"

"Three months."

"That's not a long time. Where were you before?"

She sipped her coffee. "I worked for the Smithsonian in Washington DC."

He regarded her with admiration. "Wow."

She raised an eyebrow. "He hires only the very best."

"I can see that. You seemed sceptical when we were talking about Atlantis. I take it you're not a believer?"

"I am not, no. It amazes me anyone can be."

"Why do you say that?"

"It just seems so far-fetched."

"You saw the daggers."

"But isn't it possible they could be from another ancient civilization?"

"Maybe," he said, his voice trailing. "But I hope not."

She blinked in the soft cabin light. "This is really important to you, isn't it?"

"Finding Atlantis has been my dream for most of my life."

"And you're not worried if people think you're a crank?"

He paused and thought about how to reply. "I don't care what other people think and I never have done. I think Atlantis was real, and some sort of hub civilization joining all the other ancient ones together. Just because archaeologists have never been able to link the ancient cultures of the Americas with those of Sumer or Egypt, doesn't mean it's impossible."

"No?"

"There are many unexplained coincidences."

"Such as?"

"Such as carvings in South America with a striking resemblance to those of ancient Egypt. Something must have acted as a bridge and linked these cultures together, and it's my belief that 'something' was Atlantis. All I have to do is find it."

The pilot announced they were ten minutes out and should buckle up ready for landing.

"And that journey begins now," Kirsten said.

"Absolutely."

He watched as the small jet touched down on Cuban soil and after the usual hassles at customs, the two new colleagues were standing outside in the stifling heat looking for their driver.

"Are you certain one is booked?" he asked.

She tutted. "Yes, because I'm the one who booked it. Ah – here he is now."

A man in a chauffeur's cap drove an idling black Mercedes over to the kerb, pulled the handbrake up and hopped out of the car. "Are you Dr Anderson?"

"I am."

The man looked genuinely upset. "I am Miguel from Car Cuba. I'm sorry I was not here to meet you in the arrivals lounge, but there was traffic on the way."

"You're here now," she said as he popped the trunk and wheeled their bags around to the back of the car.

Hunter opened the rear door. "After you."

"You're a true English gent," she said sarcastically.

The car rocked when the driver slammed down the trunk. He walked around and climbed inside and turned on the engine and AC unit. "Welcome to Cuba. I hope the car isn't too hot for you. It will cool down when we get going."

He pulled out of the airport and began cruising toward the capital city. Hunter counted the years since his last visit to Havana and realized grimly it was almost twenty-five. A different time, back then. Just him and Avril backpacking around the Caribbean for a few months. Cheap motels and rum and long nights on the beach.

A lot had changed since then. Avril was gone, and he'd worked hard to build a career spanning two regiments in the British Army, an Oxford archaeology doctorate and now a great job at UNESCO. Cuba had changed too. A raft of economic reforms in the early nineteen-nineties had reduced the deficit and grown exports to many countries all over the world.

"Everything looks different," he said, but there was no reply. He turned and saw Kirsten was asleep, her head lolling gently on the rear headrest. Without her glasses, he saw more clearly the way her brown eyelashes curled gently toward the rise of her cheekbones and made her look younger.

As the driver pulled up outside a large villa, Hunter thought he heard her mumble something through her slightly partly red lips. He nudged her awake. "We're here."

Her eyes flicked open and she stared at him with sleepy, jet-lagged eyes. "Sorry?"

"We're at Vazquez's mansion," he said, nodding past the driver at the large black iron gates in front of the car. "And by the looks of things, crime pays."

"Like Oskar said back in Switzerland," she said, fumbling in her bag for her glasses. "Be careful what you say in here. Sounds like Raul Vazquez is a dangerous man."

"I'll bear that in mind, but I can get pretty tetchy myself, especially after a long flight."

She looked at him over the rim of her glasses. "Max?"

"Yes?"

"Do try and take this seriously. We're talking about a three million dollar purchase for the Rorschach Foundation and doing a deal with a known gangster."

"You know me," he said with a broad smile, then added, "Actually you don't."

"No, but I'm starting to get the picture."

The gates swung open and the driver turned in the seat. "Are we going in?"

"Drive on, please," Kirsten said. "We don't want to keep Señor Vazquez waiting."

"No," the driver muttered. "You really don't."

# CHAPTER ELEVEN

The car swept around a large circular drive and pulled up outside the sprawling property's main portico entrance. The driver opened their doors and they emerged into the shade of a dozen royal palm trees. A man in a black suit stepped out of the house and greeted them. He had long hair tied back in a ponytail and a sharp, tanned face.

"Dr Anderson and Dr Hunter?"

"That's us," Hunter said. "How could you tell?"

Kirsten gave him a look and elbowed him. Turning to the man, she gave him a million dollar smile and Hunter was once again struck by her beauty. "It's a pleasure to meet you Señor Vazquez."

He laughed. "You are mistaken, Dr Anderson. My name is Mario Davila, I work for Señor Vazquez."

"I'm so sorry."

"Think nothing of it. Please, if you follow me I will take you to the artifacts. I know Señor Vazquez is very keen to make a mutually acceptable deal with Mr Rorschach."

They stepped up to join him and he showed them into a small room at the side of the house. The dark wood floorboards were polished to a sheen and potted fan palms swished back and forth under the downdraft of a vintage windmill ceiling fan, gently whirring above their heads.

Davila walked into a small room just out of sight and returned with the winged statue and a rolled-up map in his hands. "Here, do your thing, Dr Hunter."

Hunter unrolled the map and cast his eyes on it. "I'm no expert, but it looks real. Dr Anderson?"

Kirsten took a jeweller's loupe from her pocket and leaned over the desk to study the map in silence. After gently moving the small magnifying glass over the surface of the war-era map, she stood up and slipped the loupe back in her pocket. "Without a doubt, this looks like a genuine Nazi stamp and the age seems to correlate with the story. I'm not prepared to go further at this stage without chemical analysis but I can say with confidence Mr Rorschach will not be disappointed."

Davila smiled. "And the statue?"

Hunter lifted the winged statue cautiously. On a quick surface inspection, it was almost identical to the one he had found in the desert tomb outside Mosul. His head filled with memories of McCabe and the soldiers hunting him through the labyrinth.

"Let me see." He turned it over in his hands. It felt strange holding one of the three Winged Guardians so soon after McCabe had snatched the other one from him.

"Is it real?" Kirsten asked.

"It's real," he said. "But that's different from authentic. You know that, right?"

She sighed. "You know what I mean, Max."

"I need time." He turned it again, studying every carving, symbol, chip.

"Like the other one, this one has a sickle hanging from its belt. That's a good start."

"What's the significance?" she asked.

Davila sighed and leaned on the edge of the desk, slipping a toothpick between his teeth and folding his arms over his chest.

"When carving kings, the Assyrians sometimes gave them a sickle as a weapon to fight monsters. The mace on the other side of the belt represents the supreme god Ashur. The thing that's got me is that the inscription is obviously pre-early Assyrian Empire, and by a long way, by the looks of it."

"What do you mean?"

"Pictograms and alphabets evolve very slowly over time. Think about how we can read Latin script carved into tablets or buildings from two thousand years ago. With very few exceptions, it's basically the same alphabet – the same letters. These are so different from early Assyrian or Egyptian glyphs that we're talking thousands of years older, exactly like the ones I saw on the statue in the tomb at Nineveh."

"So it's authentic?" she asked.

Aware of the heavy responsibility he had to get the assessment right, he paused and took another lingering look at the statue in his hands. "The inscription is very similar in content and exactly the same in style. The size and weight are the same. It looks like the same age, and the strange rosy silver it's made from is the same. In my opinion, we just found the second of the three guardians."

Davila pulled the toothpick out of his mouth and flicked it into the bin behind the desk. "In which case, I will call Señor Vazquez and let him know the good news."

Hunter and Kirsten stood awkwardly near the window while Davila called his boss. The two men spoke in hushed Spanish for several moments and then Davila put the phone down and addressed them.

"He is very happy they have been authenticated by two such eminent experts in their fields, but he has changed his mind about the price. If Mr Rorschach wants to bring these items into his collection, he will have to pay much more for them."

Kirsten held her breath. She had been prepared for something like this. "How much more?"

"The new price is ten million dollars."

She gasped. "But Señor Vazquez made a deal! He said he would sell the winged statue and the map for three million American dollars."

Davila was unmoved by her pleas. "And now Señor Vazquez has modified the deal. He will sell you the items, but for ten million dollars."

Hunter winced. "That's not a fair price."

Davila stared at Kirsten with dark, unblinking eyes. "Well? What's it to be, Dr Anderson?"

Kirsten pushed her glasses up the bridge of her nose and contemplated the new deal Vazquez had put to her. "I'm authorized to go to ten million, but no higher."

Hunter looked at her, astonished. "Ten million? I wish that son of a bitch McCabe hadn't taken the one I found even more, now! I could sell it to Oskar and retire."

Davila spoke on the phone with his boss, nodded and ended the call.

"Is he accepting the ten million dollars?" Kirsten asked.

"It turns out Señor Vazquez no longer wants to sell the items."

Hunter huffed out a laugh. "Is he bloody kidding? We flew all the way out from Switzerland to verify them and now he doesn't want to sell them anymore!"

"But why not?" Kirsten asked. "Now he knows they're authentic."

"Because if you're willing to pay so much for them, they must have a far higher value and he wants to know what that might be."

Hunter checked his watch. "This has been a total waste of my time. If we hurry we can get the last flight back to Switzerland. I can get a flight back to Paris in the morning when we land."

"I'm afraid that's not going to happen either."

Hunter's expression grew darker. "Why not?"

Davila's response shocked them both. With no fuss or warning, he gently reached inside his jacket and pulled out a Beretta 92. Lifting it until it was pointing at Kirsten's face, a greasy smile broke on his face. "Because you're coming with me and the statue and the map. We're going on a ride together."

Kirsten couldn't hide her shock. "You can't take us prisoner!"

"I think I just did. Canosa, get in here."

A man in a trilby slipped into the room. He was holding a Makarov pistol, waist-height and an unlit cigarette was hanging from his lower lip. "You called, boss?"

"Get the car."

"Si."

Hunter's eyes drifted from the barrel of the Beretta up to the face of the man training it on Kirsten. "Where are we going? Somewhere nice, I hope."

"As a matter of fact, yes. We're going to see Señor Vazquez on his yacht. Now get moving."

Armed men forced their captives out of the house and down some concrete steps into the drive-under garage. One of them pushed an oily red button on the wall and activated a double-width roller door. As it creaked slowly upwards, a strong warm breeze blew in from outside and the smell of exhaust fumes mingled with engine oil.

Davila walked down the steps and joined them in the garage. He had slipped a linen jacket on over the top of his black shirt, but the grip of his Beretta in the shoulder holster was still partially visible when the breeze blew the hem of his jacket back. On the drive out front, more armed men were milling around.

Davila spoke to Canosa. "The Oceanus is out in the Straits so we'll need to use the tender. It's in the Hemingway Marina."

"Where's that?" Kirsten asked Hunter, keeping her voice down.

"It's out in Santa Fe," he whispered. "It's a massive marina made up of four separate canals. Many people who like to cruise spend the entire winter there."

"Keep your mouths shut," Davila said. "Unless I tell you to speak. You're not on a little UNESCO field trip anymore. Canosa, tie their hands."

"There's no need for any of this," Kirsten said. "We're academics."

"You maybe, but not him." Davila looked at Hunter. "Everyone knows all about the famous archaeologist Max Hunter, and that includes the fact he was once a soldier. Their hands, Canosa. Bind them tightly."

"Just the way I like it," Hunter said with a wink, but Kirsten was too scared to indulge him.

Davila ordered them both into the car. It was now Hunter saw the dead body of their driver, Miguel, slumped over the wheel of his car with a gunshot in his temple. Rage was rapidly replaced by a sense of calm; this was a highly dangerous situation and he had to keep his wits about him.

They climbed inside the car and Davila slid in beside them. He pulled his gun a second time and pushed the muzzle of the Beretta into Kirsten's midriff. "I am willing to bet good money that if I fire this gun it will go through you and end up burying itself in Dr Hunter's stomach. My advice is, don't do anything to make me squeeze the trigger."

"Sounds like good advice to me," Hunter said. "I promise to be a good lad until it's a fair fight."

Davila smirked. "Drive on, Canosa. Take us down to the marina."

# CHAPTER TWELVE

Gabriela Batista passed her binoculars to the man sitting next to her and thought about what she had just witnessed. Down under the dashboard, the AC unit rattled and hummed as the man raised the field glasses to his eyes and studied the people on the marina.

"Interesting," he said.

"That's what I thought. You were right, Gomez. They must be taking them out to the yacht. The man in the hat is holding the statue you told me about."

"Yeah," he said, chewing on a cocktail stick. "They're taking everything over to that bastard Vazquez. You want to go out there and see what's happening?"

"Are you kidding? Not even a storm could stop me going out there."

Gomez winked at her. "But we wait till dark, right?"

"You think I'm crazy? Of course we wait till dark."

"How long is that around here?"

The sun was low on the horizon "An hour."

"Then we haven't got long to get a boat."

"Relax, I already told you I know someone."

She threw the car into drive and cruised down a road running alongside one of the slipways. Parking up, they stepped out into the cool of the evening and took in the view. Sailing boats' masts rattled in the breeze and seagulls cried and wheeled in the sky.

"Time for some reconnaissance," said Gomez, scanning the horizon for any sign of Vazquez's men. Behind him, Gabriela spoke with an old friend about hiring his boat for the night.

*

"I'm sorry I got you into this," said Kirsten to Hunter as the tender cut across the turquoise Straits of Florida. Up ahead, on the horizon, the outline of the Oceanus appeared like a large white citadel. The American woman stared at the helipads, deck guns and towering smoke funnels with sad, blue eyes. "If I had known this was going to happen I would have advised Oskar not to send us here. He said Vazquez was dangerous, but I thought we would be safe. I guess I was wrong."

"Don't beat yourself up about it," Hunter said, glancing back at the relative safety offered by the Hemingway Marina. "We're not dead yet."

The boat skipped over the waves. At the front, Davila and Canosa shared a laugh and smoked.

Hunter turned back to Kirsten. "I never told anyone outside of the regiment about this, but once when I was on patrol in Afghanistan one of my platoon stood on an IED. It blew his legs off. The smoke hadn't even cleared when we came under sustained sniper fire so we had to drag him through the crossfire to get him to safety."

"I've heard stories like this before."

He nodded. "We lost him. Blood loss was just too great, but during the fire fight two more of my men were snatched by the enemy. We found their bodies the next day, hogtied in a ditch and…" he stopped talking. "Sorry, I've already said too much. We caught up with the men who had killed them and took them all out."

"Why are you telling me this?"

"I'm saying I think I can handle these clowns, so take it easy. They only need to make one slip, and…" he drew his finger across his throat to indicate what was on his mind.

She was shocked by the casual way he had described killing these men, but before she could respond, Hunter stared up at the giant vessel in disbelief. "Bloody hell, that's a cruise ship!"

"A *private* cruise ship," she said quietly. "A superyacht."

He leaned in closer to her and squinted at the stern of the boat. "What flag is that?"

"Liberian. It's a flag of convenience," Kirsten said. "All ships have to be registered to a country, so people like Vazquez use the countries with the weakest labor laws. They do it so they can pay the people they employ onboard as little as possible. Nearly half the ships in the world are registered to just three countries – Panama, Liberia and the Marshall Islands."

Hunter had been vaguely aware of the arrangement. "But Vazquez can still be prosecuted for his crimes even though he's in international waters, right?"

"In the end, sure. But by staying out here and moving around on the high seas in a Liberian vessel, he's making it has hard as possible for the Cuban and American authorities to get hold of him. Meanwhile, he gets on with the serious business of intimidating jurors and bribing witnesses in the trial Oskar talked about."

"Nice."

She turned to him, lowering her voice. "What do you think Vazquez has planned for us?"

He looked off the port bow. They had fallen into the Oceanus's massive shadow and Canosa was bringing the tender about. He steered the small boat up to the starboard side of the enormous ship and cut the engine. As some men up on the deck operated a davit crane to winch them on board, Hunter looked into Kirsten's eyes. "I don't know. What do you think he has in store for us?"

"Nothing good, I promise you that."

Davila shouted at her in Spanish and grabbed hold of her by the collar, dragging her to her feet. "Shut up and get on board!"

Hunter got to his feet. "You leave her alone, you bastard."

Canosa struck his neck with the grip of his pistol, knocking him down into the boat's floor. The blow felt like someone had driven a metal spike into him. He fought to stay conscious, but dizzy and disoriented, a wave of nausea overtook him and he threw up in the boat.

Canosa kicked him in the ribs and swore in Spanish. "Get up out of that vomit, you dog."

Davila was now on the private cruise ship's deck with Kirsten. "Did he just throw up in the boss's tender?"

"Yes." Canosa pushed Hunter out of the boat and he crashed down on the Oceanus's deck.

"Make sure it's cleaned immediately."

"Maybe this dog should lick it up?" Canosa said, snarling at Hunter.

"This dog has an appointment with Mr Vazquez, just like his bitch. You clean it up, Canosa, and pray I don't tell the boss how you beat this man and made him throw up in his tender."

"Yes, sir." Canosa backed down and told one of his men to get a mop and bucket.

"This way," Davila said.

They followed him into the yacht and down a long corridor before climbing a set of plush, carpeted steps.

Raul Vazquez received them like a renaissance king. He was sitting on a large velvet and gold seat at the head of a long polished table. The table was empty except for a single gold plate full of food and beside it, one gold candlestick. Vazquez reached over and lit the ivory-colored candle with a gold lighter and sat back in his chair. He wore an onyx black shirt of freshly pressed Sea Island cotton and his expensive aftershave radiated away from him like an aura.

Hunter lowered his voice and leaned closer to Kirsten. "You think this guy knows that all that glitters is not gold?"

"Ah, Mario!" Vazquez said. "I see you have brought my guests to me! Please, take a seat. You really must try this meal."

"I'd rather stand," Hunter said. "If it's all the same to you."

Vazquez made no movement. "You are missing something exquisite. It's premium beef and rock lobster with winter black truffles and Umbrian porcini mushrooms. The entire dish is served beneath a beautiful pie crust delicately covered in Florentine gold leaf."

Kirsten looked disgusted. "I think that's what they eat in Regla."

Hunter turned to her briefly, but held his tongue when Vazquez started laughing.

"Ah, the ghetto. Perhaps you should go there and tell them this pie costs ten thousand American dollars to make."

"That's nearly a quarter of a million pesos, you bastard."

"A man who is a king, must live like one to prove it. Now, why is the Rorschach Foundation willing to pay such a ridiculous sum of money for a small silver statue and an old torn Nazi map?"

Hunter and Kirsten exchanged a lingering look.

"What's the matter, cat got your tongue?"

"The Rorschach Foundation doesn't discuss its business," she said sharply.

Vazquez tutted and waved his gold knife at them. "Not good enough. Perhaps you need some time to think over my proposal."

"What proposal?" Hunter asked.

"That you tell me the truth about the winged statue and the map or I will throw you to the sharks circling this ship. Mario, take them both to the brig. I wish to finish my meal in peace – just me and this strange, winged angel Oskar Rorschach seems to covet so much."

*

Gomez sailed the boat out of the marina and headed north toward the straits. They ploughed onwards, seawater spraying up off the bow. "I should have known something like this was going to happen," he said. "I'm sorry it's all gone shit-shaped, Gabby."

"It's my fault, not yours," she said.

Gomez gently pushed the tiller and steered the boat west of the yacht. "I told you he wouldn't cause any trouble and that robbing Hunter and Anderson would be a walk in the park. Look at what happened."

"It's nothing. We just got unlucky. It happens to everyone."

He huffed out a sour laugh. "Tell me about it. Did I ever tell you about the time I was on a mission in the Gulf of Guinea?"

"No, I don't think so."

"We were protecting a team of oil explorers from the pirates who operate in that area and we got *real* unlucky."

"What happened?"

"I was on board a small ship shuttling employees and equipment out to an offshore drilling rig. We'd had a briefing in the HQ back in Accra and thought we could handle it, but when the pirates turned up, their force was three times bigger than we thought. We knew we had to call in for backup but we lost our satellite comms at the exact second the pirates came into view."

"Maybe they cut the signal?" she said. "Seems like too much of a coincidence."

"We lost a lot of good men that day, so there was an enquiry. It *was* a coincidence. In other words we just got unlucky."

"And the pirates?"

"They didn't make it home that night. Burial at sea."

She fell silent, and the rest of the trip out to the ship went without a hitch. Gomez steered the small skiff around to the bow and pulled in tight. When he was close enough, he lashed a rope around the starboard anchor chain and stopped the boat from drifting.

In the black night, the boat bobbed about on the water while he tested the anchor chain. When he was satisfied it was safe, he put his bag over his shoulder and climbed up the chain toward the anchor well. Halfway up, he smelt cigarette smoke and heard men on the deck talking in Spanish. He gave Gabriela the signal to stay where she was and tucked his head down until he felt the cold carbon-manganese chain on his cheek.

His heart beat harder in his chest. He knew how vulnerable they both were, hanging from an anchor chain. One false step that gave them away and Vazquez's men would take them out like fish in a barrel. He calmed down when he caught the amber flash of a cigarette butt sailing past him. It twisted down to the water and then the conversation on the deck above him fell silent.

*How the hell did I wind up here?* he thought.

He reached the anchor well and climbed inside and waited for Gabriela. He felt another ripple of relief when he saw her face appear at the top of the chain. He reached out and took her hand and helped her up. It felt like they had been out half the night, but when he checked his watch he saw the entire trip had only taken twelve minutes.

"I can't believe I talked myself into this," he said.

"You want the map and statue, don't you?"

"More than anything, but I don't want to die in the process."

Safely inside the anchor well, she kissed his cheek. "No one's going to die. Now, let's get moving."

# CHAPTER THIRTEEN

"So this is what a brig looks like."

Hunter looked over to Kirsten as she paced up and down her cell. There were two cells, divided by a wall of bars, and he was in the other one. "You like it?"

"Trust a psycho like Vazquez to build a jail in his floating palace."

"It's standard for big vessels like this, even cruise ships. They always have somewhere on board where they can keep unruly passengers just in case things get out of hand. These things go out to sea for weeks sometimes. You get people making trouble and you need somewhere to put them."

"I never really thought about it."

"It's usually like this – a couple of steel rooms below decks next to the security officer's cabin. You wind up in one, you get escorted off the ship at the next port and that's the end of your little cruise. On the high seas, the captain is judge and jury, believe me."

"You sound like you know a lot about it. Don't tell me you've been on one before."

He laughed. "Nah, not me, but a good pal of mine worked the cruise liners for a long time."

"And did your friend ever tell you how to escape from one of these places?"

"There's no escape. We're inside a room made of steel, and we're sitting in here twiddling our thumbs until Vazquez orders our release."

Kirsten checked her watch and continued pacing. "I can't stand just sitting here waiting for the axe to fall."

"Stop walking up and down, will you? You're making me dizzy."

"Sorry."

Hunter's eyes met hers through the bars dividing their cells. "How did you know about Regla?"

"Excuse me?"

"Back when Vazquez was stuffing his face with that pie and bragging about how much his dinner cost, you said something sarcastic. You said that's what they eat in Regla."

"Did I? I guess I was just angry. Why?"

"I thought you told me you'd never been to Cuba before , that's all."

She paused and furrowed her brow. "And I haven't. What is this, the third degree?"

He raised his palms. "I didn't mean anything by it, take it easy. It was just an observation."

"If you must know, I read about it on the plane journey here."

Hunter felt a ripple of guilt. "I'm sorry. I went to Regla when I was younger with my girlfriend and I just wondered how you knew about it."

"Rorschach Foundation employees do not arrive at a meeting without being very well briefed, especially one as important as that one."

"Of course."

"Damn it, I just can't get a break lately."

He saw obvious signs of the offense he had caused, and decided to change the subject when the security office door was smashed wide open. He and Kirsten jumped up from their bunks as a large man with fists as chunky as boxing gloves stormed into the room. A woman in her thirties came in behind him. She was holding a pistol in her hand, but looked nervous.

"Who the hell are you?" Kirsten said.

"My name is Gomez," the man said. "And this is Gabriela. We are thieves like you, here to take the statue and the map. If you tell me where they are I will get you out of here."

Kirsten was staring at the man when Hunter reached his arm though the bars and tapped her on the shoulder. "What were you just saying about never getting a break?"

"So you will help us?" Gomez asked.

"It's not as simple as that," Kirsten said. "First, I'm not a thief. I'm here to buy the statue and the map for ten million dollars for a very powerful man. I can't just let you steal them."

"Then let me take the map and you have the statue," shrugged Gomez. "The map is what's important to my employer. If you stay in here, Vazquez will kill you, for certain."

After a short discussion, Kirsten made the call. "All right, I can agree to that. We get the statue and you take the map."

Gomez laughed. "Then you are a thief after all, unless you are going to leave the ten million dollars behind when you take the statue?"

"Wait a minute," Hunter said. "No one said anything about stealing artifacts from Cuban relic smugglers. I work for UNESCO!"

"Can we just hurry the hell up?" Kirsten snapped at Gomez. "His men could come back any second."

"Maybe," Gomez said. "But not the two I just knocked out in the corridor outside this room. Where do you think we got the gun from?"

"Well played," Hunter said, turning to Kirsten. "I'm starting to like this guy already."

"Sure, but how are we getting off this damn ship even if we get the statue?" Kirsten asked. "I counted at least half a dozen lifeboats! If we take one and try and head back to the coast they'll be swarming all over us in seconds in the other boats."

"Maybe, maybe not," Gomez said. "But that's a chance we'll have to take." He took the keys from the desk and opened both cells. "We must work faster than this if we are to make this work."

"Then we'll start in the grand dining room," Hunter said. "That's where His Nibs was when he had the statue and map last."

"A good plan," Gabriela said.

They ran along the corridor and took the stairs up to the top deck. Being on a cruise ship with so few people on board was an eerie experience, but it made reaching the dining room without being seen much easier. Inside, Hunter scanned the room but saw no sign of the statue or the map. Vazquez's ten thousand dollar dinner was gone and the table cleared of all the golden plates and cutlery.

"Damn it," Kirsten said. "He's somewhere else on the ship."

"And so are the goodies," Hunter said.

Gabriela said, "So where do we start?"

"The ship's too big to search," said Gomez. "Believe me, I've done my research. We need to find someone and persuade them to tell us."

"Too late, scum."

They turned and saw two men moving toward them with pistols.

Kirsten arched an eyebrow. "Looks like our departure from the brig has been noted."

"Put your hands up and shut up," one of the men snarled. "And get out into the corridor."

Hunter led the way, arms raised. He was surprised to see how close the men with the guns were letting them get as they approached the door. When he was at the right distance, he and Gomez shared a look. Both men knew what the other was thinking.

Hunter moved first, piling his shoulder into the first man and bringing his hands down in one fluid movement. The man tried to fire but Hunter knocked the gun from his hand, powered a jab into his jaw and decked him. As his victim crashed into the floor, he turned to see Gomez lashing out with his gnarled fists at the other man. He caught the side of his face, breaking his jaw and blasting him back onto the dining table.

He struggled to get up, but Gomez grabbed hold of him and with two big bunches of his shirt in his fists, he propelled him down the length of the polished table. He flew off the end and smashed headfirst into Vazquez's golden throne.

As he staggered to his feet, Gomez was there to help him up. Taking hold of another two big fistfuls of his shirt, he spun him around and wrapped his arms around his neck until he had him in a dangerous bearhug. Squeezing his throat until the man started croaking, he leaned in close to his ear and said, "Where did Vazquez take the statue and the map?"

The Havana gangster was out of his depth. He struggled and squirmed in Gomez's muscly arms, desperately trying to pull them away from his neck as his face turned purple. "I don't know…"

Gomez strengthened his grip. "I'll keep squeezing till your eyes pop out, you dog. Where are they?"

"All right," he gasped. "He had Davila put them in the ship's safe."

"And where is that?"

"On this deck at the bow, in Señor Vazquez's private penthouse suite."

"And where the hell is that?"

The man slipped into unconsciousness and slumped to the floor. "Sorry," Gomez said. "Guess I don't know my own strength."

"We can ask directions along the way," Hunter said. "Let's move."

They left the dining room and jogged silently through the ship toward the bow, peering into rooms along the way in the hope of finding someone. When they reached the top deck and were approaching the bridge, their luck changed.

"There!" Gabriela said. "One of the ship's crew."

Up ahead, a man in a smart suit was holding some freshly pressed and folded towels and walking with purpose along the starboard deck. They ducked inside one of the cabins until he passed, and then Hunter threw his arm out, grabbed his neck and yanked him inside the room.

Throwing him up against the wall, Hunter said, "Easy way or hard way?"

Gabriela saw the confusion on his face and repeated the question in Spanish. "He says easy way."

"Where is Vazquez's penthouse suite?"

The man rattled off the directions and then Hunter gave him a look of apology. "Buenos noches, amigo."

The punch was enough to knock him out in one clean blow. Hunter dragged him over to the bed and stretched him out with his head beneath the pillows. "Let's get going."

# CHAPTER FOURTEEN

The walk-in strongroom vault in Vazquez's study was a monster of steel and iron favored by art collectors and bullion dealers. Manufactured by SafeGuard, the vault was impossible to break open unless you had the combination. As Gabriela watched Gomez fumble with the dial combination lock, she prayed the intel the unconsciousness crewman lying on the floor had supplied was good. When she heard a metallic clunk and the door clicked open half an inch, she breathed a sigh of relief.

Gomez looked amazed. "It worked."

"But this guy's going to have a headache when he wakes up," Kirsten said, nudging the crewman with the toe of her shoe.

"Hurry up, Ric," Gabriela said. She was at the study door with Hunter, keeping watch down the corridor. "We haven't got long."

"Sure thing. I'm going in."

Gomez went inside the vault and gazed around at the shelves. Each of them was stuffed full of files, folders and various ancient artifacts but no sign of what they wanted. He blew out a breath, and almost forgetting to breathe, he started searching. The heavy silence of the strongroom's interior felt almost like a weight on his shoulders as he began rifling through box files and drawers. Getting inside this place was one thing, but making a proper search of it was an altogether different kettle of fish.

"There must be thousands of documents in here. Are we all cool out there?"

"Keep going," she whispered. "We're still okay."

Hunter called over. "You making any progress?"

"Not yet. It's all just regular banking stuff, loans, maybe a quarter of a million in US dollars. Not what I want."

"It's a sodding statue eight inches high!" Hunter said.

"You're forgetting about the map, Dr Hunter," said Gabriela. "We need the map, too."

"I'm doing my best," Gomez called back. "Being in this safe isn't exactly what I dreamed of as a child."

Kirsten sighed. "And standing in here with all these weird sculptures is not what I want either. There's only so many naked stone butts you can see before – wait. I hear something."

Gomez stopped and peered around the vault door. "What do you hear?"

"I thought I heard something but it was nothing. Get back in there and find it!"

Gomez was already back in the vault and going through the files on the one remaining shelf he hadn't yet searched. Rushing was a temptation, but overlooking the map in haste wouldn't help anyone. "I need another couple of minutes."

His hands worked fast, slipping in and out of the folders, leafing through files and thumbing through endless documents. Even looking for stacks of fifty dollar bills would be easier than this. The problem with a map was how easily it could be tucked inside a pile of other papers. Sifting through the last few box files, he finally found a map and punched the air.

"Yes!"

"You found it?"

"I think so." His heart pounded in his chest until he took a closer look. "No, wait."

"What's the problem?"

"No Nazi stamp, plus wrong era and wrong location. I have to keep looking."

"Good, because I don't think we've got much longer."

Another half-minute passed, then he stepped out of the vault holding a rolled-up map in his hand and wearing a big grin on his unshaven face. "Got it."

Gabriela pulled her head back out of the gap in the door and turned back to face him. "You're certain?"

"I said I had it, didn't I?"

Hunter stepped over. "And the statue?"

"There's a floor safe," Gomez said, sighing heavily and swearing in Spanish. "I can do this, wait."

"We can't do much else, pal," Hunter said.

Gomez dropped to his belly and squished something against the safe's hinges.

"Wait, what is that?" Hunter said. "Are you carrying C4?"

"One of life's staples," Gomez said. "Everyone back."

He closed the strongroom door and they all felt a deep thud as the explosives detonated inside. A wisp of smoke drifted through the crack in the door but Gomez was through it like a ferret. They all waited a long, tense ten seconds before Gomez spoke from inside the strongroom. "All right, we have the statue." He stepped back into the study and threw the statue at Kirsten. The map was already stuffed inside his belt.

She caught it in one hand and smiled. "Mine all mine."

"We need to get out of here, Ric," Gabriela said. "That explosion will have everyone up here in seconds."

They slipped out of the study and made their way along the carpeted corridor. "This place gives me the creeps. Let's go faster," Gabriela said nervously.

"We have what we came for, Gabby," Gomez said. "Just relax."

"Relax? We just broke into Raul Vazquez's private study and stole something from his strongroom. We're talking about a man who had one of his debtors decapitated after defaulting on a thousand dollar loan. What do you think he would do to us if his men caught us in here?"

"Why don't we ask him, thieving scum?"

They froze. Up ahead, Diego Canosa stepped into the corridor. He was holding a compact machine pistol, a weapon ludicrously overpowered for such a small space, and looking at them with a shit-eating grin on his pock-marked face. "I'm sure he will be very impressed when I tell him I have caught the thieves."

He took the statue and the map and shouted at them. "Now get your hands up and get moving!"

He marched them out onto the deck and up the next set of metal steps where Mario Davila was walking in their direction. When he saw them, he smiled. "You have done well, Diego. Señor Vazquez will be pleased." He looked at the prisoners' faces. When his eyes fell on Gabriela, they lingered there. Stepping closer, he ran his forefinger through the hair tumbling down from her fringe. "What have we here?"

She flinched and Gomez raised his fist.

Canosa swung the gun right up into his face. "Tut tut, big man. Step away or eat lead."

Gomez bristled and lowered his hand, taking a step back.

"So what do we do with them, boss?" Canosa pushed the muzzle of his gun into Gabriela's temple, forcing her head over to one side. "You want me to do this one right here?"

"I think not," Davila said.

"Then what?"

"I'm surprised you don't recognize her, Diego. She is Gabriela Batista, the daughter of Esteban Batista."

Canosa's face changed shape, from angry killer to shocked apprentice. "Not the judge in Señor Vazquez's trial?"

Davila grinned and lifted Maria's long brown hair away from her face to see her better. "Yes my friend, the very same. Something tells me we stand a much better chance at getting Señor Vazquez the favorable verdict he so richly deserves if he has the judge's daughter locked away some place safe."

The two men shared a belly laugh, then Davila spoke. "I know the boss will want to speak with the people who tried to break into his ship and steal his property."

"How nice of him," Gomez said.

Davila smirked. "And if you beg him, he will kill you quickly with a bullet to the head. If you do not beg him, he will turn your last few days in this world into indescribable agony. I have seen this more times than I can remember. Do not test him."

"He certainly was a real charmer when I met him earlier," Hunter said.

"He's the most dangerous psychopath in Cuba," Gabriela said, finding some courage. "He has killed hundreds of men and women who have crossed him and yet the only crime we can nail him on is simple fraud."

"And thanks to you turning up, he'll get away with that, too."

They walked them to the foredeck where Vazquez was smoking a cigar and counting the stars. When he turned and smiled, it was as if they were old friends. "Hello, amigos!"

"We caught them, sir," Davila said. "They had broken into your safe and stolen the statue and the map, just as you said they would."

Vazquez sighed. "I'm very disappointed in you, Dr Anderson. An academic with such eminent credentials stooping so low." He turned to Gomez and Gabriela. "Tell me, do you know this scum?"

Kirsten bristled at the question. "No, of course not. Who do you think I am?"

Davila glared at her for a moment and then turned to face the thieves. "It was a bad idea coming here and trying to steal from us."

"Yes, it was," Vazquez said.

"What should I do with them?"

"Take them away," Vazquez said. "Tonight we leave for Key West and when we're out in the deep water shoot the thieves and throw them to the sharks. Hunter and Anderson will accompany us into the jungle and help us find whatever has piqued Oskar Rorschach's interest so much."

"That's plain old-fashioned murder," Hunter said.

"And who will pursue such a thing? Out here on the *mare liberum* or free seas, the captain of his vessel is judge, jury and executioner. The UN convention on the Law of the Seas declares that *no state may validly purport to subject any part of the high seas to its sovereignty.* In other words, you are mine."

"That's not true at all," Kirsten said. "If you're in international waters then you're ruled by the laws of the country where the ship is registered."

Vazquez laughed. "Yes, Liberia, one of the most corrupt countries on earth. Judges there are very happy to accept bribes, Dr Anderson, and I am more than happy to bribe them. There will be no blowback from any murders on this ship."

"You son of a bitch, Vazquez!" Kirsten said, struggling in Davila's grip.

Hunter looked at her, shocked by the sudden outburst from the mild-mannered academic he had come to know over the last couple of days. "You're not going to get away with this, Vazquez," he said calmly. "Not one of you."

"I've heard it all before," Vazquez said, taking the statue and the map from Davila. "Mario, you take the professors back to the brig. Canosa, kill the two thieves. I am bored of them now."

# CHAPTER FIFTEEN

Hunter felt the barrel of Davila's machine pistol between his shoulder blades as the Havana thug marched him back down the stairs. Kirsten was just a step ahead of him, and both their hands were raised in the air.

"I thought you were supposed to be some sort of Indiana Jones character?" she said.

"Hey," he said. "I have no control over your lurid fantasies, Dr Anderson."

"Please, give me a break. This is a complete boondoggle and I need to think."

"You brought it up."

"I'm just looking at you and wondering how we could have been taken hostage twice in one night."

"I don't know," he said. "Let me think about it for a second. Oh yeah, these guys have machine pistols and we're armed with nothing but our wits."

"If we're talking about *your* wits, then heaven help us."

"I'm just saying use your loaf for a second."

"Huh?"

"Loaf of bread, *head*."

"You talk funny," she said.

"I talk funny?" he said. "What the hell does boondoggle mean?"

Her lips tightened. "We're a great team divided by a common language, right?"

"We're a *team*?" he asked. "I'm appalled."

"You two shut up," Davila shouted. "I'm sick of listening to your crap."

"Did you hear what he just said?" Kirsten said, stopping and fixing her eyes on Hunter. "He said you should shut up. I think so, too."

"Oh, you do?"

"Uh-huh."

"Get moving and go down the damn stairs!" Davila said.

Hunter saw the look in Kirsten's eyes and knew what she was doing. He turned to Davila and gave him a man-to-man smile as he blocked his view of her. "Would you let your woman talk to you like this?"

"What?"

"Like this," he said, and ducked.

Kirsten's fist appeared out of nowhere and landed with a smack in the center of Davila's face. The strike was hard enough to fracture his nose and tip him back on his heels. As he fumbled back on the steps, Hunter piled his fist onto the exact same place, knocking him clean out.

"Good work, Dr Anderson."

"Your woman? You think I'm your woman?"

"Hey, I was improvising. Work with me here!"

She shook her head but smiled. "I guess we do work kind of well together, but right now we need to get out of here. I hear men running on the deck above us."

"Agreed," Hunter said.

They made their way down the steps to the next deck. Hunter tried a door. "Let's try in here." He reached out for the cavity pull handle and slid the heavy door open. He waved Kirsten inside and then joined her, sliding the door closed behind them. They were standing inside a luxury suite set over two floors and decorated in pale blush pink and cream paint. Beyond a polished black baby grand piano, a mahogany staircase swept up to the second floor, and the entire space was dominated by a floor to ceiling window wall looking out on a calm ocean.

"Talk about an experience *de luxe*," Kirsten said with a raised eyebrow.

Hunter pushed his ear up against the door. He heard the bodyguards trampling along the thick carpeted corridor outside the cabin and froze on the spot. "They're running along the corridor. Give it a second, just to be sure." He turned and checked out the cabin. "Whoa, this is something else. And look at the size of the bed."

"It's bigger than my first apartment," Kirsten said.

Hunter looked at her with a grin. "Are you thinking what I'm thinking?"

"That we should get going and rescue those two thieves before Canosa kills them?"

"Yeah," he said. "That's what I was thinking, too."

She frowned at him. "They rescued us, Max."

"I know, but I'm not sure we're strong enough to help them."

"Don't be so modest. You were an officer in the British Army for many years."

"A guards officer and then a helicopter pilot, not a sodding commando."

"Guards training is very demanding, plus the whole world knows all about your exploits working for UNESCO. You're a famous daredevil, but apparently only when it suits your own ends."

"And just what is that supposed to mean?"

"Maybe you'd be happier saving their lives if I got some paparazzi in to record your selfless bravery?"

"It's not like that *at all*."

"Then we get the thieves first, and then the statue and map and get out of here, in that order."

"What are you, my boss?"

She looked at him like he was stupid. "Of course, I am. You're on a contract to authenticate the statue for the Rorschach Foundation. Does that make it clearer?"

He shrugged. "When you put it like that…"

"There's no other way to put it. Don't make me start calling you Dr Hunter again."

He gave her a wry smile. "All right, we can go and get the thieves."

"Good job, Max."

He gently opened the door and peered out into the corridor. It was empty, so they made their way to the end and reached a door with a porthole in it. He looked through it and saw one of the bodyguards standing on the other side, at the bottom of a stairwell. He was flicking through his phone.

"God bless modern technology," he said. "Years ago he'd have been on guard, but now he's got bored and he's cruising around on Facebook."

"So what do we do?" she asked.

Hunter calculated the door's swing area and the position of the man's head, bowed down as he stared at the phone. "This."

He kicked the door as hard as he could and smashed it into the bodyguard's head. The impact of the steel door knocked him out cold and he fell back into the stairwell, tumbling down the top few steps.

"We do that," Kirsten said. "Of course we do."

Hunter stepped into the stairwell, hauled the man up off the steps and checked his phone.

"So, was he looking at Facebook?" she asked.

He tossed the phone down on top of the unconscious man and took his gun and two spare magazines. Checking the mag inside the grip, he said, "You don't want to know what he was looking at. C'mon, let's get out of here."

They ran to the top of the stairs and emerged on one of the higher decks. "I hear a chopper," Kirsten said.

"Me too. Sounds like Vazquez might be planning on taking a flight with the goodies."

"I'm just hoping he hasn't already killed the thieves."

"Considering they're just a couple of lousy artifact smugglers, you seem to care an awful lot for them. Are you sure you don't know them?"

Kirsten straightened up and swept some hair away from her face. "As I told Mr Davila, I have never seen them before in my life, and I resent the implication that…"

In a heartbeat, several bodyguards rounded one of the lifeboat tenders and saw them standing on the deck. Without hesitating, they raised their weapons and discharged a wild blaze of gunfire on them. Hunter elbowed Kirsten hard in the chest, forcing her back inside the corridor and then returned fire, emptying the magazine in three bursts.

The barrage of fire drove the men into the cover of the lifeboat and gave Hunter the time he needed to reload. "We're not getting up to the helipad that way."

"No shit… and that hurt by the way."

"Eh?"

"When you pushed me!"

"Are you *kidding* me? I just saved your life!"

"I'll probably have a bruise for weeks."

He shook his head. "Are you for real?"

She put her hands on her hips. "And what is *that* supposed to mean?"

A bullet pinged off the top of the iron doorway and sprayed them in a shower of bright white sparks. "Maybe we could finish this conversation later?" he said.

"I see them!" Kirsten said, peering over the rail. "They're down on the deck below."

Hunter leaned over the rail and saw Gomez and Gabriela standing against the rail on the portside. They had their hands on their heads and were standing still while Diego Canosa and five other men stood in a line in front of them.

"What are they doing?" Kirsten asked.

"They're a firing squad," Hunter said, putting a new mag into the Makarov. "They're going to shoot them and push their bodies over the rail. Here, take the gun."

"Why?"

"Because you're going to cover me. This isn't a toy, Dr Anderson. It's a Makarov semi-automatic pistol and when it bites it kills. Have you ever killed a person?"

She pulled her head back and her mouth opened a little in shock. "No, I have not killed anyone! Who do you think I am?"

"I think you're someone who might have to kill a man very soon and you'd better get used to the idea."

"You really think there's a danger of that?"

"Yes, and I think there's just as much danger of you hurting yourself. Remember to keep the safety engaged just like I told you. Don't take it off unless your life is in danger, understand?"

She nodded and hooked the gun down inside her belt. "Yes – they're pointing their guns at them! We have to do something!"

Then, Canosa raised his gun and said one word that chilled their bones.

"Fire!"

# CHAPTER SIXTEEN

With no time to tell Kirsten what he planned to do, Hunter vaulted over the rail and landed on Canosa, crumpling the gangster to the deck where he landed with a thud. The aerial attack came out of nowhere and the Cuban fired his gun involuntarily out into the sea until half the mag was gone. The other men rallied and turned their guns on Hunter.

"Get off him!" one of them shouted.

Hunter climbed off the unconscious Canosa and raised his hands. Glancing at Gomez and Gabriela, both of them returned a silent nod of thanks. Seconds later, all of them jumped out of their skin when a series of shots was fired from above; bullets chewed into the deck and the men scrambled for cover.

Hunter stared up and saw Kirsten with the gun in her hand. She swept the muzzle across the deck and kept the men pinned down. "Don't just stand there, damn it!" she called out. "Get out of there! This thing's only got eight shots!"

In the chaos, the men had forgotten to take Canosa's gun. Hunter wrenched it from his unconscious grip and ran with Gomez and Gabriela away from the men to the cover of another lifeboat farther astern.

"Thank you for saving us," Gabriela said as she slammed down next to him.

"Forget about it," Hunter said. "You saved our lives and we saved yours. Now we're even."

Kirsten sprinted down the stairs and dived down beside them. "Way too hot up there," she said quickly. "Vazquez's men all over the place and I think the Bell's about to take off."

"Damn it," Gabriela said. "He still has the statue and the map!"

"We need to worry more about ourselves right now," Hunter said. "His men are regrouping and heading right for us!"

Vazquez's bodyguards advanced along the deck, firing on them in controlled but aggressive bursts. Hunter fired back, unloading Canosa's Makarov into the nearest man and killing him on the spot. He crashed down to the deck in a bloody heap as the other men dived for cover.

Hunter dropped the empty Makarov, snatched up the dying man's weapon and checked the state of the mag. The gun was a Brügger & Thomet APC9 submachine gun and the mag was over half full. Smacking it back into the weapon's body he spun around and sprayed Vazquez's men full of lead.

The weapon jerked and bucked in his grip as he swept the muzzle from side to side and took out everyone in sight. Used by personal security details, it had all the firepower and accuracy he needed to get himself and the others down to the tender and back to the coast.

"More on the way!" Kirsten leaned half out of a bulkhead door and fired on another man, planting three shots in his chest and knocking him over the rail. He crashed into the deck below with a wet crunch, bouncing once and thumping to a rest. "But not anymore!"

Hunter gave her a double take. "Good shot."

"Beginner's luck, I guess," she said, goofily waving the muzzle at him.

"Whoa! Point that thing to the ground!"

"Sorry."

"Holy crap…" Hunter's eyes rolled. "Listen, we should retreat to the stern before either they, or *you* kill one of us."

"Hey!" she said.

"Agreed," Gomez said, snatching an MP5 compact machine pistol from one of the dead men. "This way."

The Cuban thief led them past a wine bar and a two-tier restaurant on the way to the quarterdeck, but when they turned the corner they found themselves confronted by ten more armed men. They were dressed like the rest of Vazquez's personal security detail in smart black suits and polished shoes, and they were armed with concealed pistols.

"About time!" one of them shouted. "We've been waiting for you scum to steal a lifeboat tender for ages."

Hunter moved to fire his weapon, reaching down and swinging the Brügger & Thomet up into the aim. He was stopped by the sound of Gomez's MP5 as he opened fire on the men.

Kirsten took cover behind the stern of one of the tenders and joined him, firing on the men alongside Gomez until they had been reduced to a heap of shredded, blood-soaked clothes and shattered bones. Hunter took up a position of cover beside the cartographer and looked on with disbelief as the two of them killed every last man.

When the shooting had stopped, Gomez slung the MP5 over his shoulder and busied himself with the task of lowering one of the motorized tenders down into the sea. Hunter noticed Kirsten was trying to avoid him. "More beginner's luck, right?"

"I suppose it must be," she said. "The thief really did most of the work."

"Are you sure Mr Rorschach hired you just for your cartographic skills?"

"And what is that supposed to mean?"

"You know what it means."

"Quick!" Gomez called out. "More men on their way – they're climbing down the stairs from the promenade deck forward of this position. We need to get in this thing right now."

Davila was above them now, and casually dropped a grenade into the tender Gomez had lowered. When it exploded, it blasted the small boat into matchwood and embers.

"Shit," Hunter said. "Wait here."

"No!" Gabriela yelled.

"What the hell is he doing?" said Gomez.

Hunter broke cover and sprinted down the length of the deck like the devil, with the bullets of Vazquez's bodyguards nipping at his heels. As he went, he raked each of the lifeboats with lead blasting chunks out of them and blowing holes through their hulls. When the last boat was wrecked, he returned the same way, under heavy fire, and crashed down into Kirsten.

"Dr Hunter!"

"Sorry," he said, pulling his head out of her lap. "An honest mistake."

"That's the lifeboats all trashed," Gabriela said. "So what do we do now?"

Hunter grinned. "We go down to the next deck and borrow Vazquez's personal tender. Follow me."

He ran hard and dropped down through a hatch to the deck below, the Brügger & Thomet gripped in his hand and pointing ahead. Swinging around, he saw the coast was clear. "C'mon!"

The others dropped down beside him and they made for the tender, moving swiftly through the humid moonlit night until they reached their destination. Kirsten climbed in first while Hunter and Gomez kept watch. Gabriela started to climb in next, but then a shot roared from above and shocked them all. Then another round, and then a full burst of automatic fire.

"No!" cried Gomez, surging toward Gabriela.

It was too late. The bullets raked across her upper body, ripping into her stomach and chest and heart and blasting an explosive cloud of blood onto the white-painted bulkhead behind her. The Cuban woman collapsed to her knees, the life slipping from her horrified eyes by the time she crashed onto the floor.

Hunter and Kirsten shared a look of incredulity as Gomez changed course and headed for Mario Davila on the deck above.

"Get back!" the Cuban gangster yelled, grinning. "Or I shoot again!"

Gomez froze on the spot, the terrifically loud gunshot still ringing out in the confined space. "That was murder, you bastard. You just murdered an innocent woman with two kids waiting at home in their beds."

"She wasn't innocent," Davila said coolly. "She boarded this ship illegally and tried to steal my employer's personal property. She was a thief."

Gomez charged forward, but Davila raised the smoking gun once again, this time pointing it at his face. "I mean it, scumbag."

"More men on the way!" Kirsten shouted. "We have to go!"

Gomez's enraged face twisted with hate and terror as he moved his eyes from Davila to the dead woman on the deck. Suddenly, his head dropped and he made for the lifeboat, climbing in just behind Hunter who now hit the button on the davit crane and lowered it into the water.

"Kill them all!"

With the sound of Davila screaming above, they hit the water and Hunter fired up the outboard motor. Dropping the propellers into the water and turning away from the ship, his mind raced with what had just happened. He had lost the statue and the map and watched a woman's brutal cold-blooded murder.

"They're firing!" Gomez yelled. "Get down!"

Hunter increased the throttle and dipped his head down inside the tender's hull. Peering back up at the ship, he saw a dozen or more men lined up on the deck firing automatic weapons at them. The rounds pocked the rising-falling surface of the black sea all around them, but they were a moving target in the dark and already hundreds of feet away.

"I think we're away," he said at last.

"And so is Vazquez," Kirsten said.

Overhead on the far side of the ship, they saw Vazquez's chopper swoop down over the sea and head back to the Cuban coast. "There goes the statue and the map," Hunter said. "Damn it."

"We failed," Kirsten said.

"And a good woman got killed," Gomez said bitterly. "For this, Vazquez will pay with his life. I swear."

"I never even got any time to study the damn thing." Hunter smashed his fist into the side of the boat. "Just like with McCabe! And I doubt I ever will."

"That's not exactly true," said a stern-faced Gomez, rummaging around in his pocket and pulling out a Sony

RX011. The black digital camera was no bigger than a box of matches. "I have photos of the statue and the map on here, from every angle."

Hunter was shocked. "When the buggering hell did you have time to do that?"

"In the strongroom," he said. "Just in case something like this happened."

"What the hell?" Hunter said. "Let me look at the photos."

Gomez handed the camera over and the archaeologist held it away from the dashboard lights. He studied it for a few seconds as the boat rose and fell with Kirsten at the helm.

"El Salvador," he said triumphantly. "Whatever this is, it's in El Salvador. Specifically, the mountains in the east." He swiped across to the pictures of the statue.

Amy saw his frown. "What's the problem?"

"Not sure," he said. "Something's bothering me and I don't know what it is. I'll need to spend more time on it, but the map says El Salvador."

"Really?" Kirsten said.

"Sure," he said. "Don't look so surprised. There are lots of important pre-Columbian archaeological sites in El Salvador, including, most famously Tazumal, but none exactly in the location on this map. Any one of them might be hiding the third Winged Guardian."

"The question is," Kirsten said, looking out across the water, "what the hell did the Nazis want with these statues?"

Hunter handed Gomez the camera, paused and then gave them each a crooked smile. "Listen, I know something is going on here that I don't know about, and I think someone needs to start talking."

Kirsten's eyes were still looking across the water at the lights on the ship's deck and then the moonlight bouncing and dancing on the black water all around them. Turning to Hunter, she sighed. "All right, but not here and not now."

# CHAPTER SEVENTEEN

The following morning, the jet screamed away from José Martí International Airport and banked hard to the north en route to its first airway. Hunter had barely been in Cuba more than a few hours and already he was on another plane, but it was a life he knew well. He had travelled all over the world in the army, commanding men on exercise and in combat, and his archaeological career had proved to be even more adventurous.

He relaxed in his seat and stared out at the sugarcane plantations and verdant cassava fields of Pinar del Rio. A perfect golden line of beach divided the rich greens of the crops from the vibrant, sparkling blue of the sea, but there was something else on his mind. When Kirsten unbuckled her belt and gave him a smile, he decided to call her out on what she had said the night before.

"Why are you looking at me like that?" she asked.

"It's time to 'fess up, Dr Anderson."

She hesitated for a second. "I don't know what you mean."

"C'mon – back on the tender last night you told me you'd let me in on your little secret. I thought about that a lot when I was asleep last night, and what with you being so quiet today, I was wondering if you maybe changed your mind?"

Silence. Hunter unbuckled his belt and smiled at Gomez. "What about you?"

"Me?"

"Yeah, you have anything you'd like to get off your chest? I don't know Oskar Rorschach well, but I'm sure he doesn't allow Cuban thieves on his private jets, Nazi maps in their pockets or not."

Gomez looked at Kirsten, bushy eyebrows rising. "I think maybe we're busted, Amy."

The corner of Hunter's mouth twisted up into a curious smirk. "Amy?"

She glared at Gomez. "Well, we're busted *now*, thanks to you. I thought we agreed no real names?"

The big man showed his palms. "Hey, I'm just saying. This guy is onto us."

Hunter rested his forearm on the arm of the chair and leaned over toward the young woman sitting on the opposite side of the aisle. "Yeah, *Amy*. I'm onto you, so why not give me the whole story?"

She turned to the other man and sighed. "Sal, some coffee, please."

The man pushed up out of his seat and patted her on the shoulder. "Good call."

"Sal?" Hunter asked.

The man turned as he walked. "I'll let the boss explain. How do you like your coffee?"

"Dash of milk, no sugar."

"Consider it done, but you should know you're a big girl for not taking it black."

The man wandered up to the galley. Nestled in between the main exit and the cockpit, the Citation offered a compact galley capable of producing tea, coffee or small meals and snacks. He headed up there and fussed around with the coffee machine while Amy thought about what to say.

"No need to hem and haw," Hunter said. "Just let it all out. I'm listening."

She pursed her lips. "You know, you can be really annoying sometimes."

"That's what my therapist used to say."

"Used to say?"

"Yeah. Sadly, he topped himself right after one of our sessions."

"Funny."

"I thought so, thanks." He let the moment pass. "Look, I didn't need Gomez the Map Thief over there to work out there was something going on here."

"Was I that obvious?"

"First, I've worked with a lot of academics, including some map historians and cartographers. These are very clever people, but we're talking about the sort of people who can't be trusted to plug in a toaster or tie their own shoelaces, never mind handle a weapon. Not only did you know how to use the gun I gave you, but you handled it too well for a beginner."

"I tried not to."

"Second, you also knew precisely how many rounds a Makarov semi-automatic pistol carries. I never told you that. You also knew guards training was so tough. I asked myself, how would an American cartographer specializing in ancient maps know that?"

"I might have read about it in the Rorschach briefing notes."

Hunter let it hang. "Third, I know you said you read about Cuba on the flight from Switzerland, but I still thought the comment about Regla was odd. I presume you've been there?"

"Twice, on business."

He nodded. "Fourth, you were able to anticipate what Gomez over there was going to do in a fire fight. This told me you'd met before. People behave very different under that sort of pressure and it's impossible to know what they're going to do next – unless you know them."

"Yeah…" her voice trailed away into the hum of the jet's cabin. "Is that it?"

"Fifth, back on the deck you told me the Bell was getting ready to take off. I knew it was a Bell from its silhouette which I saw on the tender on the way over to the ship. My excuse is I'm a helicopter pilot. It's possible you are a cartographer with an enduring interest in rotary aircraft, but

I doubt it. I'm guessing you know your aircraft from some sort of formal training?"

She nodded. "Uh-huh."

"I thought so. I think it's time you told me the whole truth and nothing but the truth."

"Sounds like a good plan to me," the man said, returning and handing out the coffees. "What do you think, Amy?"

She sighed and took a second out to sip the coffee. As the western coast of Cuba faded behind them, so did their old, fake identities. "My name is Special Agent Amy Fox and I work for a branch of the FBI that handles matters of antiquity. I've been working undercover at the Rorschach Foundation for several months keeping him under surveillance, and I just recently returned there after a few days in DC reporting to my boss."

Hunter smiled. "All starting to make sense."

"And this is Sal Blanco. He works on my team."

Sal wiped his paw on his jeans and thrust it across the aisle. "Good to meet you, Max."

"Good to meet you, too, Sal. I'm guessing you're no thief."

"Your gut instinct serves you well. I've been a soldier, a mercenary and a semi-professional wrestler but I have never been a thief."

"Sal *catches* thieves," Amy said. "We all do. That's the mission of our team. We intercept and sometimes infiltrate large organized criminal networks working in the antiquities market and secure the artifacts and jewels they steal and trade."

Hunter sipped his coffee and pushed back on the soft leather. "How big is the team?"

"Not big," Amy said. "There's the director, James Gates, and then me, Sal, Quinn, Jodie and Ben."

"Six. How cosy."

Amy rounded on him. "We're not a joke, Max. We've hunted down some of the biggest looters and artifact thieves in the world."

"And we work hard," Sal grumbled. "Damn hard, and usually without any public recognition or thanks. You might be surprised by some of the stuff we've come across."

"And vice versa," Hunter said, rising to the challenge. "I'm no slouch when it comes to archaeology."

"Which is why I advised Rorschach to hire you – not because he needed you, but because we did."

"So this was all a set-up right from the very start. The interview in Switzerland, the viewing of the map in Vazquez's Old Havana mansion, the rescue from the yacht. All of it, stage-managed."

Sal laughed. "You could say that – except for the rescue from the yacht."

Amy sighed. "Things changed when Rorschach briefed you about Vazquez. It was the first time I'd even heard he was dealing with him. We had to think fast, so we cooked up a new plan."

Sal sipped some coffee. "The original plan was to stage a robbery at your hotel in Havana and take the statue and map from there. That way Amy could supply Rorschach the paperwork from the Cuban police and the whole thing could be written off as a regular hotel room robbery. When Gabby and I saw Vazquez's thugs taking you down to the marina at gunpoint, we knew we had to change plan fast."

A long silence. Hunter said, "Tell me about the dead woman. Did you know her well?"

"I knew her," Blanco said. "She was a private investigator who I worked with before in Cuba and some other neighboring countries. We were good friends, but she only ever knew me under my fake identity as Gomez."

Hunter dipped his head for a second and stared at the carpet before fixing his eyes up on Blanco's angry face. "I'm sorry for your loss."

"Feel sorry for Mario Davila, because he's going to pay for her death."

"So what now?" Hunter changed the subject. "I guess it's not Dr Kirsten Anderson or Ricardo Gomez anymore?"

"No," she said. "You can call me Amy."

"And I go by Sal."

"And I'm Max," he said with a cautious smile. "But then you already knew that."

"We didn't deceive you for kicks, Max," Amy said. "It was serious government business."

He set his coffee cup down on the table and raised his palms. "You misled me, yes, but you did what you had to do. What I want to know now is, what's next?"

"We're meeting with Director Gates and the rest of the team in San Salvador," Amy said flatly. "The decision to use the Nazi map to try and find the third Winged Guardian has already been made. You can join us if you want or you can go your own way when we land. The US Government will pay for your flight back to Paris."

Hunter tapped his chin with his forefinger and furrowed his brow. "Let me see, go back to my office in UNESCO and write out reports for my boss, or help you find a statue that might lead us to the discovery of Atlantis, my lifelong dream. That's tough."

"Atta boy," said Blanco, punching the air in excitement.

Amy pulled out her phone. "I'll tell Jim to expect you."

# CHAPTER EIGHTEEN

The Apostle observed the High Circle as they entered the chamber. The procession was silent and sombre, each of their faces hidden in the folds and shadows of their sumptuous velvet cloaks. Outside the castle walls, a tepid wind picked at the canopies of the fir trees and whisked the first fallen leaves of autumn into chaotic ochre spirals.

Within the stone walls, a less pastoral scene was unfolding. Two of the Creed's disciples were dragging a terrified, shaking man into the chamber. They had gagged him and bound his hands behind his back. He was perspiring profusely and beads of sweat ran down over his eyebrows and trickled down his cheeks like tears.

"Remus," the Apostle said quietly. "Kneel before the High Circle."

Before the man had a chance to obey, the two disciples pushed down on his shoulders and forced him to his knees.

The Apostle ran his fingers along the plump quilting of his throne's cushion, then stared down at Remus from the rostrum until the captive thought his eyes might burn two smoldering holes in his tortured soul.

"You have breached the Creed's code, Remus."

Remus looked up at him promptly, and began mumbling through the cloth gag. When the Apostle snapped his fingers, one of the disciples removed it and the begging began.

"Please, I meant no harm, I..."

One raised finger from the Apostle was enough to induce a cold, terrifying silence into the castle chamber. Even the broken sobs receded into the dark respect now dominating the men clustered around the Creed's second in command.

"You have breached the Creed's sacred code, and the Magus is very disappointed in you. You have incurred his displeasure, and he has ordered me to relay that to you."

"Please, Teacher! Spare my life!"

"Cato and Cassius," the Apostle said, addressing the disciples. "Take a step away from Remus."

They obeyed, stepping back with a graceful bow of their heads. The flourish was noted by the Apostle who now returned his attention to the man trembling and crying on the floor. "I am also very disappointed in you, Remus."

A peal of distant thunder rumbled outside.

"I will repent!" he screamed.

"It is too late for any of that. You betrayed our sacred trust. You must now reckon with the Chimera."

"No!" His wretched screams clawed at the walls and tore at the ears of the solemn-faces hidden in the shadows. "Please, Teacher! Anything but that!"

Here, they all knew his pain. Each man and woman knew about the fire-breathing monster from Lycia, described by

Homer in the Iliad. Could it be true? A hideous, monstrous beast with a lion's body and a goat's head and a tail that grew into a snake with a snapping, fanged mouth at its end. Only the Magus and a few selected disciples really knew what was below the trap door, deep in the castle's dungeon.

Driven almost to madness by the thought of it, Remus's pleas grew more desperate. "I beg the High Circle's forg—."

The Apostle threw a lever beside his chair and opened the trap door. Remus screamed all the way to the bottom of the pit, stopped only by the force of the fall breaking his legs. Sobs of pain grew louder, then cries of rage. When the deep, rasping roar of the Chimera was heard, the Apostle retracted the lever and the trap door swung shut.

He turned to the man on his right. "See the bones are never found, Draco."

"As you wish, Teacher."

Beyond the rostrum, Cato and Cassius were sliding a Persian rug back over the trap door. The Apostle smiled thinly and looked over their heads through the window. It looked like a heavy storm was about to blow in.

# CHAPTER NINETEEN

In the west of El Salvador's capital city, the Crowne Plaza Hotel nestles in the old town on the slopes of the San Salvador volcano. Known as Quezaltepeque to the indigenous peoples of the land, the volcano's last eruption was over one hundred years ago in 1917. The lake inside it evaporated to leave the desiccated bowl still visible today.

Hunter took one last look at the ridge running around the top of its crater and stepped back inside the air-conditioned conference room. As Amy had promised back on the plane, her FBI team were here, sitting around the long table beneath the whirring ceiling fans and waiting to hear his briefing on the statues and map. In the center of the table was a box identical to the one he had seen back in Rorschach's grand dining salon.

James Gates was last to arrive. He was a lean man with a narrow face and cool grey eyes and dazzling white hair parted precisely on the left. He wore a plain black suit and white shirt, and now he took the suit jacket off and gave Hunter a long handshake.

"I understand you fought alongside two of my team."

"It was nothing," Hunter said. "Besides, they helped me more than I helped them."

Gates fell silent, impressed by the modesty. "Nevertheless, you might not have made it without each other, so good job. Take a seat."

Hunter hesitated, but then sat down. After so long in the army, he was accustomed to senior officers giving him orders. The only problem was, Gates wasn't his superior.

"You wear your irritation well," Gates said with a smile.

"I'm sorry?"

"My telling you to take a seat looks like it annoyed you."

"You're very observant."

"And also very busy, Dr Hunter. We have no time for formalities and even less for a dick-measuring contest. You've come in on this mission as part of an FBI team and that makes me your boss."

"Actually, it makes *me* your boss," Amy said. "At least in the field."

"True," Gates said. "And that's where you're spending most of your time, so Amy's the boss. Think of me more as a sort of god."

Hunter couldn't help but grin. "Got it."

"Good," Gates said. "Now, before you start your briefing, let me introduce you to the rest of the team. As you know, my name is—"

"God, I know, You just told me."

A wry smile. "I'm glad you were listening. You can also call me James Gates. I'm the Director. You've already met Amy Fox, my lead agent and Sal Blanco. He's the man who can get things done. Let's leave it at that.

Hunter nodded and smiled.

"Sitting beside him is Jodie Priest, another field operative. Broken home, car thief and juvie led to a career breaking into cars and apartments until she got caught. Did I miss anything Jodie?"

"That's my life."

"Great. The goth with the impressive frown beside her is Quinn Mosley, our IT expert."

Hunter took in the young woman with the black eye shadow and black lipstick.

"She has a SAT score of 1600 and at least three degrees but we only know that because she brags about it. She's also known as Ghost, the world-famous hacker. At the end is Ben Lewis, our resident historian. I like him better than all the others because he's an ex-Marine, which is only one down from US Navy where I spent the best years of my life. They all report to Amy."

"Great to meet you all."

The team offered polite smiles and Gates cleared his throat. "Team, this is Dr Max Hunter. He's a former officer in the British Army and a trained helicopter pilot with plenty of field experience. By formal academic training at Oxford he's also a Palaeolithic Archaeologist, but more recently he has specialized in ancient weapons and symbols, is that right, Dr Hunter?"

"Sounds about right," he said. "Anything from the Stone Age to the Dark Ages has my attention."

"You know why they were called the Dark Ages?" Lewis said, suppressing a smile.

Hunter's reply was instant. "Because there were so many knights. There's not an

archaeology joke I haven't heard ten times before and you should *never* take up poker. Director Gates, shall we begin?"

"Please, Dr Hunter," Gates said with a sympathetic glance at Ben. "The floor is yours."

"Then we start at the beginning." He gestured at the wooden box containing the mysterious blades. "May I?"

Gates looked at Lewis. "Please."

The historian pushed the box to the end of the table, but didn't realize its base was a smooth green velvet. It sped along the smooth laminate surface of the conference desk, raising every eyebrow in the room. Hunter stepped in and swept it up into his arms just before it crashed to the floor.

"Good one, Ben," Quinn said.

"I guess I don't know my own strength." He started to roll up his shirt sleeve. "Here, check my muscles."

"In your dreams."

"Take it easy, Ben," Gates said. "These are priceless artifacts. Right, Dr Hunter?"

Hunter put the box back on the table and clicked the lid open. Taking a dagger with a red stone handle, he held it up for all to see and gently turned it in his hand. "Without a doubt, these are exactly the same as those Rorschach has, and simply in material terms, they would command a very hefty price at auction, but it goes much further than that."

"So, we're rich?" Lewis said.

Hunter set the blade down. "This is about more than money, and let me explain why. In their construction, the blades of these daggers are a mysterious alloy created from gold, copper and what Plato described as orichalcum."

"I heard of that once." Jodie said. "But isn't it a myth?"

Hunter grinned. "As I explained to Special Agent Fox, it's hard to say. It's written about in Plato's *Critias*, one of his later dialogues, and also in another I discovered recently called *Diocles*, in which he also describes the three Winged Guardians of Atlantis. That's what started all this. I agree it's not much, but it's all we have. I think these daggers, and the winged statues are from Atlantis."

Gates stepped into the stunned silence. "While half the team was getting shot at in Cuba, I had some tests done on the daggers. We found that while the blades are forged from this strange alloy, the metal running around the pommel had extremely high concentrations of iron and cobalt in it. It was, literally, like nothing on earth."

"You can't mean it's an alien artifact?" Amy said.

"Yes and no. Yes, it came from out of this world, but no, it wasn't made by aliens. The current theory is that it came from the metal of a crashed meteorite. Samples of metal from meteorites known to have crashed in Egypt show very similar levels of iron and cobalt."

Amy shifted in her seat. "Very similar, but not the same?"

"No, not the same."

Quinn twiddled her pen, determined not to look fazed. "So, that means the metal you're talking about wasn't made from the crashed meteorite."

"Probably not, which means…"

"Which means aliens made it," Lewis said.

"Which *means*," Gates said, "that it probably came from another meteorite with slightly different metallic properties. Either way, there's never been a meteorite crash-land anywhere on earth with anywhere near the metallic composition of these blades – or the statues, if they're made of the same material. At least, not one that has ever been found. Dr Hunter?"

Hunter was thinking. "It's my theory that the orichalcum in the blade alloy, along with the crazy iron and cobalt levels you found in the pommel, probably all come from a meteorite crash in an unknown site, probably in Atlantis."

"This is getting heavy," Lewis said.

Amy broke into another strained silence. "What about the photos of the statue and map Sal took back on the yacht, Max?"

Hunter held up printed copies of the photos. "You can see from this picture that there's a lot of water damage on the map, but it seems to be indicating that there's a kind of settlement or maybe even something more substantial in a very remote section of the Montecristo Cloud Forest in the east of El Salvador."

"What do you mean by settlement?" Gates asked.

"As I say, there's water-damage and smudging, but some of the notes on the map indicate that Himmler's Ahnenerbe team were able to translate some of the inscriptions on the base of the Acassuso Idol, also known as the 'Winged Guardian' we found in Vazquez's strongroom. The translation implies a substantial settlement in a hidden valley called the Scorpion Ravine, as marked right here on the map. More like a lost civilization really, including pyramids."

Amy noted the shock on the faces of her team members. "You said back on the plane that something about the pictures was bothering you, Max."

Hunter smiled. "It was, but it's not any more. Back on the tender was *not* the greatest environment to study the images Sal took, but I've had time to think about it since. The problem was a technical one. The symbols on the statue are like some sort of cross between Assyrian hieroglyphics and Egyptian hieroglyphics. To me, it's like a new language, and bear in mind I'm not the world's greatest Egyptologist to start with."

"You surprise me," Amy said, arching a sarcastic eyebrow.

"I'm sure I do," he said with a grin. "Anyway, I've done my best, and from what I can tell, the Ahnenerbe made a mistake when translating the inscriptions for their little map. This is not hard to do – hieroglyphics like these depend massively on context. The same sign can mean something quite different if put in a different place in the sentence. Also, some glyphs are logograms, which represent a word, and others are ideograms, which represent ideas, but we're more interested in the contextual thing."

Jodie groaned. "This is making my head spin."

Hunter smiled. "I think the Nazis confused a syllabary sequence for a logographic one."

"Stupid Nazis," Quinn said.

"Yeah, stupid Nazis," said Hunter, pointing at the picture. "Their map indicates that the lost city is reached at the southern end of the ravine at a location the ancients called the scorpion's tail, but this is because the translator thinks this key symbol here means tail. I think it does, too, but not when combined with this glyph beside it. From the brief glimpse I got of the inscriptions on the base of the Mosul statue, I think this compound glyph means *north.* In other words, anyone following the map precisely is going to the wrong end of the ravine, in the south."

"They're looking in the wrong place?" Gates asked.

"I think so, but we won't be. We have to go to the north of the Scorpion Ravine."

"And we have enemies everywhere," Gates said. "We know from Dr Hunter's account of Mosul that this Brodie McCabe character is working for someone named Gaius, but we don't know who he answers to, if anyone." He left a long, weighty pause. "It could be Rorschach."

More silence. No one knew exactly what to say.

Except Jodie. "This is all batshit crazy, dude."

"No, it's kinda cool," said Quinn.

"It's your next stop," Gates said. "And be careful – we also all know Vazquez and his thugs are out there somewhere, searching for the third Winged Guardian. They're dangerous."

"And don't underestimate McCabe," Hunter said. "Maybe that Gaius freak will show his face again, too."

"Or even Rorschach," Amy said. "If that's who's tugging McCabe's strings."

Gates's smile was fading fast. "Just watch your backs."

# CHAPTER TWENTY

High in the El Salvadorian mountains, Montecristo Cloud Forest is a high-altitude jungle teeming with tropical life. Pumas, toucans, spider monkeys, two-fingered anteaters and striped owls all live in the premontane forest, in a world unchanged since the dawn of time.

Sprawling over the borders into Guatemala and Honduras, the rainforest's high altitude causes a fine cloud-mist to hang over it for much of the time, and gives the entire wilderness an eerie prehistoric atmosphere. Directed by their guides, Gerardo and Fidel, the team drove deeper into the wilderness and the mist grew thicker.

"I'm half expecting a T-Rex to come out of nowhere," Jodie said. "This place gives me the creeps."

"Me too," said Lewis. "I want my mommy."

Jodie lifted her middle finger and held it an inch from his face. "Get lost, Benedict."

Fidel laughed. "It's not always like this."

"Wait," Amy said. "I think I see something."

Hunter pulled himself up beside her in the moving truck and rested his hands on the driver's headrest to keep his balance. "Where are you looking?"

Blanco changed down into second gear to navigate the rutted track more safely.

"Right there, just off to the right of us."

"I don't see anything," Jodie said, staring into the misty jungle.

"Me neither," said Gerardo. "Oh..."

As the hood of the 4x4 inched forward, the outline of a dead man slowly emerged from the shadows of the vines and laurels. He was wearing a moisture-wicking khaki shirt and camo fatigues, but they all recognized Diego Canosa's face when they saw it from the briefing back in San Salvador.

"Maybe it was a hunting accident," Quinn said naively.

"No. There's no hunting in this park," Amy said. "The government banned it outright a few years ago. I don't know who's firing weapons but I doubt it's hunters – the park has armed guards looking out for them."

"Poachers, maybe?" asked Jodie.

"I don't think so," Hunter said, pointing. "Look over there."

Meters to the left of the corpse was another dead man. "I know that face, too," Blanco said, slowing the truck and braking to a stop. "He was also on Vazquez's ship."

"And there's another one farther off the track," Jodie said in a sombre tone. "That makes at least three."

"Four," Hunter said. "Look over there."

Amy gasped. "Davila's dead?"

"I hope so," Hunter said. "Because someone shot him in the face three times."

"Good," growled Blanco. "He was the bastard who shot Gabriela. The only problem is, I wanted to kill him."

"Guys," Amy said. "I see Raul Vazquez over there to the right. Major gunshot wounds to the face and neck." She lowered her voice to a whisper. "What the hell happened here?"

Blanco drove farther down the track and killed the engine. He leaned his head over the side of the truck and stared down at Davila's dead body. After a long pause, he said, "These guys were real assholes, Amy. Not just that, they were ruthless and tooled up like a small army. And they knew how to use their weapons, too. They defended Vazquez's cruise ship very professionally. I'd say they were mostly ex-army, maybe even special ops down on their luck."

"I agree," Hunter said. "I've fought alongside special forces on the battlefield and some of these guys moved in the same way. I think I have the same question as Sal."

"Right," Amy said. "If these guys were so good, who the hell could have made such a mess of them?"

"You think this was McCabe?" Blanco asked Hunter.

"Maybe, but whoever it was," Hunter said, "we have to presume they now have the Winged Guardian and the map that was in Vazquez's possession."

"Not good," Amy said. "A new and more dangerous enemy."

"No, not good." Blanco swung his arm off the top of the door and turned in his seat. "I'm tired. Who wants to take over?"

"I will." Gerardo and Blanco switched seats and the El Salvadorian guide turned the ignition key. The truck grumbled back to life and he revved it a few times. Everyone was grateful when the eerie silence of the fresh open grave all around them was gone.

"C'mon, let's get out of here," Hunter said. "We still have a long drive to reach the coordinates on the map and it looks like we're already losing the race."

Blanco slapped a mosquito head-net over his hat and pulled it down over his face. "I'm getting some sleep. Don't wake me unless someone's shooting at us, and even then think very hard about exactly how much danger my life is in. If it's sixty-forty, let me sleep."

Amy rolled her eyes. "Sweet dreams, Sal."

*

"Sal, wake up."

Blanco heard the words but they were vague and muffled. He opened one eye and saw Quinn leaning over him. She was shaking him gently by the shoulder.

"What happened to sweet dreams?" he asked.

"Ask Amy, she said it."

He opened the other eye and pulled the mosquito net away from his face. Shuffling up on the rear seat, he yawned and stretched his arms. "You remember what I said about that sixty-forty thing, right?"

"And right now it's more like seventy-thirty," Lewis said. He was sitting on the rearmost seat next to Quinn and looking rattled.

"Anyone care to explain what's going on?"

"We have company, Sal." Amy sounded as nervous as Lewis looked. "A Jeep and what looks like an old army truck have been following us for the last fifteen minutes."

"Tourists?"

"Gerardo says he's never seen tourists in an army truck before."

"Nor me," Fidel said. "This is very unusual."

"How the hell did we get ahead of them?" Blanco asked.

"They must have gotten lost," said Fidel. "It's not hard in this jungle."

Blanco turned and looked in between Lewis and Jodie at the small convoy traveling behind them. The lead Jeep was driving down into the ditch they had navigated moments earlier, splashing mud up onto the side of the track. The engine roared as it climbed back up the other side. It steered to the left to use a shallower gradient on its way back up to level ground and Blanco saw a man in the front passenger seat.

"Not seen tourists in a military truck before, huh?"

Gerardo said, "No, señor. I think we have trouble."

"Judging by the guy up front with a submachine gun hanging out of the window, I'd be tempted to agree with you."

Amy gasped. "They're armed?"

Blanco rolled up his sleeves and twisted his hat into a more comfortable position. Sleep had pushed it over to the left and made him look like a drunken sailor, but he was all set now.

"I'd say heavily," he said.

"And we know it's not Vazquez." Quinn slapped a mosquito and cursed. "Eww! Is there anything more gross than nature?"

Hunter was riding in the middle just behind Gerardo. He dipped his head and glanced in the side mirror. "Too far away – anyone got any bins?"

"Bins?" Amy said.

"Binoculars."

"Sure, here." She passed him a pair from a bag on the back seat.

"Thanks, and take it easy Gerardo – I want to see what's going on." He watched the Jeep pull up onto the level where it parked and waited for the truck to catch up. When the larger vehicle steered to the left to find the easier slope, Hunter saw what he had feared. Sitting in the passenger seat in the truck's cabin with his arm hanging lazily over the door and his hand tapping the hot steel was an old friend.

"We're in trouble," he said. "It's bloody McCabe. Get going, Gerardo. As fast as the track allows."

Their driver speeded up and steered around some ruts in the track to make better progress, but behind them, the truck was out of the ditch and pulling up beside the jeep. Some of the men got out, followed by McCabe.

"They've stopped," Quinn said. "And I'm in the back seat. That's called drawing the shortest straw, right?"

"Guys," Lewis said. "The guy in the big hat is drawing a handgun. Why is his nose all smashed in?"

Hunter flicked his head around and saw McCabe aiming a pistol directly at them. "We had a disagreement in Iraq recently."

"Is this a joke?" Quinn said.

"It's no joke," said Hunter, tapping Gerardo on the shoulder. "Faster, my friend, and everyone else get down!"

The bullet smashed the rear window, ripped a split in the headrest and punctured a perfect hole in the back of Gerardo's head before blasting the front of his skull off on the way out.

Amy screamed and recoiled back in her chair as far as she could go. A peaceful drive through the jungle had turned into a nightmare. The dead man slumped forward against the wheel and the truck began to swerve off the track toward the trees.

Hunter sprang into action, unbuckling his belt and clambering in between the two front seats as pieces of yellow seat stuffing rained down like snowflakes in front of the blood-splattered windshield.

"What the hell is happening?" Quinn said.

"Driver just got shot."

"I worked that bit out."

"Then why ask the sodding question in the first place?"

"I don't know, I..."

A second bullet obliterated the driver's side mirror just as Hunter was trying to get control of the vehicle. There wasn't enough space for him to get into a position where he could pull the driver out of the way, so that left only one option. He leaned over the dead man and opened the driver's door. Steering the truck with his right hand, he pushed him out onto the dirt track and slipped down into the driver's seat.

"Sorry, Gerardo," he said, slamming the door shut and stamping on the gas. "It's not personal."

"How could you do that?"

He flicked his head around for a second. "Eh?"

"That poor man."

"We're being shot at, Amy! We have to get away!"

"Not just being shot at," Blanco said, leaning awkwardly over the middle seat and looking between Lewis and Quinn through the shattered rear window. "They're getting a GPMG out of the Jeep and setting up it up on the hood."

"Not good," Hunter said. "That is so not good."

"They're firing!" Lewis said.

Quinn screamed, crunching into a ball with her hands over her head and bringing her knees up to her face in one move.

"Get off the track, Max!" Amy screamed.

Rounds peppered the back of their truck, punching holes in the tailgate and blowing out the rear right tire. They all felt it collapse down to the right in response as Hunter struggled to control the vehicle.

More gunfire, chattering behind them. Puffs of smoke from the muzzle of the GPMG back on the jungle track. Fifty mil rounds from the belt-fed weapon traced through the steamy air and pocked the track behind them.

Amy screamed as terror coursed through her veins. "Get off the damn track, Max! Now!"

Hunter steered to the left and ploughed the truck into the jungle.

# CHAPTER TWENTY-ONE

"Brace! Brace! Brace!"

The engine roared like a scalded pig as the truck bounced and swerved down a long muddy slope. Hunter's sweaty hands held the wheel tight and steered the truck to the right to try and keep it from flipping.

"Quinn!" Amy yelled. "My bag's in the back! Get it quick – it's got the satphone in it."

Quinn turned and looked. "I can't see it!"

Ripping through the undergrowth, the truck's battered grille ate up vines, orchids, and ferns like it was a hungry panther. When they hit a patch of moss, it skidded wildly and finally tipped, crashing over onto its side and sliding uncontrollably down the rest of the slope. It came to a rest on a ledge overhanging a large valley.

Quinn spoke first. "Is it just me, or does this place suck?"

After a long silence, Lewis groaned. "It's not just you."

Slowly, they felt the truck tip forward and then come back again.

Jodie reached out and grabbed the back of a seat. "What the hell was that?"

Hunter stared out of the windshield in horror. "We're hanging over the edge of a cliff."

"What the hell?" Quinn said, panicked. "How far down is it?"

"Very far," Fidel said.

"How far?!"

"You don't want to know," Hunter said. "Everyone just stay calm."

"I'm calm in a fucking bath, Hunter!" Jodie said, her voice gradually getting louder. "Not hanging over the edge of a cliff in the middle of the damn jungle!"

"We have to get out of here," he said. "This is not good at all. The good news is, I don't think we're in immediate danger of an explosion because I can't smell petrol – but we might still have broken a fuel line."

"Gas," Amy said.

"Petrol."

"Gas."

"Let's go," Blanco said, punching open the door now above his head. "Whatever you want to call it, if it ignites, all that's left of us is seven black skeletons. Plus, this thing could go over the edge at any time. We can climb out through what is now the top and get away before anything unpleasant happens. Start at the front and work backward to keep the center of gravity at the back."

Hunter opened his door in the same way, threw his bag up through the hole and then pulled himself up. When he got up on top he moved to the back and waited for the others. Blanco was next.

"Where did you learn to drive, Max?"

"Who says I ever learned?"

Blanco laughed and helped pull Lewis and Quinn up out of the truck. Fidel climbed out on his own and Hunter reached down and pulled Amy and Jodie up. One by one they climbed down over the back of the truck and stepped down onto the jungle floor. The radiator was steaming and the blown out tire was still spinning around from the velocity of the crash.

Quinn checked her bag. "Laptop's okay. I know that's all I care about."

"Everyone else all right?" Amy asked.

A round of dazed nods was the answer as they pulled the last of their packs off the back of the truck and swung them over their shoulders. The area was still covered in the thick mist that made the cloud forest so unique, and the humidity was rising.

Jodie kicked a clump of mud and it struck the back of the truck. "Could today get any worse?"

The truck creaked and groaned. When it tipped forward they all expected it to swing back again, but it just kept on going until it went right over the edge, disappearing from sight in a haze of dirt and shredded plants and steamy mist.

In the long silence that followed, no one knew quite what to say.

Except Quinn. "Awkward."

"It was finished anyway," Blanco said. "Right?"

"For sure," Hunter said.

"Damn it," Amy said. "My bag looks like it got crushed by the damn truck! The satphone is in there!"

She pulled her squashed bag out of the mud but the phone was obviously wrecked. Undeterred by its condition, she tried to bring it back to life by desperately drying it off and wiping the mud and silt away from the speaker. When she turned it on, it made a sad squealing noise, crackled for a few seconds and then died. "It's no good. We're on our own now."

"Damn it," Blanco said. "And that means we're *really* on our own. This is pretty unforgiving terrain and I'd say we're at least three days' hike back to anywhere with a phone."

"We can do without the phone," Hunter said. "My army training included some time in the jungle in Belize. That's not too dissimilar from this. I'm guessing the US Army trains you guys in jungle warfare, am I right, Sal?"

"Schofield Barracks," he said. "Near Honolulu in Hawaii. That's where the Jungle Operations Training Center is located and yes, I spent some time there. I even learned how to rub two sticks together to make an annoying noise and make a pretty veil out of a mosquito net."

"Good job, soldier," Hunter said. "I knew there was more to you than meets the eye."

"And Ben here was a marine," Amy said. "So the odds are in our favor."

Behind them, Quinn sighed and turned away from the group, visibly deflating.

Hunter and Amy exchanged a look, and he walked over to her. Putting his arm around the goth's shoulder, he wheeled her around so they were facing away from the ledge. "You're not to blame for this, Quinn."

She frowned and kicked a pebble into the undergrowth. "Whatever I do, I always just screw it up. I can do computers, but that's it. I get asked to find a bag with a satphone in it and I screw it up, just like I screw everything up. Just like I screwed up all my jobs and just like how I screwed up college. I'm just a damn screw-up, Max. That's me. If you want something screwed-up then give me a call. I work twenty-four seven at very reasonable rates."

Hunter watched her young face scrunch up as she fought hard to stop crying. She was trying to deal with some serious issues deep down inside and he wanted to help her if he could, but this wasn't the time or the place.

"The truck was flying around all over the place," he said. "No one could have found the bag in those conditions."

"You're just saying that."

He opened his mouth to speak, but beside him, Lewis spoke up.

"How far do you reckon we came?" He was staring up the slope, squinting.

"Easily five hundred meters," Hunter said.

"Yards," Amy said.

"Meters."

"Either way," Blanco said, picking up his bag and hoisting it over his shoulder. "Whatever you want to call it,

I doubt McCabe and his men are coming down the same way. For now at least, I'd say we're safe from the threat they pose."

"Agreed," Amy said. "But which way to the coordinates from here?"

Hunter had walked away from the group and was standing on the edge of the cliff with his map and compass. "The lost city," he announced proudly, raising his right arm and pointing out across the misty valley, "is right over there. Am I right Fidel?"

He handed the photo of the Nazi map to the surviving guide. Fidel studied it for a few moments, then looked up at the undulating ribs on the far side of the ravine. "Si. If this map is right, then it is where you say it is."

"In that case, we'd better get going. Not long till dark and McCabe is already ahead of us. He now has two of the three Winged Guardians and the Nazi map."

"Where is this place we're heading to?" Jodie asked.

"If you look over there," Hunter said. "You can see where the track we were on bends around and then dips down into the ravine. To be honest, we'd have been leaving the truck behind at some point and hiking the rest of the trip anyway."

"Which is great until we start talking about how we're getting out of here after we find the place," Jodie said.

Amy picked up her bag. "And we'll talk about that when it's time to talk about it."

One by one, the dejected team followed Hunter back down into the jungle.

# CHAPTER TWENTY-TWO

They made their way down the slope and after a while, their humor returned. Chatting and laughing, Hunter started to feel like part of the team. After a few miles, Amy brought up the subject she had been sitting on for so long.

"So that was McCabe, huh? Just what the hell's the deal between you and him?"

They were alone at the front of the team, sharing some warm water from his canteen in the humid heat. Hunter took in her no-nonsense face and decided honesty was the best policy. "We were in the army together."

"Uh-huh, and?"

He shrugged. "And he's an arsehole."

Amy watched him for any sign there might be more. "Don't play games."

"It's ancient history."

"Coming from an archaeologist, that's cute."

"I don't want to talk about it."

She pulled up to a stop. The rest of the team were only minutes behind them. "Not an option, soldier. It's obvious the waters between you two run deep and he just tried to kill all of us, not just you, so now you're going to talk about it, whether you like it or not."

"Hey, I'm not in your little team yet, so you don't get to order me around."

"Yet? That's a tad presumptuous."

"You brought me into this little escapade when you hired me for Rorschach, not the other way around. Try and remember that."

She put her hands on her hips. "Are you going to tell me what's up with you and McCabe, or keep avoiding the subject like you are right now?"

"Fine, but you asked for it," he muttered. "McCabe and I go way back to the very beginning. We went to Sandhurst together, which is the British equivalent of West Point."

"I know that."

"I'm just saying."

"Fine."

"Fine, then.

"Keep talkin', Max."

"We both applied for the Grenadier Guards, which is the most senior guards regiment in the British Army Order of Precedence. They were established in 1656 to protect King Charles II when he was in exile in Bruges."

"Is there a reason for the military history lecture?"

He fought back a smile. "Yes. McCabe also applied to join it, but he didn't get in. He got his second choice, the Scots Guards. A fine regiment, but not the one he wanted. That was when things started to go sour, and they got worse from there. We met again in Afghanistan when our regiments were deployed there during the war, and some things happened that I don't want to talk about right now. The point is, those things drove us further apart."

"You really do have a history with this guy, then."

Hunter watched the team as they made their way through the jungle. Blanco was up front with his machete, but Jodie was no slouch with a blade either. She hacked at the undergrowth like it was personal.

"After a few deployments, he left the army and studied archaeology at Cambridge. We'd spoken about our shared love of the subject at Sandhurst, and I'd told him I might study it if I left the army. When I quit the Guards and did just that at Oxford, he accused me of copying him and we fell out all over again. That's when the real rivalry started."

"How so?"

"An arms race developed between us, each trying to best the other with our academic research, each trying to organize the most exciting excavations and each of us more determined to make the biggest discovery. It got crazy, and dangerous."

"Ah yes, the lethal dangers of the academic staff room."

"I'm serious," he said, but unable to resist a grin. "I'm talking about hiring local thugs to trash digs out in the sticks of some pretty lawless countries, accusations of faking evidence, you name it."

"You did that?"

"Of course not," he said. "But he did it to me."

"He sounds kind of insane."

"We're from very different backgrounds. Brodie is from a very old and wealthy family. They expected a lot of him, and never shied away from telling him so. His father was a Brigadier in the SAS and his mother was in the House of Commons for many years. It was different for me. My background was pretty ordinary, and I had to work like the devil to get whatever I wanted. It wasn't just handed to me on a silver platter because of family connections."

"You're right about the weight of family expectations."

"You have experience of this?"

"Forget about it," she said, backtracking. "Go on."

"Anyway, that's why McCabe was so enraged about not getting his choice of regiment. He presumed his family connections would pull the right strings and get him in and they didn't. Not that time, at least, and they didn't do him any favors at Cambridge, either. Then, his mother was caught up in a major parliamentary scandal involving fiddling her expenses and the family name was ruined."

"I remember reading about that in the papers, but it didn't get much coverage in the US."

"It was a major shitstorm in the UK," Hunter said. "And Abilene McCabe was right in the middle of it. She resigned from the Cabinet and left Government in disgrace. I'm guessing it would have been about that time that Brodie started stealing artifacts from his digs and selling them to fences to sell on to smugglers.

"What an asshole."

"At some point, he graduated and cut out the middlemen, becoming a full-on thief of ancient artifacts. I guess under so much pressure, the rage finally hammered him into the ground like an old twisted nail. Exactly how he ended up working for a man like Gaius is anyone's guess."

"It's *our* guess, you mean," she said. "We need to know who Gaius is working for, and whether that's Rorschach or not. Right now, McCabe is our only serious lead."

"I know, I know..." he paused. "Anyway, now you know the deal between me and Brodie McCabe."

"Thanks, Max," she said. "And thanks for what you did earlier today back at the crash site."

"What did I do?"

"When you spoke to Quinn. I know how she comes across but she's really fragile. She's totally out of her depth here. It was nice of you to say what you did."

"She'll be fine," he said. "Just some dented pride, that's all."

"Still, you didn't have to say it."

"Forget about it." He looked at her, took his pack off his shoulder and dropped it on the floor.

"What are you doing?"

"Calling it a day. It's getting late and we're not hiking through this jungle at night, so this is where we make camp."

# CHAPTER TWENTY-THREE

As evening fell over their makeshift camp, the temperature dropped down to ten degrees Celsius, surprising Jodie. She slipped her denim jacket over her shoulders and shivered. "I thought the rainforest was supposed to be hot."

"It is," Hunter said. "But we're over six thousand feet up, hence the mist."

She looked unimpressed by the explanation. "If we're going to be here all damn night, maybe one of you big tough army types could build a fire? I can break into any car or apartment you dare me to, but there's no way I'm rubbing sticks together."

"We don't do that anymore," Hunter said. "Not since Uncle Zippo joined the party."

"Whatever. Just make something that'll warm my hands up."

"I hear that," Quinn said. Like Jodie, she pulled a jacket out of her bag and threw it over the top of her Stone Temple Pilots t-shirt. "I thought these places were supposed to be hot, too. What's so funny, Hunter?"

"I thought you were some kind of know-it-all genius."

"I know about computers. After that, I don't know squat and I don't care."

"Fair enough."

"Any word on something to eat?" Jodie asked.

Blanco looked serious as he rummaged around in his pack. "Coming right up." He balanced a pan on rocks around the fire and tipped some beans inside it. When they began sizzling, he pulled a pack of crackers from his pack and opened them up. "Nothing like cooking over an open fire."

Jodie was still warming her hands, and peered down at the beans suspiciously. "If you say so."

"Trust me," the New Yorker said as he spooned out some portions of beans and some crackers into some tin bowls. "After the day we just had, this is going to taste better than anything you ever ate before in your whole life."

They ate the modest meal in the glow of the fire's embers. The aroma of the beans mingled with the smell of mosquito repellent and burning charcoal. Above them, the moon rose over a tropical canopy thick with flying insects.

"I'm almost starting to enjoy myself," said Lewis.

"Is that you, or just the crackers talking?" Blanco said.

Fidel laughed. "That's funny."

"No, I mean it."

Jodie gave him a sideways glance. "Have you been smoking the sofa stuffing again?"

"No, I always loved camping. I was a marine, remember. It kind of helps if you like camping. I love it."

"Me too," Quinn said to a host of shocked faces.

Lewis poked the fire. "Really?"

"Sure," she shrugged. "Just us and the cicadas and the starlight. Oh yeah, and an army of psychos trying to kill us with machine guns. Truly delightful."

"Talking of which," Hunter said. "I'm bothered by how McCabe got in the park in the first place."

Amy warmed her hands on the bowl of beans she was holding. "How so?"

"For one thing, getting in this park isn't like visiting any of the other parks in El Salvador," Hunter said. "And staying overnight is usually a big no-no. I bet it took your director some serious high-level trading to get us in so fast, right?"

Amy nodded. "A lot of phone calls."

Fidel swallowed a mouthful of beans and drank some water. "It's true. The authorities usually require a lot of notice and personal details for this park. Licence plates of all vehicles coming in, names of everyone and passport details, plus the exact length of time you're planning on spending in the park."

"Wow," Quinn said. "Sounds like they have something to hide in here. What's the betting they know about the pyramids we're trying to find?"

"I think it's more likely they're trying to protect the environment, schmuckle," Lewis said.

"Ben's right," Fidel said. "They have a lot of problems with pollution here like pesticides from the local cotton fields. During the rainy season there are large deaths of fish and birds in the park's Jocotal Lake. They don't want endless numbers of tourists coming in and ruining the place even more."

Blanco said, "But I think Max is trying to say that this McCabe must have some pretty high-level contacts, right?"

Hunter nodded. "Yes, but I know him and I can't think of anyone he would know in the El Salvadorian parks department. I mean, he might have a connection, but it just seems weird."

Jodie changed the subject and set her bowl down. "You know what, Sal?"

The man from Brooklyn smiled. "That was the best thing you ever ate?"

"Oh no," she said. "It tasted like shit, but I was going to say this place could be quite romantic."

"Thanks, Jojo," he said. "You really think this place is romantic?"

"Sure," Quinn said. "Except for the flies and mosquito bites and humidity and sweat and headaches and getting shot at."

"He wasn't asking you, Morticia."

They heard something rustling in the undergrowth. Hunter pulled his knife and leapt to his feet ready for anything. "It's nothing," he said. "Just an animal."

Blanco followed the creature's path as it vanished back into the jungle. "It's an agouti," he said. "Along with Macaws, it's the only thing on earth that can open a Brazil nut without a tool."

"Whoa, Salvatore," Amy said. "That's enough Discovery Channel already."

He gave the gruff but honest laugh Hunter was already starting to warm to. "You got it, and remember it's Sal, unless you want me to tell our new friend what Amy stands for?"

"You wouldn't dare."

He shrugged. "Try me."

"Leave it, Sal."

"I thought Amy stood for Amy?" Hunter said, grinning.

"You'd think," Jodie said. "But you'd be wrong."

"Can we move on, please?" Amy said.

Another grizzly laugh. "Anything you say."

The fire crackled and popped. Embers floated up into the darkness and then higher into the silvery moonlit canopy. The threat of McCabe and his men was real, but as the night grew older they started to feel sleepy and more relaxed.

Jodie's voice broke the silence. This time, she sounded less cynical than usual. "You really think Atlantis was a real place?"

Hunter's reply was instant. "No doubt in my heart. I've spent most of my life studying it and what started out as a fascinating myth in my childhood gradually turned into something I'm convinced is out there."

"But what would it mean?" she asked. "I mean, if it's real."

The others sat in silence, waiting for Hunter's response. When it came, it shocked them all.

"It would mean the end of everything humanity knows. Right now, we think we know everything about our pasts and where we come from. About where our civilizations started and how they began. The second I find Atlantis, all of that changes forever. The foundations of humanity are rocked to the core."

"How so?"

He lifted his eyes from the fire and fixed them on her. "Are you kidding? If we find Atlantis, not only do we find evidence of a totally new civilization stretching back thousands of years older than anything we currently know, but we also find out we're not anywhere near as clever as we think we are. How the hell do we get to the age of satellites and not know every inch of our own planet?"

"I guess."

"After Atlantis, everything changes," he went on. "If it's older than Sumer, we have to rewrite the story of human history. And we have to ask just how the hell did such a civilization ever end?"

She shivered. "You're starting to freak me out."

"Me too," Quinn said. "I'm hitting the hay. If my life's like one percent in danger, then wake me up. No wait – half a percent."

Lewis laughed. "Not sixty-forty?"

"You heard me, Marine. You can do probabilities right?"

"Not really," he said. "I'm a historian."

Jodie looked at her watch. "It's late. I'm turning in."

"Jodie's right," Amy said. "It's late and we have a long hike in the morning if we're going to reach Scorpion Ravine. We need to get some sleep."

"We need a night watch," Hunter said. "I'll go first and we'll change every two hours."

Now Amy checked her watch. "I'll do midnight till two."

"I'll sit with you," said Fidel.

"I'll do two till four," Blanco said. "I'm usually playing poker at that hour anyway."

"Then it looks like I'm four till six," Lewis said. "Former Marine here, guys. No stranger to night watches."

Jodie went to throw some water on the fire but Blanco stopped her. "Keep it going. Not only do you need your water, but the smoke will keep the mosquitos away."

"Won't it help this McCabe dude find us?"

"He'd have to be almost right on top of us to see it," Hunter said, his voice trailing away as he stared into the fire. "Get some sleep. It's okay. We rise at daybreak and go to the ravine. If there really is a lost city hidden away there, our lives are about to change in a big way."

# CHAPTER TWENTY-FOUR

The dawn was cold. Hunter splashed his face with water and rearranged his pack ready for the day's hike to the ravine. They had made it through the night without McCabe attacking them, but that only made him think his old enemy had beaten him to the lost city. He drank some water and made his pack comfortable on his back. When everyone else was ready, they broke camp and headed through the jungle with the sun at their backs.

Within minutes, the day heated up. Amy's feet were slipping around inside her boots and her socks and shirt were slick with sweat. The heat and humidity worked together to crush her spirits and the winding jungle path seemed never to end. For the first time since the mission started, she wondered if she was doing the right thing.

She felt the straps of her pack cutting into her shoulder and hoisted it up higher to get it into a more comfortable position. It wasn't heavy – like most of the others she was only carrying water, some energy bars, a few cans of insect repellent and her gun and some spare ammo – but the heat had sapped her strength. It was beginning to feel like someone had sneaked a ten pound dumbbell inside it.

They stopped for a quick lunch and some more water and then resumed their hike through the undergrowth. There were no trails here, no paths or tracks. Just thick tropical jungle requiring endless hacking with their machetes. By the time they reached the ravine, they were all exhausted.

"I need a long rest," Quinn said.

"But you're not going to get one," Hunter said. He was pointing to a cave in the cliffs at the bottom of the ravine's north side. McCabe's truck was parked up in a clearing and night had brought a new development: two heavy-duty black hawk helicopters were sitting in a clearing in the sunshine, their blades still whirring slowly. Positioned outside one of them in the clearing was a black metal chest. "He's called in back-up after yesterday's skirmish, but by the looks of it they haven't been here long. How the hell did they get permission to bring those choppers into the park?"

"I doubt they got permission, Max," Amy said.

Fidel waved a mosquito away. "They would never get permission. They are here illegally."

"And what's in the chest?" Jodie asked.

"Beats me," shrugged Hunter. "Who are those guys with him?"

Amy and Blanco exchanged a quick glance. Amy said, "They're heavily armed and they have two choppers. That's all that matters right now."

"No, it's not," Hunter said. "What also matters is that I was right – they're not looking in the right place! McCabe is making the same mistake as the Nazis!"

"Are you sure?" Amy looked at him with hope in her eyes.

"Sure I'm sure. Did I not tell you that I'm twice the archaeologist that he is?"

She fixed him in the eye with a look of mock-admiration on her face. "You did, yes. In fact, you're like a god to us."

"Thanks, but make it *four* times the archaeologist. McCabe is doing just what I thought he would and trying to enter the ravine in the south. We have an advantage."

"So where should we go now?" Lewis asked.

"Farther to the north," Hunter said, pointing away from the McCabe crew. "Down there in that gulley is my best guess."

"Then let's get on with it," Amy said, adjusting her pack. "It won't take them long to work out their mistake and there are just too many of them to fight."

Hunter pointed at the choppers and grinned. "At least we found a way out of here."

"We sure did," Blanco said. "But getting to them might be a problem – they're being watched by a couple of armed guards."

"We'll cross that bridge when we come to it," Hunter said. "For now, let's just see if we can get inside the ravine and find the lost city before they do."

They moved away from McCabe and followed the gradient down to the bottom of the north end of the ravine. Still no tracks, and the work was heavy and draining. Machetes swung and hands grabbed at fistfuls of undergrowth as they cleared a path to the gulley at the base of Scorpion Ravine.

Hunter pulled the printed photo of the map from his pocket and took another look at it. "This is it. This has to be it. That's the overhang drawn here – see how it looks like a Scorpion's claw?"

"Not really," Quinn said. "And by the way, I want to go back to my apartment."

"Noted," Amy said. "Max?"

He smiled. "This must be the entrance, Amy. See the split in the rock?" He moved closer, clearing vines and weeds as he went until he found what looked like the entrance to a chambered long barrow. Two stone posts stood either side of a narrow entrance blocked by a roughly hewn boulder. Balanced on top of the posts, a heavy capstone was wedging the boulder in place. Above the boulder, a slim fissure widened just enough for him to angle a flashlight beam down into it and see what was inside.

"Some sort of tunnel," he said.

Fidel climbed up beside him, and said in awe, "I have never seen anything like this before in my entire life!"

"That boulder looks pretty chunky," Lewis said.

"We can move it if we work together," said Hunter. "If Sal and I can lift the capstone, Ben and Jodie should be able to roll out the boulder blocking the entrance."

"Feeling strong?" Lewis asked Jodie.

"Always."

Hunter and Blanco hefted the capstone up an inch giving Lewis and Jodie enough room to crawl underneath and heave the boulder forward. They rolled it away from the entrance and overturned it, collapsing down into the undergrowth when they had finished. The effort of moving the heavy boulder had made the Californian girl lightheaded. "That was heavier than your music collection, Quinn."

"Bite me, Barbie."

"Hey!"

"But we're in," Amy said, raising her voice. "That's the main thing."

Lewis clapped his hands together. "Just cannot wait to investigate these caverns. I'm taking a selfie for Meg."

Hunter and Blanco lowered the capstone back down with a couple of loud grunts and a puff of light dust. The Londoner gave the top of the flat rock a loving tap. Peering down underneath it and seeing the hole Lewis and Jodie had created by moving the rock, he gave a toothy grin to the rest of the team. "I'm going first. No arguments."

He threw his bag down and climbed in after it, descending the sloped shaft feet first. At the bottom he swept his flashlight around his new home and saw he was standing in a small entrance chamber flanked by two smaller transept chambers. At the end of the entrance chamber, three archways gave way to dark tunnels. Each one was marked with a symbol set into its keystone.

Calling up to the rest of the team, he told them the coast was clear and they followed him down. Amy was first, making her way down the slope like a child on a playground slide until she landed at the bottom next to Hunter.

"Having fun?" he asked.

She got to her feet and dusted off her backside. "If I were, I'd never let anyone know."

The rest of the team arrived. "Which tunnel do we go down?" Jodie asked.

"This one." Hunter angled his flashlight beam over to the central archway and illuminated the keystone. They all stared up at the carving, shocked.

"Wait, is that a bas-relief bear?" Lewis asked.

"It's high-relief," Hunter said. "And it's a polar bear."

Amy gasped and leaned in closer, standing on tiptoes to get closer to the keystone. "My God, it really is a polar bear. How old is this carving, Max?"

"Thousands of years old."

"But how is that possible?' she asked.

"It's insane," said Fidel.

"Yeah," Jodie said. "Exactly how could anyone in El Salvador, thousands of years ago, know what a polar bear looked like?"

"Maybe they traveled," Blanco said, but the tone of his voice told everyone he didn't believe his own theory.

"If they traveled to the Arctic, then they came home through Africa," Lewis said, shining his flashlight beam at the keystone on the right-hand tunnel. "Because if that isn't an elephant, I'll hand my PhD back into Yale."

"This is freaking me out," Jodie said. "There are no damn polar bears or elephants in El Salvador, right?"

"No," Hunter said. "And neither have there ever been."

Quinn's voice stabbed the tension. "If a polar bear and an elephant are freaking you out, wait till you see what's on the keystone over here on the left."

They turned and saw what looked like a Chinese dragon twisting in flight and breathing fire.

Jodie took a step back. "Okay, did we just walk into the damn Twilight Zone?"

"No," Hunter said darkly. "But we need to get a move on. Don't forget about McCabe."

"Wait, you said we should follow the central tunnel," Quinn said. "What's so special about the polar bear?"

"We're not interested in the polar bear," Hunter said. "These animals were probably objects of worship, but they're not significant. If you look either side of the capstone you'll see some other glyphs carved into the rock. The ones beside the dragon indicate some sort of armory and the ones next to the elephant suggest something like an infirmary."

"And the polar bear?"

"I'm coming to that. If we want to find the main city then we should follow the polar bear, because that's what the symbols indicate. We're looking for something like a place of worship with an altar or something like that. That's where we're going to find the third winged statue."

Quinn nodded. "I'm not going to argue with that."

Outside the chamber they heard the sound of men trampling through the jungle and arguing in English and Spanish.

"Damn it," Hunter said. "McCabe finally found the right place to look."

"And he'd have found the trail we made too," Blanco said. "So he already knows we're here."

"Let's get going," Hunter said. "With some luck, it'll take him a long time to decipher the symbols in the keystones. Make sure to cover your tracks as we head down into the tunnel."

Hunter led the way, jogging down the tunnel with his flashlight sweeping over the ground ahead of him as he searched for traps. Behind them, they heard the sound of McCabe's voice. He was calling out to them in the darkness, goading them to break their cover and return to him.

"Stay quiet everyone," Hunter said. "He's trying to get us to reveal what tunnel to use."

"I say let him work it out for himself," said Lewis.

Hunter gave him a sideways glance as they walked through the darkness. "Plus, if we go back there he'll probably kill us all."

"There's that, too."

"Yup."

They set off once again, making their way down a shallow gradient and always aware they were going deeper underground. Another half hour passed as they followed the twisting, turning tunnel taking them deeper inside the earth.

Then Blanco's deep voice broke the silence. "Wait, what the hell is that up ahead?"

"What do you see, Sal?" Amy asked, her voice echoing in the tunnel.

"My God," he said. "It's a damn pyramid, just like you said, Max."

Hunter stepped ahead of the group and turned his flashlight beam up into a vast cavernous space. They had thought they were deep underground, but instead, the cavern's roof was a seething mass of vines and roots. "We found it," he said quietly. "And it looks like we're not underground anymore, but in another ravine."

"One completely covered over with plants," Amy said shocked.

Blanco looked at them with awe on his face. "And did I mention the giant pyramid?"

"Yeah," Amy said. "Let's go take a look at that, right Max?"

But Hunter was already walking forward, mesmerized by the lost city in front of him.

# CHAPTER TWENTY-FIVE

The rest of the team stepped toward him until they were standing on a ledge covered in rubble and debris. Hunter swept his flashlight beam across the ground at their feet. "Look out for the loose stones. They're probably caused by the earthquakes."

Blanco kicked some of the smaller rocks and they tumbled over the edge into the black. He followed their passage with his flashlight beam. Fifty meters below them was a rugged cleft, channelling down toward a deep inner gorge.

At the bottom, they got a better look at the unmistakable outline of a vast and awe-inspiring pyramid. As they searched the area with their flashlights, more details started to emerge from the gloom. Four stone edges trailed away from the pyramid's apex and stretched down into a dusty and barely visible network of streets and alleys.

"Damn," Amy said. "Would you look at that?"

"That thing has to be bigger than the Great Pyramid at Giza, right, Max?"

But Hunter was speechless. His eyes crawled all over the confusing images he was seeing below, lit periodically by the random sweeping patterns of the team's flashlight beams.

"You okay, Max?" Amy asked, touching his elbow.

Startled, he looked across at her. "Yeah, sure. I just can't believe we found it. It's the most incredible thing I ever saw." He passed the beam up over the dense latticework of tropical plants knitted over the top of them where the sky should be. Vines and bromeliads twisting and writhing and hiding the entire lost city from the rest of the world for endless centuries. "No wonder we never found it with any sodding satellites."

Blanco jabbed a meaty finger down at the pyramid. "We need to get down there, Max. Your old army buddy is right on our asses, but if we get the statue, I still think we've got a chance to get out of here alive."

"He's right." Hunter removed his hat and wiped sweat from his brow. Slapping the hat back down he took a deep breath. "Brodie's getting more insane by the year. I honestly think he'll murder us all if it means getting the statue."

"Exactly," Fidel said. "Look what he did to Gerardo. We need to move."

Hunter peered over the ledge. Sweeping his flashlight from right to left he found what looked like their only chance – a narrow crumbling path twisting down into the darkness. Looking back over his shoulder he saw six faces looking back at him, scared yet full of hope and excitement.

"We all good?" he asked.

"Never felt better," Amy said.

"Don't worry about me," said Blanco. "I'm always up for a challenge."

"Me too," said Fidel.

Lewis, Jodie and Quinn looked less certain until they heard the eerie echo of McCabe's voice barking orders at his men back in the tunnel.

"Let's do this," Lewis said.

Quinn shuddered. "You twisted my arm."

Jodie's eyes sparkled. "There could be treasure down there, right?"

"Once a thief, always a thief," Quinn said.

"Probably," Hunter said, leading them down. "Unless it's already been looted."

A few minutes later, the path became clearer and wider and took them straight to the base of the pyramid. Towering above them, it dominated the entire space. From down here at street level they were able to see that most of the roads in the lost city led to one of the four sides of its base.

"Is that the entrance?" Lewis asked.

Hunter looked to where he was shining his flashlight and nodded. "I think so. Let's take a closer look."

When he brought his foot up and finally stepped on the lowest step at the pyramid's base, he felt something like a jolt of electricity go through him.

"What is it?" Amy asked.

"Just nerves, I think," he said. "I feel like Neil Armstrong or something."

He led the team up the steps to a rectangular slab built into the side of the giant edifice's south side. Moss grew in the interstices at the edge of the slab, but when he slid his hand over the smooth stones in the center, he saw the same carved symbols he had discovered back inside the tomb under the Gates of Nineveh.

"We're in the right place," he said, blowing a thick layer of dust from the symbols. "And the good news is I can read what's written here because I've seen it before, back in Iraq."

Amy stepped closer to him until they brushed shoulders. "Really?"

"Uh-huh. If I push them in the correct order this slab should move away and reveal an entrance. Ra, Osiris, Set…"

"Wait, aren't they Egyptian gods?" Quinn asked.

As the slab ground open, Hunter looked over his shoulder at her. "Sure, didn't you hear what I just said? I saw these same symbols in Iraq. Clearly they're not just Egyptian gods, but much older than that. Those names are just the Egyptian words for them. No doubt the people who built this pyramid had other names for them."

"But how the hell can a picture of Osiris be carved into a stone slab on a pyramid in the middle of a ravine in El Salvador?" Quinn asked. "I know enough to know that is just plain old crazy."

Jodie rolled her eyes. "That ship sailed when we found the world's biggest pyramid hidden here, dude."

"No time for this," Hunter said. "I haven't got all the answers, but I know a big deal when I see one. We need to get in here and get the statue before McCabe. The Q and A session is at the hotel if we get out alive."

"Please say when we get out alive," Quinn said.

"Fine, *when* we get out alive. Let's move."

The short tunnel from the entrance opened into a landing at the top of a flight of stone steps. Hunter led the way to the bottom, where he was shocked to see a perfectly flat pool of water stretching out into the shadows of a stone antechamber. Dotted across them were thirteen steppingstones.

"Did not expect that."

"What is it?" Fidel asked.

"We have to cross them to get to the other side, I guess."

Amy looked at him. "And you were top of your class?"

He turned and sighed. "You want to go first?"

"No."

"That's what I thought."

Holding on to the wall, Hunter stepped down onto the first stone. It instantly gave way and he grabbed hold of the wall to stop himself tumbling in. At the same time, darts fired out of the ceiling above them and punctured the surface of the water where the steppingstone had been.

"That was uncalled for," he said. "And very unwelcoming."

"So what now?" Quinn asked.

"We go through the water," he replied. "No other way."

Taking care not to tread on any more of the steppingstones, Hunter led them cross the pool, knee-deep in the freezing, muddy water. Amy was right behind him, at the head of her team, her legs slowly going numb.

"I see another antechamber," Hunter called back. "It looks natural."

"I really should not be in a place like this," Quinn mumbled. "I'm just not built for it. I bet there isn't even any Wi-Fi down here."

"Are you kidding?" Hunter said. "This place is hundreds of feet inside a ravine and —"

"She's kidding, Max," Amy said.

"Ahh."

They made it through the final antechamber and found a larger chamber with stone walls covered in bas-relief depictions of various gods from ancient Egypt and Sumer. There were others even Hunter didn't recognize. With no time to study them, they quickly crossed the chamber to a door on the other side and opened it onto what looked like some sort of treasury.

"Whoa," Quinn said. "You got your treasure, Jodie."

Hunter struggled to process what he was seeing. Endless piles of gold and silver ornaments and jewellery sparkled in their flashlight beams. As they moved the beams around the room and tried to take it all in, the beams threw shadows from the mysterious cache up on the walls, adding to the eerie atmosphere.

Hunter walked deeper into the room. Amy saw his eyes were staring at something, unblinking and almost wild. When she called out to him, he didn't hear her.

"And there it is," he muttered. "The third Winged Guardian."

Sweeping his flashlight beam up through the treasure onto what looked like an altar, he illuminated the strange peachy-silver angel for all to see. As he reached up and took hold of it, a low, hideous howling noise filled the chamber.

Fidel made the sign of the cross over his chest and head. "I don't like this, Dr Hunter. I think we should get of here. I think we have angered something ancient and dark."

"Relax, Fidel," Hunter said. "This angel was sitting on some sort of hole. When I picked it up, I broke a kind of seal and allowed air to flow from the main entrance to whatever the hell is down there."

"Sure," Amy said. "But what *is* down there?"

Hunter shrugged and angled his beam down into the hole. "Beats me. Maybe we should check it out?"

"Well I'm not stupid enough to stick my hand in that thing, that's for damn sure."

Hunter could hardly blame her for that. He stared back inside the hole and scratched at the stubble on his chin. "Yeah."

"It's still howling," Jodie said. "Not liking that."

"We need to go, Max!" Blanco called out. "We got what we came for."

"Okay," Hunter said, turning. "We should be able to…"

He froze.

"What is it?" Amy asked.

Hunter said nothing, but raised his flashlight higher on the wall behind the altar. When they saw it, everyone gasped.

"Holy crap," Lewis said. "Is that a statue of an Egyptian pharaoh?"

"Hunter?" Amy asked.

He was walking toward it, his boots crunching on uncut emeralds and diamonds. "Yes, it is. Ramesses X to be exact, and he seems to be in front of a model of some sort of landscape. Get some pictures right away."

"Is that significant?" Jodie asked as Blanco took photos of the statue from every angle.

"We just found a statue of an Egyptian pharaoh in El Salvador, nutsack," Quinn said. "What do you think?"

Jodie squared up to her and pushed hard against her shoulders, forcing the young goth to step back and regain her balance. "I think you should shut your stupid little vampire face."

"Enough!" Amy said.

"What's that in its hand?" Blanco walked over and pulled a papyrus from its stone fingers. He handed it to Hunter who unrolled it. "This is way over my head. I'm no expert on Egyptology, guys," he said, scanning through even more indecipherable hieroglyphs. "But I know a man who is. We need to take this to him. Finding references to gods is one thing, but Ramesses X was only three thousand years ago. This means whoever built this place was travelling to and from Egypt as recently as then."

"I want to leave," Quinn said, still scowling at Jodie. "Right now. I joined this team – correction – I was blackmailed into joining this team for my computer skills.

How the hell I ended up in the freaking land that time forgot, I neither know nor care."

"She's right," Lewis said. "We should go. We have what we want. At least this way we can get away before McCabe gets here."

Amy's face fell as she pointed to the entrance. "We're too late."

Hunter turned and saw the face of Brodie McCabe move into the light of one of his team's lanterns, cold and blue. As he moved into the chamber, a dozen men armed with submachine guns scrambled into the room and flanked him.

"Brodie, you just keep turning up like a bad penny. How many more times, I ask myself?"

"This will be last, Max. Put the statue and the papyrus down on the ground, raise your hands and turn around."

Hunter shuffled to his left, inching closer to the Ramesses statue's outstretched arm. "Like I said in Mosul, you bastard – if you want to kill me, then have the balls to look into my eyes. Go ahead and shoot."

"Whoa there chief," Jodie said. "You save that shit for when you're on your own."

"Have it your way," McCabe sneered. "Kill them all."

The men raised their guns but Hunter moved faster, heaving down on the statue's arm and triggering a secret exit. The chamber rumbled and shook and McCabe and his men took a few steps back. Just behind Hunter, a stone block slid aside to reveal the entrance to a secret tunnel.

"Don't just look at it!" he yelled to the team. "Get going!"

No one on the team hesitated or asked him how he knew about the hidden passageway behind the statue. In a hail of bullets, they raced into the tunnel and vanished into the darkness.

# CHAPTER TWENTY-SIX

At the end of the tunnel, Hunter broke through the undergrowth and emerged into a thick mist. It enveloped him like steam in a sauna, and then Fidel tumbled out of the split in the rock and crashed into his back. Behind them inside the hidden ravine, they heard more gunshots echoing in the tunnels and the sound of McCabe's ranting.

"He doesn't sound very pleased, amigo," Fidel said.

"He never does."

"How did you know about the hidden tunnel?" he asked.

"I saw the exact same statue in Iraq," Hunter said. "Only difference was the head. It was Nergal there, and Ramesses here, but the hand was clearly a lever in both places. Never mind that, Fidel – which way back to where we saw the choppers?"

The El Salvadorian guide pointed into the mist just off to their left. "I think if we go this way we can get to that position in a few minutes, but what about the guards?"

"We'll deal with that when we get there."

Amy and Quinn climbed out of the hole, reaching up to the rugged edges of the rocks with trembling hands as they heaved themselves out into the jungle. Jodie and Lewis were next with a puffing red-faced Blanco at the rear.

"Those damn guys nearly shot my ass off!" he said.

Quinn leaned back and looked at his behind. "Maybe if you didn't leave them such a big target area…"

"Enough with the funny," Amy said as Blanco crunched down into a swathe of mist-cloaked ferns.

"Yeah," the big man said. "I'm very proud of my ass."

"And now back to reality," Hunter said. "Be in no doubt, when McCabe catches up with us, he will kill us all."

"Reassuring," Lewis said.

"And if he gets this." Hunter waved the statue. "He gets the hat-trick – all three Winged Guardians – so can we make tracks over to the chopper and get the fuck out of here?"

Quinn squinted at him. "I object to the profanity, Dr Hunter. Seriously. I'm putting in a written complaint about you to UNESCO."

"Anything that makes your motor hum, honey," he said, "but you have to be alive to write your little complaint, right?"

"Sure."

A bullet pinged off the rock behind her head and cut up into the misty canopy with a tinny whistling sound. Quinn started and nearly jumped out of her skin. "Holy fuck!"

"Now can we go?" Hunter said, grabbing her by the hand and yanking her away from the hole. "And by the way, I'll be putting in a written complaint about your language to Director Gates."

They sprinted down the length of the ravine, vanishing like ghosts in the ancient cloud forest by the time McCabe reached the tunnel entrance. As his men piled out behind him, he ordered them to open fire along the path they had beaten in the jungle.

As soon as he heard the gunfire, Fidel darted off to his left. "This way my friends!"

With McCabe and his crew on their tails, they followed the guide deeper into the trees until pulling up in a small clearing. "I think we lost them," Amy called out, her chest rising and falling with the effort of the run.

"No way," Blanco said, desperately scanning the trees. "They're out there somewhere and we need to get to the other side of this clearing or we're sitting ducks."

They heard a sustained burst of gunfire chattering in the trees to their west. Disoriented by the mist and their desperate flight from Scorpion Ravine, even Hunter was confused. "I thought they were on our other side."

"No, that's right," Blanco said. "They should be over there."

More gunfire, closer now.

"Get down," Hunter warned.

Hunter drew his pistol and threw himself to the jungle floor. Landing with a soft thud in the moist, loamy dirt, he wiped the sweat from his eyes and tried to work out where the men had gone.

"You see them?" Jodie whispered. She had landed beside him and was holding her pistol in both her hands.

"Not yet, anyone?"

A gun exploded off to their right and a bullet ripped through the undergrowth surrounding them. They reacted fast, rolling around to face the direction of attack.

"Still can't see the bastards," Blanco said.

Fidel carefully got to his knees. "If I was a little higher I might just be able to see them."

"No! Get down!"

Hunter reached out for him but it was too late. A short crackle of gunfire and some tracer lines in the mist and then a line of bullets exploded out of their guide's back and blasted him off his feet. He crashed down into the dirt on his back, facing the canopy with wide, staring eyes. He started to mumble a Spanish prayer but died with the words on his lips.

Jodie gasped. "Someone's running away into the jungle!"

Hunter and Blanco fired into the trees at the fleeing man. Their rounds tore through tropical ferns and orchids and buried themselves in the trunk of a giant forest oak, but the man got away.

"Damn it!" Hunter said.

"Son of a bitch took Fidel out," Jodie said, respectfully closing the dead man's eyes. "Now we don't have a guide."

"We know where the choppers are," Amy said. "I'm more interested in how these guys are always one step ahead of us. Oh, and just who the hell they are!"

"We know who they are," Blanco said grimly.

To underscore the bleak comment, the croaky call of a toucan echoed in the dripping canopy high above them.

"Let's not go there," Amy said, starting to walk again. "It's not what we need right now."

"That's because it's a crock," Jodie said.

"What's a crock?" Hunter asked, following her. "If you know something I don't about McCabe's new friends, now's the time to tell me!"

"Not now," Amy said. "Besides, we don't know if McCabe and Gaius are working for Rorschach or not. It's a working assumption."

Jodie gave a dismissive laugh. "I never bought into Jim's bullshit theory about who's pulling Rorschach's strings, anyway. He lets his imagination run away with him sometimes. The idea a secret society hidden in some German mountain can deploy the sort of guys who can take special ops like this at the drop of a hat is just ridiculous."

"I wish I had your confidence," Amy said.

"Then who the hell took out Vazquez's men?" said Blanco, reloading his rifle. "Those guys were the real deal and now they're spread all over the jungle floor with so many gunshot and knife wounds they look like a barbecue platter."

"Damn it, Sal," Jodie said. "Leave that shit in your head next time."

Amy winced. "Yeah, and before I forget, Sal, can I just thank you for that image?"

"Be my guest."

Jodie ripped off her jacket, revealing a drenched tank-top and sun-tanned arms glistening with sweat. "Fuck this place already."

"I see one of McCabe's choppers!" Hunter yelled. "And just two guards."

Blanco sniffed. "One each, right?"

"How much?" Hunter said.

Quinn looked confused. "How much what?"

"To bet on who takes his man down first," Blanco said, lifting his paw to Hunter. "Fifty dollars."

"American or Mexico?"

"Funny. US."

"A done deal." Hunter said.

"Why not just shoot them?" Jodie asked.

"And risk giving our position away to McCabe?" Hunter said. "They'd be all over this clearing before we even had the blades whirring. Everyone stay low. We still don't know where McCabe and the others are."

Hunter used the cover of the trees for as long as they lasted, but the choppers were in a clearing. When he broke cover, he kept one of the giant transport helicopters in between him and the guard and then tracked around the outside of the aircraft until he was behind the man's back. Up close now, he scanned his weapons: an assault rifle over his shoulder and on his belt two holsters – a gun and combat knife.

He crept forward, pulling his combat knife but the man turned and shook his rifle from his shoulder and swung it around in Hunter's face. He had no time, and threw the knife at the man. It spun silently through the air and the blade buried itself in his chest. In shock, the man fired and got off a single round. The bullet gouged a hole in the heel of Hunter's palm but broke no bones.

As the guard grunted in pain and reached for the knife's handle, Hunter rushed him and took out the knife. The guard blinked several times, working his mouth but saying nothing. Hunter grabbed his head and twisted it, instantly breaking his neck. Looking across the makeshift airfield, he saw Blanco's guard crumpling to the ground, dead.

"Who was first?" he said.

Blanco shrugged. "Beats me. Let's call it even. What about the other chopper?"

"We blow it up when we're airborne." Hunter turned and called back to the team in the tree line. "All clear, everyone in the chopper. I'll fire her up."

"Wait," Blanco said. "You're not flying with a wounded hand, Max. Let me take this one."

Hunter looked at the blood pouring from his hand. "It's just a flesh wound."

"Do as he says, Max." It was Amy. "That's an order."

Blanco shrugged. "It's not wise to cross the boss."

Hunter had a smartass reply all ready, but when he looked up and saw the look on Amy's face, he changed tack. "I guess not. Everyone inside now!"

# CHAPTER TWENTY-SEVEN

Blanco raced through the pre-flight checks and started the engine. Amy climbed into the seat beside him up front, while Hunter, Jodie, Quinn and Lewis sat in the rear compartment and quickly buckled up their seatbelts. The brusque Brooklynite flashed his eyes over the instrument panel and then raised the collective, lifting the helicopter slowly out of the clearing.

He turned the chopper in the air until it faced the other helicopter and fired the chin-mounted Gatling gun in a remorseless burst of fire. The rounds made short work of the grounded chopper's thin metal skin and when they reached the gas tank a spark ignited the kerosene and blew the aircraft all over the clearing. Chunks of burning metal rained down on the jungle as McCabe and his men burst out of the trees.

"That's you done, Brodie," Hunter laughed, looking down at the bullet-raked heaps of twisted fuselage beneath them.

"Thank God," Jodie said.

"We're not out of it yet," Blanco told her. "They're getting something out of the metal chest we saw on the edge of the clearing."

"What the hell now?" Amy said.

"It's a drone," said Hunter, peering out of the window as he wrapped a bandage from the first aid kit around his hand. When it was airborne, he turned to Amy and said, "And it's going to move a lot faster than this old bird."

"Maybe we can lose it in the mist?" she asked.

He shook his head. "We can try, but we have to presume it's fitted with heat-seeking technology. It'll fix onto our heat signature and stay right on our arses. You hear that, Sal?"

"I hear you."

"So what do we do?" Amy asked. "Just wait until it blows us out of the sky?"

Blanco chuckled. "Hey, you're forgetting who's flying this thing. I'm a US Army helicopter pilot with years of combat experience under my belt. I'm not about to let these guys take us out just like that." He snapped his fingers to underline the point. "I have a plan."

"Hunter's First Law," Hunter said. "Always have a plan."

"And would you like to share your plan with the rest of us?" Amy asked.

A burst of sustained fire to their right; these were no warning shots. The quadcopter drone was aiming to kill, and then the operator swooped the machine down out of the sky until it was level with them. They all knew what was coming next.

Blanco tipped the chopper down and hard to the right. They felt their stomachs turn as the helicopter barrelled into a narrow valley, levelled out and skimming just meters over the top of the canopy.

Amy gasped. "Quinn, can you hack the drone?"

"Damn it, I hope so," Lewis said.

Quinn sighed. "While making dangerously low passes through the El Salvadorian mountains in a speeding helicopter?"

"Too much?"

"Not at all," she said, casually running a hand over her short, raven black hair. "I'm still wondering when you're going to give me a challenge." The pale young woman pulled her GPD Pocket laptop out of her bag and pulled it open. The tiny computer was only slightly bigger than a smartphone but contained a much faster Intel CPU and a physical keyboard, favored by hackers. "Just keep me alive long enough to do it."

Blanco levelled the aircraft. "That's a deal!"

"I'll buy that for a dollar fifty," said Jodie.

As the grey hat hacker's fingers danced over the keys, they all heard the sound of more gunfire chattering from behind them.

"They're firing again!" Amy said.

Blanco said nothing. He had seen the drone lining up to take another shot and was already taking evasive action. He swung the chopper hard to the left and banked around in a tight arc before descending into another narrow valley and a thicker bank of mist.

Amy leaned forward as far as her belt would allow. "Whoa, can you fly this thing in that kind of weather?"

"I guess we're about to find out," he said through his helmet headset. "How's that hacking coming on, Quinn?"

"I'm getting there, Sal. It's not easy. Some of these new drones are based on dragonfly neurons. That's how they're so agile, but fear not – I'm using the same kind of exploit we smashed that Vegas security system with."

Blanco gave a quick thumbs up. "That was a great night, let's hope it works this time."

"Does what happened in Vegas have to stay in Vegas, or is someone going to tell what's going on?" Hunter asked.

"Brief the newbie, Amy," Quinn said, fingers still tapping on the tiny keyboard. "I'm too busy, also I don't care if he knows or not."

"Thanks," Hunter said.

The chopper rolled in some turbulence as more of the drone's bullets traced past them and vanished in the mist on their starboard side. Amy was gripping her armrest like her life depended on it when she turned to Max. "Quinn overloaded the security system at a major casino in Las Vegas a few weeks ago by sending thousands of consecutive Wi-Fi connection requests into it. Each one of the requests was attempting to take control of the system which resulted in the central processing unit crashing and shutting down the system."

"It was a work of genius," Blanco said, piloting the helicopter up out of a valley and around the top of one of the range's mist-cloaked peaks. "But can you do it this time, Quinn?"

"Not that way, no," she said, frowning. "I already got into the drone using a brute force attack and injected a rootkit. Right now I'm sending some data packets in an attempt to overload the drone's flight app buffer's capacity allocation."

"If I knew what any of that meant," Hunter said, "I bet I'd be even more impressed than I am right now."

"Save your wonder," Quinn said sarcastically. "Because that didn't work either."

"And they're bringing the drone right behind us again," Blanco said.

"Give me time, Sal."

"I'm doing my best, but we're running out of places to hide." Blanco steered the chopper down into a misty ravine. "And right now our lives are hanging on a pretty shaky ground proximity warning system older than you, Quinn."

"I'm not done yet," she said calmly. "I'm programming my laptop to mimic the drone."

"What does that do?" Hunter asked.

Jodie screamed when more turbulence rocked them from side to side. "I hate flying!"

"We don't second-guess the genius, Hunter," Quinn said. "We simply obey it without question. Damn, I thought you said this guy had been briefed, Amy?"

"Special Agent Fox seems to have overlooked telling me about the north face of your personality disorder," Hunter said. "Mount Ego."

Quinn ignored him. "Okay, Sal, hang on just a second longer. I'm sending a whole bunch of fake data packets back to the drone's controller and… holy crap! Can't you keep this thing stable?"

"We're getting shot by a drone, Quinn!"

She rolled her eyes. "Fuck's sake, everyone's got an excuse."

"Are you done yet?" Lewis said.

Hunter laughed. "With the moaning or the hacking?"

She snapped the laptop shut. "Both, and you can all thank me later."

They all looked out of the starboard windows and watched the drone drop away from the side of the helicopter and streak down toward the canopy. It broke through the treetops and then exploded in a massive fireball, muted by the thick mist drifting over the forest.

"Beautiful work, Quinn," Blanco said.

"What did you do?" asked Hunter.

"I broke the comms link between the controller and the drone and caused it to go into safe mode, which means an automatic landing."

"So why did it blow up?"

She slipped her laptop back into her bag and crossed her arms over her chest. Once again, she seemed to get smaller, all folded away in the creases of her baggy black hoodie. Slumping down in her seat, she pulled her hood over her face and closed her eyes. "Because I wanted it to."

"No one screws with Quinn Mosley," Amy said.

Hunter looked at the young goth and thought he saw the ghost of a smile through the black lipstick. "Good job. You saved our lives."

"Can't a girl get some peace and quiet around here?" she said. "I'm trying to sleep."

Blanco zoomed up out of the mist and rounded another peak before turning the helicopter to the southwest. "We're going back to San Salvador," he said through the headset. "We did it, folks."

"Yes we did!" Amy said. "Good job, everyone."

Hunter was frowning.

"Max?"

"Maybe now you can tell me just who the hell you all think McCabe, Gaius and Rorschach are working for?"

A tense silence filled the headsets and everyone except Hunter shared an uncertain look with one another. Amy's voice broke the silence, crackling with static but clear enough to understand. "Yeah… we need to talk."

# CHAPTER TWENTY-EIGHT

Their last night in El Salvador was spent in a bad part of town. Deep inside the gang-controlled neighbourhood of Zacamil, they stayed in a cheap motel tucked away behind one of the city's many housing projects. Hunter was drying his hair with a thin bleach-smelling towel when he stepped out of the shower room and saw the rest of the team waiting for him.

The attack in the jungle had hit everyone hard and when he saw them chatting quietly among themselves, he suddenly felt like an outsider again. "Guess it's a good job I decided to put my trousers on," he quipped.

"Pants," Amy said.

"Trousers."

"Pants."

"Whatever you want to call them," Blanco said. "Max was right to ask about who we think Rorschach is working for."

"I *am* right," Hunter said. "In fact, I'm rarely wrong."

"Talk about ego," Amy said.

"Thanks – we can talk about it later," Hunter said. "I'd like that. But now I want to know who was helping Brodie McCabe hunt me through the jungle. They seem like quite the upgrade from his usual goons. Right now I'm finding it pretty crazy that McCabe and our friend Gaius might be working for Rorschach, never mind who *he* answers to."

Quiet, reserved and almost shy, Amy now looked at him earnestly. "If you think that's crazy, then wait until you find out who we think Rorschach's working for."

"You're making me nervous," he said with a smile. "Should I sit down?"

"Maybe." She patted the end of the bed, beside her.

"I don't know," he said. "If the news is that heavy maybe I need to sit on the toilet instead."

Lewis laughed, but the rest of the team were stony-faced.

"Sorry," he said, leaning against the TV cabinet. "I'm listening."

"Good," Amy said. "Because this is no joke. We think Oskar Rorschach is working for the Illuminati."

Hunter paused in the silence and then fell about laughing.

She looked genuinely offended. "What's so funny?"

"You're not being serious?"

"Yes, I am," she said, her face hardening.

"But they don't even exist," he said. "You might as well have told me our nemesis is the Joker."

"It's not true that they don't exist," she replied. "Sure, thanks to a series of high profile adventure novels and movies, the name is bandied about far too often these days. The fictional story that has grown up around the word is outrageous, and while the powers that be want us to believe the truth is more prosaic, the reality could be much darker."

Hunter tossed the towel on one of the beds. "Wait – you really are suggesting the Illuminati are actually a thing, aren't you?"

"Oh, they're definitely a thing," Quinn said. "There's no doubt of that. They were formally founded in 1776 by Adam Weishaupt, a professor of law and philosophy at the University of Ingolstadt. Some say today they're headquartered under Denver Airport."

Hunter was starting to wish he had sat down. Instead, he unscrewed the top from a bottle of water and took a long, slow sip. His eyes fell on his bag just behind Amy on the bed. The top was open and the head and wingtips of the precious Winged Guardian were just visible, shining brilliantly in the room's greasy lamplight. He passed a hand over his face and collected his thoughts. "You guys aren't yanking my chain, are you?"

"No," Amy said. "Director Gates is a retired US naval intelligence officer with a distinguished combat record. He rarely goes in for chain-yanking, especially when vital national security is concerned."

"All right, I'm sorry. You were telling me about the Illuminati. Trying to convince me they're real."

"They *were* real," Amy said. "We think they're something a little different now."

"I don't understand."

"The history is simple. Weishaupt formed the original society at the end of the Age of Enlightenment, and he intended the society to be based on the principles so important to that time – wisdom and knowledge and what have you. That's why he used the Owl of Minerva as the society's symbol."

"The Owl of what?"

She arched an eyebrow. "I see someone never read his Hegel."

"Are you still talking in English?"

"Minerva was the Roman goddess of wisdom and perspicacity."

"Now I know it's not English."

"She went to a very good school," Quinn said. "Like all blue bloods."

"The *point* is," Amy continued, "Weishaupt intended the Illuminati to be a society of and for the enlightened, hence the Owl of Minerva. As Hegel once wrote, *The owl of Minerva spreads its wings only with the falling of the dusk.* Or in other words, only when something has passed can you really understand what it was all about."

"I get it," Lewis said. "Like the way you don't know if you got a bad chili dog until later that night."

"Yes, Ben," Amy said. "I believe that is what Hegel was getting at. Some believe that despite Weishaupt's best intentions to create a society for the promotion of enlightenment principles, the group was infiltrated by another much older and sinister force. They crept into the society covertly until they controlled it and then redirected the entire group to work for their own ends."

Hunter set his water down and pulled out a chair from under the desk. "So what happened to Weishaupt?"

"The original Order of the Illuminati was banned and he was exiled to the palace of Duke Ernest II of Saxe-Coburg-Gotha, whose Illuminati name was Quintus Severus."

"All this sounds very cloak and dagger to me."

"It was – they'd been banned," Quinn said.

Amy continued. "He died in his eighties and the membership of the Order was dispersed – or so we are told. As I say, the truth is that the Order was never broken up and simply went underground, calling themselves the Creed. They used their banishment as cover to move out of sight and continue to grow in number and influence. Today they are more powerful than ever and run what is essentially a shadow network behind the scenes of many of the world's biggest governments."

"Including the US?"

"Let's not go there," Amy said. "Not right now."

Hunter sighed. "Isn't this a little heavy for such a nice sunny evening?"

"It gets heavier when you ask just why the hell do they want to find Atlantis?" Blanco asked.

Hunter leaned back in his chair and folded his hands behind his head. "And heavier still when you ask why my life just got turned into a Dan Brown novel? Who else knows about this?"

"About Rorschach possibly being part of the Creed?" Amy asked.

"Yeah."

"No one, at least not as far as we know. As of this moment, the rest of the world thinks Oskar Rorschach is nothing more than a Swiss business magnate and philanthropist with an abiding interest in ancient civilizations. We know better because we intercepted emails from his account in Switzerland. He was sending them to known members of the Creed."

Hunter looked like he wanted to take a strong drink or three. "So he's a major league player in the world's most notorious secret society. Wow."

"We're not a hundred percent on Rorschach yet," Amy said. "But we've almost got him. Like I say, we know he's been engaging in an extensive email correspondence with key members of the group in Germany, Sweden, England and the US. We have no direct proof he is in the Creed but the evidence is starting to stack up against him. If we're right, he's what they call the Apostle, and we think Gaius works for him as what they call a disciple. We think Gaius probably hired McCabe to help him find the statues for the Creed."

"And that's why you were undercover at the Rorschach Foundation?"

"That's right."

A hushed silence descended on the briefing room.

"Earth to Hunter?" Jodie said. "You still with us, buddy?"

He blew out a long breath and shook his head in shock. "I've done a lot of digs and seen a lot of stuff, but if we're talking about secret societies and crazed devotees calling themselves disciples, then I'm starting to feel out of my depth."

"I get that," Amy said.

Blanco smiled. "Tell me about it."

"So now you know what we're really up against," Amy said. "I hope you can see why it's so important that we find out what they want with Atlantis."

Hunter nodded silently, still struggling to believe McCabe could be part of such an organization. "I'm still in. I've wanted to find Atlantis my whole life and I'm not letting McCabe frighten me off, no matter who he's working for."

"But…" Amy said.

"But I'm going to need to run this past my boss."

"I'm your boss," she said with a smirk.

"You know who I mean," he said. "Juliette Bonnaire at UNESCO. This is a major development and she needs to be briefed."

"That's fine with us," she said, breathing a sigh of relief. "I'm glad you're staying on board, Max, because we really need you right now."

He shook his head. "No, you really need my old doctorate supervisor."

The team shared an uncomfortable look. "Why?"

"Because I've been trying to work out the glyphs on the papyrus we found in the lost city back in Scorpion Ravine and I'm just not getting anywhere."

"But I thought you were the greatest man alive?" Jodie said.

"Hardly," he said with a disarming smile. "Just *one* of the greatest. The truth is I'm not an expert in early Egyptian hieroglyphs, but like I said back in the ravine, I know a man who is. He's called Professor Julian Walters and he's the greatest Egyptologist on the planet. But there's a problem. I remember what you said about how long it took you to vet and approve me for coming inside the team. I'm worried about how long we're going to have to wait while you do that for Julian. He's a miserable old bastard but I think we could really use him."

"He'll say no," Amy said confidently.

"And how do you know that?"

"Because we already asked him." She took in his shocked expression. "That's right, you were our second choice."

"You really know how to make a man feel special. Did Julian really say no?"

"Not in so many words," Blanco said. "His vocabulary was much richer. We got the impression he doesn't like to be bothered much."

"I could have told you that. He took a year's sabbatical from Oxford a year or so ago and moved to Arizona. After a few months watering his cactus collection and photographing the pueblo ruins he took a job with the

Louvre in Paris. Put it this way, I was his best student and the last time I contacted him he told me to get lost."

"We really need him, Max. He's our best chance right now."

"Again, thanks for building up my confidence and self-esteem."

"Will you talk to him and get him on board?"

Hunter lifted his head and stared up at the nicotine-stained ceiling. After a few seconds thinking about it, he looked back at the team. "I'll speak to him, but knowing now that he already said no, I'm not promising anything."

A round of high-fives went around the room. Amy took out her phone and started to make a call.

"What are you doing?" Lewis asked.

"If Max has to meet with Professor Bonnaire at UNESCO and then talk to Professor Walters at the Louvre, we need to get to Paris as fast as possible. I presume no one has any objections to a short trip to the City of Lights?"

When she saw there were no objections, she hit the speed dial and called Director Gates.

# CHAPTER TWENTY-NINE

"Good to see you, Max."

Hunter wandered over to Juliette's desk and shook her hand. "Always a pleasure."

"And I see you have some introductions to make."

"This is Amy Fox, Sal Blanco, Jodie Priest, Dr Ben Lewis and the inimitable Quinn Mosley," he said. "They work for a covert branch of the FBI concerned with antiquities crime."

"Pleased to meet you all," she said. "And welcome to Paris and UNESCO. I understand you saved Dr Hunter's life during a dangerous helicopter chase, Special Agent Mosley. Thank you."

The young woman shrugged and looked down at her trainers. Hunter was interested to see a vague trace of embarrassment on her face. "You got any coffee?" she said.

"Please, have a seat. I have already ordered coffee."

"Cool."

Quinn crashed down in the seat farthest from Juliette's desk and stared forlornly out of the window at the Paris drizzle. Hands stuffed deep in her pockets and her hood pulled up over her head as usual, she was barely visible at all.

Juliette arched an eyebrow, her perfect sense of professional etiquette untouched by the young woman's rudeness. "I see why they call you the Ghost."

"It's just *Ghost*," she mumbled through her black-painted lips. "Not *the* Ghost. I'm not drawn by Marvel and I'd look like shit in Spandex."

Hunter moved to talk but Amy caught his eye and cautioned against it. Juliette stared at him with wide eyes, just two old friends sharing a silent, private joke before getting back to business. Then, she softly clapped her hands together and sat down behind her desk. "Anyway, thank heavens you are safe. Now, you must tell me what happened in El Salvador."

As the drizzle ran down the windowpanes, Hunter recounted to his boss everything that had happened to him in Cuba and El Salvador. From the fire fight on Vazquez's private cruise ship to his brutal slaying in the jungles of El Salvador and the discovery of the third winged statue in the mysterious cloud-forest's lost city.

Juliette raised an eyebrow and pushed back in her leather chair. "This sounds insane even for you, Max. I trust your ego came through unscathed."

"There's more," he said. "But yes, it did, and thanks for asking."

"You're more than welcome," she said, leaning forwards and resting her elbows on her desk once again. Cupping her chin in her hand, she said, "What do you mean when you say there's more?"

"Amy?" Hunter said. "I think maybe this might sound less crazy coming from you."

She gave him a look and then fixed her sharp eyes on Juliette. "We believe Brodie McCabe is working for Oskar Rorschach."

"That's impossible." She dismissed the notion with an arrogant wave of her hand. "I know both men and I find it impossible to believe they could work with each other. They are… comme le jour et la nuit."

"Huh?" Jodie said.

"Like day and night," Hunter said. "Chalk and cheese."

"But nonetheless they *are* working with one another," Amy said. "And they mean business."

"Non, that's the most insane thing I ever heard in my life."

"You'd think…" Hunter said.

"What does that mean?" Juliette asked.

"It means pour yourself a cognac, Julie," he said drily. "Because what comes next isn't going to be easy to take."

Juliette was hard to rattle. She picked a fountain pen off the top of some papers and started to twirl it around her fingers. "Try me."

"We believe Rorschach is a member of a secret society called the Creed," Amy said bluntly. "They inherited a vast empire of power and connections from the Illuminati when it was banned in the late eighteenth century."

Juliette started to laugh but held it in check. "This is a joke, n'est-ce pas?"

Hunter tensed. "No joke, Julie."

"I have known Oskar Rorschach for twenty years," she said. "Not only is he one of the world's foremost collectors of antiquities who knows the market better than anyone, but he is also the kindest and most generous man I have ever met. Now you sit here and tell me he's some sort of supervillain in the Illuminati. This is nonsense."

"It's not nonsense," Amy said. "And they're called the Creed now."

"Max, don't tell me you believe this?"

"I saw Brodie out in the jungle, Julie. He was fighting alongside some bloody fierce and determined men, and they were incredibly well armed and trained. Only someone with serious reach and wealth could buy men like that."

"That could be a lot of people."

"We have emails," Amy said. "Emails between McCabe and Rorschach, and emails between Rorschach and known members of the Creed – senior members. We're telling you the truth."

Hunter clapped his hands together, startling everyone. "And that's your friendly morning briefing."

She held her breath in for a few seconds and then blew it out in a long, slow stream as she considered what she had been told. Everyone in the room felt the tension dissipate a little when she smiled and tossed her pen on the desk. "Bien, in that case, it is more important than ever that we beat them to Atlantis, non?"

"Damn straight," Amy said.

"And to that end," Hunter said. "I was thinking about talking to Julian."

Juliette gave a shrill laugh. "Julian Walters? This time I *know* you are making a joke."

"Wrong again. I need his help. I know what I said in the briefing sounds insane, but we found artifacts with early Egyptian glyphs on them in the El Salvadorian complex. We both know Julian is by far the world's leading authority on them. I can make sense of them in a loose way, but all I can gather is a rough idea. They're pointing to something they call the Gate of the Gods but where is still a mystery."

She shrugged. "You know Julian. He's not exactly described as an easy-going man."

"And he's already told us to get lost," Amy said.

"Then you are wasting your time."

"No, we're not." Hunter pulled the statue out of his bag. "Not when he sees this. He told Amy and the team to get lost before we had this, but when he sees it he'll get behind us, I just know it. He's still at the Louvre, right?"

She nodded, wide eyes staring at the statue. "Yes. He works mostly alone there, which is good, because no one else would work with him."

"Not anymore," Hunter said, stuffing the statue back in his bag. "He's working with us now."

"Then I will call him for you and make an appointment," Juliette said. "But I wouldn't expect miracles."

Hunter's face broke into a broad, bright smile as he leaned back in his chair and folded his arms behind his head. "Who needs miracles when I'm around?"

Amy rolled her eyes. "Heaven help us all."

"For now, let's just make do with Julian."

Blanco's thick Brooklyn accent filled the room. "But can we trust this guy?"

"Trust him, yes." Juliette picked up the phone and started dialling. "Like him? Impossible."

# CHAPTER THIRTY

Gaius watched the cloaked Apostle closely as he walked into the study. From somewhere behind him he heard the sound of a deep, low organ playing and then he saw his hands, stained red with blood. The Teacher stepped into a small room and Gaius heard running water and smelled soap. When his glorious mentor emerged back into the study, the cloak was gone and the hands were washed clean of the blood.

Whose blood? Gaius knew better than to ask.

"You have an update for me, Gaius?"

"Yes, Teacher."

The smell of sandalwood soap wafted over him as the Apostle walked to his ornate mahogany desk and set about leafing through a stack of paperwork.

"Well?"

"McCabe and the disciples failed to retrieve the third Winged Guardian in El Salvador."

The Apostle tensed and immediately lost interest in his papers. "Hunter has it?"

"Yes, Teacher." He added hastily, "But we have the other two."

"We need the third."

"I know. There's more."

The Apostle frowned. "Speak."

"McCabe believes Hunter and his team found something else in the El Salvador lost city."

"What?"

"He's not certain, but he believes a statue in the complex was holding some sort of map."

"This is not good enough. Where are they now?"

Gaius watched a swallow wheeling in the sky outside the Apostle's window, high above the oxbow lake beyond the castle. "In Paris."

"At UNESCO?"

Gaius nodded once. "Yes. Our contact there has just told us they are to seek further advice relating to the map they found in Scorpion Ravine."

The Apostle closed his eyes and listened to the organ. Gaius thought maybe it was a Bach cantata, but he was untutored in classical music. After a long, pregnant pause, the Apostle opened his eyes. "Hunter is to be intercepted in Paris. I want the third Winged Guardian and I want whatever they found in El Salvador. Is that clear?"

"Yes, Teacher. It will be done."

"It had better be done," he growled. "The Chimera's appetite is insatiable, Gaius."

Gaius tried to hide a hard swallow. "Yes, my Teacher."

"Absolutely, terrifyingly insatiable."

"Your orders will be carried out at once."

"Go, Gaius. Fly like the phoenix! This time the spoils-of-war are unimaginably glorious."

Gaius bowed and left the room. As he walked down the corridor, the sound of the organ receded behind him, and the sordid smell of soap and blood mixed together with the thought of the Chimera. Suddenly he felt sick to the bottom of his stomach.

# CHAPTER THIRTY-ONE

The Louvre is one of the most famous museums in the world. The former palace is also one of the most famous buildings, with a blend of architectural styles ranging from gothic through renaissance into baroque, all reflecting its long and complex history. Originally protected by a dry moat and stone counterscarps, the site today hums with thousands of international tourists all desperate to see its countless artifacts and artwork.

Hunter had been here before with Avril, but that was a long time ago. The two of them strolled hand in hand along this very sidewalk, washed in the sunset with the prospect of a great evening ahead of them. Now, as he walked through the eastern end of the Tuileries Garden and turned left into the museum's main courtyard, he was reminded of those early days, and all the promises the two of them had made to each other and then broken.

Walking past the famous Louvre Pyramid, he was reminded of the importance of their quest. His career had taken him to many of the most interesting places on earth, but since meeting Amy in Switzerland everything had changed. The significance of pyramids to ancient cultures wasn't something that surprised any archaeologist; they could be found all over the world in one form or another. He considered Sacsayhuamán in the Peruvian Andes, or Teotihuacán in Mexico; Ji'An in northeastern China and the ninth century Borobudur Temple in Java, but it was their connection to Atlantis that enthralled him.

"I hope Professor Walters is able to help us," Amy said.

"You realize Julian is the biggest sceptic on earth?" Hunter said. "He nearly threw me off my doctorate when I started asking serious questions about Atlantis."

"He also happens to be the greatest Egyptologist in the world," Amy said.

"You don't have to tell me that. He taught me most of what I know. I'm just saying, get ready for a rough ride."

They stepped through the entrance and walked to the front desk. Hunter spoke in French and was given directions to his old mentor's office. The museum was approaching closing time and the corridors and exhibition rooms were slowly emptying of tourists as they made their way across the enormous palace.

Outside the office, Hunter straightened his shirt and relaxed his shoulders. He turned to the team standing behind him and gave them a smile. "Anyone got a Prozac?"

The door swished open before anyone could answer. A tall man was almost totally filling the space where the door had been moments earlier.

Hunter extended a hand. "It's great to see you, Julian."

"Max. Are you getting fatter?"

Hunter's smile faded. "And thanks for taking the time out to see us."

The tall English archaeologist was dressed well, as Hunter had expected, in a pale cream linen suit and a black shirt. His bright blue eyes sparkled in the soft light of the corridor.

"Hey, as the Americans say – it's your dime."

Hunter withdrew his unshaken hand. "Your new job hasn't mellowed you," he muttered.

"What was that?"

"I wondered how your new job is going?"

"It's work," he snapped. "Work is work. It goes along." He flattened his hand and pushed it through the air in front of him. "It's not like retirement. That doesn't go anywhere. It just sits there while you get older. Trust me, I tried it for a year in Arizona."

Hunter nodded and gave a cheery laugh. "Excellent, let me introduce you to everyone. This is Special Agent Amy Fox, the Assistant Director of the FBI's Antiquities and Heritage Office. Special Agents Sal Blanco, Jodie Priest, Ben Lewis and Quinn Mosley are part of her team. They're based in Washington DC."

"Really? Walters said. "I had no idea the FBI was based there. Anyway, come in."

This time Hunter's laugh was more strained. As Walters walked back over to his desk, Hunter lowered his voice so only Amy could hear. "I told you."

"He'd better be worth it, Max."

Walters's voice boomed from the other side of the office. "I hope you've got something worth my time, Max. Busy man here."

They took their seats. Amy had learned enough about their new addition not to push him too hard, and when she spoke it was in a straight, businesslike tone. They were paying him a great deal of money for his time, after all. "As you know, Professor, we're in some trouble and we need your help."

"Yes, you called me a few weeks ago and I told you to bugger off. I gather this time you actually have something interesting to show me?"

"Yes," Amy said. "We located some artifacts in El Salvador."

"Montecristo," he said. "Bonnaire already told me on the phone." He ignored Amy now and turned to Hunter. "What are we talking about, Max? Pre-Columbian Mayan?"

"Try Twentieth Dynasty Egyptian."

Walters nearly smiled. "I'm sorry, what?"

"You heard me."

"What I heard is not possible, so try telling me again. Use your words, Max. Start from the beginning."

Hunter and Amy shared a glance of mutual sympathy before the Londoner bravely continued. "The beginning? Fine. You recall *Diocles*, the supplement to Plato's *Critias* that I found in the dig in Athens a few months ago?"

"Who could forget? You practically hired a skywriter to tell the world you'd found it."

Amy smirked. "That does *not* sound like the Max I know."

Hunter coughed. "Anyway, inside the document I found a further description of Atlantis, including an intriguing reference to three winged guardians. Plato described them as angelic in appearance and made from something similar to silver, but with a rose-blush. Instantly I knew he must be describing orichalcum."

Julian sighed. "Oh, Max, when are you going to grow up and leave this Atlantis stuff behind? With some hard work and a lot of luck you could be a half-decent archaeologist."

Hunter heard Jodie stifle a laugh behind him. "Gee, *thanks*, Julian."

Amy stepped in. "As unbelievable as it sounds, we found the statues Plato wrote about in *Diocles.*"

Walters perked up. "Max?"

"As I was saying," Hunter said lazily. "The document led me to a labyrinth beneath the Tomb of Jonah at the Gates of Nineveh and I found one of the winged statues."

"Bugger me with a honey dipper," Walters said. "I apologize for what I said before, Max. You could easily be a three-quarter decent archaeologist."

Hunter gave a warm, sarcastic smile. "Again, thank you."

"May I see this statue?"

"No, it was stolen on site by Brodie McCabe."

"McCabe? I didn't know he had it in him. Stealing it is the only way he'd ever get his hands on it. He'd never find it. He's sloppier at research than you are."

Hunter turned to Amy with another smile. "I'm more of a field archaeologist."

"Anyway," Walters boomed. "Do carry on with your tale of derring-do and adventure. I'm gripped."

"If you insist," Hunter said. "After discovering the statue, I was invited to the home of Oskar Rorschach."

Walters's smile faded and he sat up in his seat. "What did he want?"

"To show me some very interesting ceremonial daggers and some photographs of a winged statue. All of the artifacts in the pictures had strong parallels to the workmanship I saw on the statue in Mosul."

"Fascinating. More, please."

"Rorschach was sent the daggers and the picture of the winged statue by a black market relics dealer named Raul Vazquez. He wanted to sell them to him and Rorschach wanted me to go down there and conduct a pre-sale authentication."

"Which you did."

"Which I did, and nearly got my head blown off in the process. While I was down there, I met my new friends here, and alongside the second winged statue we also saw a Nazi map Vazquez was hiding in his little floating strongroom. Vazquez got away with the statue and the map but we got photos. They were easy to decipher and it led us to a lost city in El Salvador where we found another almost identical statue. Vazquez and his men were slaughtered by McCabe on site.

Hunter reached into his bag, pulled out the statue and set it on Walters's desk. The old man gasped and reached forward to pick it up.

"So, McCabe got the winged statue in Iraq and the one from Vazquez, but you got the one from the El Salvadorian city?"

"Correct, and as you can see, it ain't silver."

Walters turned it over in his hands and it sparkled in the light. "My God, this is incredible – but what has it to do with Twentieth Dynasty Egypt?"

"In the lost city, we also found a life-size statue of Ramesses X guarding some sort of model, which I believe will give us the clue to the location of Atlantis. Here's a picture."

Quinn took her laptop from her bag and flicked across to the pictures. "We uploaded them from Sal's camera onto this. They're all right there."

Walters looked at her with suspicion as he took the device. "Oh my..."

"Exactly," Hunter said. "If you know how Egyptian artifacts from a thousand years before Christ ended up in a lost city in the El Salvador jungle, I'd love to hear it."

"I have no idea."

"Atlantis, Julian." Hunter's eyes were almost wild with something resembling greed. "It's the only explanation. Only an ancient highly-advanced civilization based somewhere in the center of these locations could explain this. We know the ancient Egyptians and the ancient Maya did not have the capability to travel such vast distances, which is the only other explanation. Atlantis, Julian. Atlantis."

Walters shook his head, but couldn't take his eyes off the statue and Quinn's laptop. "I don't know, but…"

"I need your help, Julian. I've tried to translate the glyphs on the Ramesses statue and they seem to be talking about how the statue was a gift from the gods, and something else called the Gate of the Gods. I think a full translation will reveal not only the location of Ramesses's tomb but maybe even Atlantis. Can you help us?"

"I think so, but I'll need time."

"That's the one thing we just don't have," Amy said.

Walters looked at her, confused. "What do you mean? If Max is right and there is an Atlantis, then it's been there for thousands and thousands of years. Another few days won't make any difference to anything."

Amy said, "We think McCabe is stealing the statues for an order placed by Oskar Rorschach, and we think Rorschach is working for an Illuminati group called the Creed."

Walters set both the statue and the miniature laptop down. "And to think you almost had me…"

"It's true, Julian," Hunter said, his patience running thinner by the second. "Listen to what she's telling you. Be a gentleman."

Walters gave his former protégé a wry look. "Do go on, Special Agent Fox."

"As I say, we believe Rorschach belongs to a highly secretive organization called the Creed. The FBI has been tracking this for a long time and at first we thought they were simply trying to control the world's antiquities market. Since Max came on board, we now think they're trying to locate Atlantis. We don't know why."

Walters paled. "Tell me more about this *Creed.*"

"We believe they were formed by the same man who formed the Illuminati."

Walters shook his head again. "No, I never heard so much drivel in all my life."

Hunter looked at his old mentor. "Please, Julian – just hear her out. It's not as crazy as it sounds."

"All right, I'm listening. But it had better be good. I have a serious reputation in this academic discipline and I'm not going to blow it all on the kind of thing you see in an adventure movie."

"The founder of the Illuminati was a man named Adam—."

"Adam Weishaupt," Walters said.

"You know."

He sighed. "Who doesn't know that in 2019? We've had about fifty movies based on this since that damn book came out."

"Fine, and in that case you'll probably know that Weishaupt angered the authorities when his society became too powerful and its members began infiltrating all the top positions of government in Bavaria and beyond."

"Yes, I know that also."

"So they banned the Illuminati and Weishaupt was exiled to Gotha, a small town in central Germany, where he was patronized by the Duke of Saxe-Gotha-Altenburg, Ernest II."

Walters had started to relax now. "Go on."

"When he was living under the patronage of the duke, he continued to work and write on the subject of the enlightenment until he died there in 1830. Many of his writings centerd on the persecution of the Illuminati by the Bavarian Government, but what most people don't realize is that another secret society called the Creed simply replaced the vacuum left by them after it was banned."

"What evidence do you have for this?"

"Scant evidence, but enough."

Walters nodded thoughtfully, and when he spoke, his tone was less hostile. "What has any of this to do with my presence being necessary in all this? Right now I'm struggling to see what links an eighteenth century European illuminist society with the jungles of the El Salvadorian highlands and Paris. You might say I'm in need of enlightenment."

Walters chuckled at his own joke as Amy thought carefully about her reply.

"As I have already tried to explain to you, we believe the Creed is still at work today, and continues to exert covert influence over many governments and other powerful institutions."

"So this is about the Creed pulling the levers of power behind the scenes after all?"

"It's not about what they're already doing, Julian," Hunter said. "It's about what they're going to do next. We're telling you this because your life could be in danger."

"Finally, something exciting," he said wearily. After a long pause, he said, "Fine, leave this with me and I'll look at it."

Amy got up from her seat. "We can't leave this with you. It's FBI property and it's staying with me."

Walters face crumpled with anger. "You come in here begging me for a favor and then tell me you don't trust me? Get out of my office."

"Whoa," Hunter said. "Take it easy. I'm sure Amy simply meant we can't leave the statue with you. Right Amy?"

"Well..."

"I'm sure we trust Professor Walters to keep copies of all the pictures we took."

"Yes," she said, still uncertain. "Copies."

Walters smiled. "In that case I'll get to work right away. If you could piss off out of my office and give me some peace, that would be most conducive to my studies. Be back here tonight at ten and I'll tell you what I know."

"At ten?" Amy said, surprised.

"You're right," Walters said. "Make it midnight."

"And what the hell are we supposed to do in the meantime?" Jodie asked noisily.

"I have somewhere we can go," Hunter said, reluctantly.

"Nowhere the Creed can find us, I hope?" asked Quinn.

Hunter shook his head. "No one knows about this place but me."

# CHAPTER THIRTY-TWO

When Hunter opened the door to his old apartment, he saw nothing but ghosts. He hadn't been in here since the day he and Avril had broken up and gone their separate ways, and it looked like she had stayed away, too.

Nothing was as he remembered it. Furniture mostly gone and bare floorboards everywhere. Walls stripped of photos. It looked bigger, untouched and now covered in a thin layer of dust. If he closed his eyes and concentrated hard enough, he could hear her voice as she sang in the kitchen. He stepped inside, swallowing down any feelings he had for his past life, and tossed the keys on the hall table.

"Come in, everyone. We should be safe in here, at least for a few hours. The place was never registered in my name."

"I've heard of minimalism but this is ridiculous," Quinn said.

"I don't live here," Hunter said. "I live across town, but something tells me Rorschach and the Creed might know about that place by now. This was always in Avril's name."

"Who is she?" Quinn asked.

Amy gave her a sharp look. "We don't need to know everything about Dr Hunter's life, do we?"

"No," he said tersely. "You don't."

He led them into the main living space where an old sofa and some tattered cushions were in the middle of an otherwise empty room. There was a standard lamp standing beside it, its cable curled around its base like a snake. Once, he had sat in this room and talked about starting a family with Avril, now it looked like an abandoned warehouse. His past fought back up to the surface. An international childhood as his father chased his dreams had turned into a wild drunken adolescence, and then here in Paris, the golden years.

"Everything okay?" Amy asked.

"All good," he said. "Totally fine. Happy. I want a drink."

She understood. "Me too. Maybe we could get something to eat too."

"Good call, boss," Blanco said. "I'm famished."

Hunter walked over to the French doors. The key was still in the lock. He turned it and stepped out onto the balcony. He'd forgotten how good the view was from here. He sighed and stepped back inside. "All right, I'll be back."

"I'm coming with you," Amy said.

"Whatever you like."

*

When Hunter and Amy returned with the takeout and wine, the atmosphere had changed. Jodie had found candles and placed them in strategic places around the room and Quinn and Lewis and turned two packing boxes into makeshift seats opposite the couch.

Making a generous sweeping motion with his hand, Blanco said, "Home Sweet Home" as they walked past him into the living room.

Soon after, with cartons of deep-fry chili beef and Hokkien noodles set out on the floor, and Amy busy pouring large quantities of pinot noir into some plastic picnic glasses they had bought with the wine, Blanco surprised everyone.

"I have a good idea."

"And that is?"

"Let's play truth or dare."

"I don't know," Quinn said. "I'd rather hear the *good* idea you said you had, not that one."

"C'mon, truth or dare."

Amy pulled her head back and stared at him. "Seriously?"

"We should play truth or dare. What's the matter, afraid?"

"In your dreams, old man."

He chuckled. "Then you go first. Truth or dare?"

"Truth."

Blanco rose to the challenge. "Biggest joy and biggest regret."

Amy went quiet. "My biggest joy was the day I got into the FBI. My biggest regret was never being able to tell Dad."

When Hunter saw the look on her face, he didn't have to ask why.

"All right, Sal," Amy said fiercely. "Truth or dare."

"You think I'm nuts? Truth."

"Biggest blessing and biggest tragedy."

"Biggest blessing is my daughters, no question."

"And tragedy?"

"There are no tragedies in my past," Blanco said honestly. "Just plain old-fashioned hard workers like my parents. Pops worked eighteen hours a day in the restaurant, and Mom took great care of us all. My childhood was in a golden era, and I'll never forget it. Poor bastards now with their damn iPads and YouTube stars and cyber-bullying. When I was six, I used to…"

"Ride a bike all morning and play ball till sunset in Marine Park," Amy and Jodie said at the same time. "We know."

The big man from Brooklyn just grinned. "Did I tell that story before?"

"Yeah, about a million times," Jodie said, fingers wrapping around her wine glass and lifting it to her smiling mouth. "But I like to hear you say it."

Blanco clasped his hands and looked down at his boots. "Yeah, I guess I miss those days. I miss Mom and Pops, too." He looked up at Quinn. "You know, kiddo, you really ought to speak to your parents because one day it'll be too late."

"I don't talk about my family," she said, changing the subject. "Truth or dare, Ben?"

"Truth."

"Are you frightened about becoming a father?"

He answered immediately. "Yes, of course I am. I worry about Megan giving birth, I worry about failing her or the baby. Yeah, I'm frightened. Now your turn. Truth or dare, Quinn?"

"Are you kidding? No one knows the truth about Ghost," she said defiantly. "I pick dare."

"In that case," Lewis said. "Kiss Jodie."

"Oh for *God's* sake," Amy said. "Are you like seven years old? I thought you were a Yale-educated historian."

"Also a former marine," he said proudly. "That never goes away."

"No, it's fine," Jodie said, winking at Quinn. "I will if you will."

Quinn shrugged and slid over to Jodie. When the two of them kissed, Lewis fumbled for his iPhone camera but Blanco reached out and stopped him. "Nu-huh, Ben."

"Damn it."

Jodie and Quinn parted lips and the goth turned to the young historian. "Happy now?"

"Hell, yeah."

Jodie shook her head. "Pathetic."

"Maybe you can show us how to be more mature," Amy said. "Truth or dare, Jodie?"

She looked at Lewis with disgust. "Truth."

"Worst moment in your life," Lewis said quickly.

"That's easy." Jodie choked back some unwanted emotion. "I was doing just great until my dad got fired from his job at the local cemetery."

"What happened?"

"He actually buried someone in the wrong plot."

"Not good."

"It was a grave mistake."

Amy threw a cushion at her. "Damn it, I thought you were being serious."

Jodie shrugged. "You don't want me to get serious, and believe me, talking about my past will bring this party down in a big way." She ripped the plastic wrap off a Gauloises pack and pulled out a cigarette. Sliding the tip onto her lip, she lit it with a match and sucked deeply. "That's much better."

"You still haven't answered," Lewis said.

She shrugged. "Worst moment? Not much to say. Dad walked out when I was eleven, I went off the rails and Mom couldn't control me. I got caught stealing a neighbor's car and crashing it through a gas station store and they sent me to juvie for three years."

Hunter looked at her in the low light. She looked younger now, and even slightly vulnerable. No longer the cynical apartment thief but a young woman cut loose by her parents in her most fragile years and left to fend for herself. He hated it, but he felt sorry for her. "Did it work?"

"Are you kidding?" she said bitterly. "The only thing Juvenile Hall ever taught me was how to take drugs, pick pockets and break through just about any lock they ever made. When I got out of that place I was a much more dedicated criminal than the girl who walked into it."

"Then, how did you wind up working for Amy?"

"Same way Quinn did – I got caught trying to knock her off, only in my case it was her house in DC. She was going to call the cops but I talked her out of it with my usual charm."

After a long pause, Amy sipped some wine and looked through the candlelight to Hunter. "What about you, stranger? Truth or dare."

"I don't know about that," Hunter said. "You guys all know each other; you all have a lot in common. I'm the outsider."

Amy said, "It's true we have a lot in common, but…"

Quinn interrupted her, laughing. "Are you kidding? We get along because we have nothing in common, Amy. You couldn't get a better bunch of misfits if you advertised on Craigslist. Look at you. You're from an FBI family of New England blue bloods with more ethics than the Catholic church. Sal is a streetfighter-turned-soldier-turned merc from Brooklyn whose parents ran a pizza parlor. Jodie is damn thief with a record as long as your arm and Lewis is the kind of asshole who eats broccoli smoothies."

"Drink," he said. "You drink them."

In the laughter, Amy said, "Truth or dare, Max. You're not getting away with it."

"In that case, truth."

Quinn jumped in. "Who was Avril?"

"You don't have to answer that, Max," Amy said, scowling at the goth.

"It's okay, Amy." Hunter took some wine and blew out a breath. "Avril was my fiancée. We met here in Paris when I was doing some post-doc work. We fell in love and it was fast and furious. Then one day she left me, just told me it was over and walked out. I almost left Paris and went home, but I'd got the job at UNESCO by then. It's a big city and I've not seen her since. Not much else to say about me and tragedy. There's my mother, I guess but now's not the time."

"I'm sorry," Amy asked. "And so is Quinn. Right, Quinn?"

Quinn rolled her eyes, stuffed a cigarette in her mouth and got up off the floor. "I'm going for a smoke."

"Aren't you going to tell me anything about you at all?" Hunter asked her.

"I picked dare, Hunter."

"I know, but…"

"Listen, no one gets to know about Ghost," she said. "That's just the way I like it."

After she had padded out of the room, he looked at Amy. "You must have researched her past before you hired her?"

Jodie huffed out a short, cynical laugh. "Yeah, right."

"I tried," Amy said. "But she's Ghost, remember? She scrubbed every last bit of her history off the internet before we had a chance to check her out."

"So you just took her word for it?"

"I know enough about her," she said. "Besides, she was looking at a long time behind bars when we caught her."

Hunter considered what she said. “Is Quinn Mosley even her real name?”

“Maybe, maybe not,” said Jodie.

“There’s a birth certificate,” Amy said. “I know that much, but…”

“But she could have worked her magic on that, too,” Lewis said. “In a world run by computers, the hacker controls the past, present and future.”

“A scary thought, right?” Blanco said.

Hunter looked at his watch and changed the subject. “Nearly midnight, guys. Time to see Julian.”

# CHAPTER THIRTY-THREE

Approaching midnight and the Louvre was a very different place. After being ushered though security with passes arranged by Walters, they found themselves walking along eerie, low-lit corridors lined with renaissance art and sculptures. Going further back in time, their heels clipped on the black and white tiles of a vast hall filled with classical statues whose stony eyes seemed to follow them as they made their way to the other side.

They stepped into a stairway with an impressive vaulted ceiling and walked up to the next floor where Walters's office was located. Turning a corner in the corridor, they immediately realized something was wrong. Halfway down the corridor, bright light from the office was spilling out onto a floor strewn with loose papers.

Hunter suddenly wished he was armed. Raising his hand to stop the others, he took a few cautious steps forward, peered inside the office and took in the carnage. Books and box files were ripped from shelves, the desk was upturned and Walters's personal collection of Egyptian ceramics was smashed up and littering the floor.

"What's up, Max?" Amy called.

"You'd better come and see for yourselves."

They stepped into the trashed office and tried to take it all in.

"Damn," Jodie said, breaking the shocked silence. "They got to old misery chops."

"Now's not the time," Amy said. "Max and Walters are close, remember?"

"If they got Julian," Hunter said. "We have to presume they got the photos, and with Julian's knowledge, it won't be long before they know the location of the Ramesses tomb."

"Not good," Quinn said.

Hunter smashed his fist into the wall. "Bollocks! How could we have let this happen? Any hope we had of finding Atlantis is dead on the vine."

"This is awful," Amy said. "I'm so sorry, Max."

"This is getting creepier by the second," Quinn said. "He most probably had something really important to tell you before they kidnapped his ass."

"Quinn, please," Blanco said.

"Sorry."

"Wait," Jodie said. "Anyone else hear that?"

"What?" Lewis asked.

"Nothing. I thought I heard something but I was..."

"I hear it, too," Amy said. "Faint, but it's definitely something."

"Is it Lewis's brain working?" asked Quinn. 'If so, talk about a glitch in the matrix."

"That's funny coming from a douchenuts like you."

Then they heard a man screaming for help from somewhere beneath them in the palace. All of them recognized the terrified voice of Julian Walters.

"Julian!" Hunter said. "He's still in the Louvre!"

He bolted from the office, scanning up and down the corridor to locate the sound of his old mentor's screams. "This way!"

Galvanized by the professor's kidnapping, Hunter and the team ran back along the corridor and dxown the stairs. When they reached the hall with the statues they heard more screams coming from a room to their right. They sprinted to the room and found themselves staring at the Colossal statue of Ramesses II. He stared back, impassive and inscrutable.

"Behind the statue!" Lewis called out.

Hunter saw Walters now, badly beaten with a black eye and a cut on his cheek. A number of men in black were forcing him through a fire escape, but before they pushed him through, he caught his old friend's eye.

"Julian!"

"Don't worry about me!" he called out. "Run for your lives!"

One of the men punched him in the stomach and he doubled over. Another turned and pointed a pistol at them. "Get back!"

"Professor!" Amy cried out.

"We're not letting them take you, Julian," Hunter called out.

Walters swung his fist and struck one of the men in the face, cutting him. "Don't worry Max, save yourselves! I'm old… next time you listen to the Mozart horn concerto, think of me and the old days. Köchel 18!"

"Shut up!" Another hefty punch in his stomach and over he went, coughing and spluttering and then one of the disciples stopped, two dark eyes staring at them. Slowly, he raised a steady arm and pointed at Hunter.

"Stay away from us."

"Who the hell are you?" Hunter asked.

The man said nothing, and slipped away into the shadows slamming the door behind him.

"What the hell just happened?" Quinn said.

Amy blew out a deep breath. "They took the professor."

"Not yet, they didn't," Hunter said. "I'm going after him."

"And you're not going alone, stranger," Amy said.

"Fine, I'll take Jodie. I might need her skills, but no one else. We can't put the entire team's lives at risk. Everyone else get back to the apartment, get the kit and wait for us to call." He threw Blanco the key. "If you guys are right and this is the work of the Creed, something tells me the police aren't going to be on our side."

He didn't wait for a response. When he kicked the fire door's panic bar and rushed out into the night he found himself standing in the rain. The Sully Wing was situated in the north-western section of the original palace and now they were standing in the main courtyard in front of the famous glass pyramid.

Looking beyond the famous landmark, Jodie saw a black Peugeot parked up on the roundabout next to the smaller inverted pyramid. "There!" she cried. "They're putting him that car. Thank God it's not a damn helicopter, or we'd be really screwed."

"We're still kinda screwed, Jodie. We don't have a car."

The Peugeot screamed away to the west, screeching beneath an archway on the palace's south side. "Oh, ye of little faith," she said, breaking into a run. "You coming or not?"

Hunter was already pounding along the asphalt after her, and by the time he'd caught up she was already racing under the arch and looking up and down the Quai François Mitterand until she found what she was looking for; parked up on the side of the road in the middle of a long line of cars was an old Fiat.

"This is our ride."

She pulled a small case from an inside pocket and selected something that looked like an attachment to a Swiss army knife. She extended it and slid it down between the window glass and the rubber seal. A small *clunk* and she flung the door open.

They both moved for the driver's door.

"What are you doing?" she asked.

"Driving."

"I think not, Hunter. Get your ass into the passenger seat."

He swallowed his argument when he saw a wild look in her eyes. Over her shoulder, the black Peugeot was racing west across the Pont du Carrouse, crossing the River Seine and heading into the seventh arrondissement. "I hope you know what you're doing."

"How many cars have you stolen and gotten away from the cops in?"

"Zero."

"Then shut your yap and do as I say."

"You know what you're doing, right?"

"Stole my neighbor's Chevy when I was a kid. That was the first of dozens, so yeah."

She climbed into the Fiat and took less than a minute to hot-wire the ignition while Hunter buckled up in the passenger seat. When she revved the engine and tore away along the bridge in pursuit of the Peugeot, he watched the young thief effortlessly changing the gears and dipping the clutch, swerving off the bridge and giving chase along the quiet midnight streets. She weaved in and out of the light traffic, the streetlights flickering on her determined face, and speeded up until they hit fifty and drove deeper into the Left Bank.

Skidding around a tight bend, she pulled a cigarette from her pocket and fired it up. Ahead of them the rear lights of the Peugeot slipped out of sight around a bend, but she was on it, dumping down into second gear and taking the corner at speed. The engine growled as she breathed out the smoke and smiled. "Now we're cooking with gas, right?"

From the look of pure delight on her face, he guessed they were cooking with gas.

"I guess so, just make sure you don't lose him. The streets in this district are narrow and dangerous. It's like a labyrinth."

"Then hold on to your ass with both hands, Hunter, because this is going to get real."

# CHAPTER THIRTY-FOUR

Up ahead, the Peugeot was making good progress south along the Rue du Bac before swerving without warning onto the Boulevard Saint Germain. Even at this time of night, the traffic here was heavier, but Jodie was calm. She spun the cheap plastic wheel, worn smooth by years of use, hard to the right and booted the throttle hard.

The Fiat surged forward but she had steered too hard and they were heading for a parked car on the north side of the boulevard. She caught the skid in a heartbeat and corrected their course with a speedy spin of the wheel back to the left.

Hunter hung on for his life, not knowing whether he was blown away by her driving or scared out of his wits. When the Peugeot's rear lights flashed over to the left in a neon blur, he knew where it was headed. "They're going down the Rue Saint-Dominique."

"Means jack shit to me, Hunter."

"It's a very busy road."

"Busier is better. Cops watching on CCTV have a tougher time tracking us."

The engine roared. Streetlights flashed on the wet hood and the wipers raced back and forth across the rain-slick glass.

"I guess you really do know what you're doing."

Jodie said nothing. She was glancing in the rear view mirror with a furrowed brow on her face. "Damn it to hell."

"What's up?"

"Looks like the traffic didn't save us after all. Cops on our ass."

Hunter's mind raced to process the information. He had a well-earned reputation for being a daredevil among the archaeological community and he was a decorated soldier but he'd never crossed the police before. Suddenly, he was looking at a criminal record for car theft and probably a dozen more charges he couldn't even think of. When the police car sirens and lights went on, his heart started to pound.

"Shit," he said. "Do we pull over?"

Jodie huffed out a weary laugh. "You really are new to this."

"If you mean car theft, then yes."

"No, we don't pull over, Hunter." She spoke quietly, never taking her eyes off the car in front which was now ripping across the road inside the park south of Les Invalides. When the Peugeot turned left and headed south, she spun the wheel and their car turned in the same direction. "If we pull over we go directly to jail and your friend is dead."

Hunter leaned forward and checked the side mirror. It was coated with rainwater but the flashing blue lights were clear enough. Flopping back into his seat, he saw the enormous Eiffel Tower looming up ahead. "But they'll call for backup and catch us that way. Then we get done for failing to stop, too."

"I wouldn't worry about failing to stop, dude," she said coolly. "You left polite society when you stole this car with me outside the museum."

He nodded, finally starting to see things the way she saw them. "I guess we have nothing to lose then."

"I know I don't."

She hit the gas. Beneath their feet, the tires raced along the slick asphalt, flicking wild arcs of water up the side of the car and over the mudguards. The Peugeot left the road, broke through a low fence and ploughed across the Champs de Mars. Jodie was undeterred by the attempt to lose her. She changed down and piled the Fiat over the kerb in pursuit, striking a metal trash bin and swerving back around onto a broad gravel path.

"We're gaining on them!" Hunter said.

"Not for long."

He watched as a black figure began to climb out of the rear window. When his entire upper body was sticking out in the rain, he raised a compact machine pistol in the air. Hunter recognized it at once as a Heckler & Koch MP7. When the orange muzzle flash lit the night, he had already grabbed the wheel and forced the car off the path.

Jodie gasped, a rare display of fear, and then the right-hand corner of the hood struck a plane tree and ended the pursuit. The Fiat spun around one-eighty degrees and came to a rest just off one of the footpaths, main-beams lighting the rainfall and steam pouring out of a hole in the radiator.

"We have to get out of here," Hunter said, fumbling with his belt.

Seconds after they pushed open their doors and staggered out of the wreck, they knew it was over. Blue lights flashed and then the yellow main-beams of half a dozen police cars lit them up like two convicts trying to escape from Alcatraz. Doors opened and men yelled and leapt from the cars.

"Don't move!" one of the policemen screamed. He was gripping a pistol in both hands and using the top of his car door to stabilize the aim.

"Damn it, he knows who we are," Hunter said.

"How do you know?" Jodie looked at him. "Got it – he spoke in English. He shouldn't know we speak English."

"Which means he got Amy and the rest of the team."

"Put your hands up!"

The man walked over to him and cuffed his hands behind his back. "Dr Hunter, I am arresting you for the murder of Julian Walters. You have the right to notify the British consul and to call an attorney and…"

"Murder? What the hell? He's been kidnapped! We were trying to rescue him!"

"I would recommend you say nothing, Dr Hunter. You are in a lot of trouble."

As the cuffs bit into his wrists, the words melted into a blur. To his left he saw two policemen pushing Jodie into the second car. Her hair was soaked with rain and sticking to her face but she was calm and unmoved. She looked vulnerable yet somehow even harder, with a steely look in her eyes, and then she was gone.

"You too, Dr Hunter."

He felt the policeman's hand on his head as he guided him down into the back seat of the police car. Somewhere in the Paris night, the Creed had Julian and their hunt for Atlantis was moving forward faster than ever.

His, he thought glumly, had just come to an end.

# CHAPTER THIRTY-FIVE

Hunter was expecting to be taken to one of the city's many police stations for a lengthy and difficult interrogation, so he was surprised when the police car drove back to the Louvre and parked up in front of the pyramid. When the second car carrying Jodie pulled up beside them, a policeman got out of the car and opened his door.

"Get out, please."

He obeyed the order and climbed out into the night. The rain had lessened to a lighter drizzle, but the air was still warm. Jodie was also ordered out of the other car and then the police flanked them as they transferred them inside the palace. In a solemn procession, they marched them upstairs, right past Walters's smashed office and into the Department of Egyptian Antiquities.

Having made their way past the final police cordon, he now followed the officers down a corridor. Hands in cuffs and shoes clicking on the polished parquet flooring of the antiquities wing, he was too shocked even to glance at the exquisite artifacts and artwork flanking him as he made his way toward the giant Ramesses II statue.

"Wait here," the policeman said. "Both of you."

Hunter watched him walk across the room to a man in a serious trench coat. They spoke for a few moments and then the man in the coat wandered over to them.

"I am Inspector Fabius of the Central Directorate of the Judicial Police."

"Why have you charged us with murder?" Hunter struggled to keep his voice low.

"Just calm down, Dr Hunter."

"Calm down?" Hunter said. "And where the hell are the rest of our friends?"

"Your friends are being questioned in another room in the palace. Tell me what happened here tonight."

Hunter calmed himself. Taking a look at Jodie, he saw she had already done just that. She was standing quietly with her hands cuffed behind her back and staring at the wall. He guessed she had experience of this part of the chase, too.

"We met with Professor Walters earlier today and handed him some important archaeological findings we wanted his help deciphering. He accepted our request and asked to meet us here at midnight."

Fabius raised an eyebrow. "A little unorthodox."

"Only if you don't know Julian."

The inspector dipped his head, accepting this was possible. "Continue."

"When we got here tonight we never had a chance to see him. His office was trashed and then we heard him scream for help. When we got to him, a group of men were dragging him out of the museum. They piled him into a black car and took off. We gave chase."

"In a stolen car."

"Yes, in a stolen car, but we lost them. Now we don't know where he is and your men have charged us with murder. What makes you think he was murdered?"

"We had our reasons."

Hunter felt tension building in his neck. "That's what I know. What do *you* know?"

"Not much, just that someone broke into the museum a half hour ago and took him. We think maybe the kidnappers found him in his office, but he escaped and tried to get away. They eventually caught up with him here in the Egyptian Antiquities section and after a fight they may have harmed him or even killed him and moved the body. We found blood on the floor and wall and even some splattered up the Ramesses statue. Look here."

Hunter looked where he was pointing and saw the blood. Squinting, he took another step forward.

"That's far enough," said Fabius, raising his hand to stop him going any farther. "We cannot let you contaminate the scene of the crime."

"I understand," he said. "But Julian wasn't murdered. He fought with the men when they were taking him and punched one of them in the face. It's his blood, not Julian's."

"Of course, we will run tests."

Hunter sighed. "If you check the museum's security cameras, you'll see we're telling the truth about when we arrived. There must be evidence of the black car on the tapes somewhere."

"We have already checked it. The black car arrived here an hour ago. Where were you an hour ago?"

"In an apartment on the Left Bank with the rest of my team. I'm sorry if that ruins your little theory about who snatched my friend."

Fabius smiled. "I have no theories yet, Monsieur Hunter. I got here less than thirty minutes ago and have not even begun my investigation. It is not every day a man is murdered in the Louvre, at least not outside of the pages of an adventure novel."

"For the last time, he wasn't murdered, but his life is in danger. You have to issue an all ports warning."

"Don't tell me how to do my job."

Hunter nodded, but his mind was wandering. How had the Apostle tracked down Julian so fast after their first meeting? Amy hadn't posed as Kirsten and reported into the Rorschach Foundation to tell them they were going to meet him, and he had told only Juliette at UNESCO. For the first time, he started to question the integrity of the other team members.

More detectives and police officers walked into the room, followed by Amy and the rest of the team. When he saw her face, he felt a strange sense of relief he hadn't expected. "Are you okay?"

"I think so. I gather they got away?"

"We did our best," he said. "Jodie drives like a rally champion."

"I know."

"I can't believe he's been snatched," Hunter said. "And it's all my fault."

"What are you talking about?" she asked.

"Isn't it obvious? If I hadn't dragged him into this nightmare, he wouldn't have been working on my crackpot theories."

The team were tired and stressed, and it only got worse. Fabius made them wait hours until he had checked their story. When he reappeared in the antiquities department and walked over to them, they were ready to drop.

"You are free to go," he said.

Amy stood. "All of us?"

"Oui." He ordered a policeman to remove their cuffs. "We checked the tapes and we are content that Professor Walters is still alive and that you are not responsible for his kidnapping. But Dr Hunter and Special Agent Priest will be charged separately with car theft."

Hunter accepted the downgrading of the charges happily. "I suppose I should count myself lucky."

Fabius gave a suspicious smile. "Yes, you really should. Do not leave the European Union."

They wandered out into the drizzle, lost, dazed and confused. Somewhere to the east, the sun was breaking through some clouds above the city's eastern skyline. After a long silence, Quinn spoke first. "Is that the end of this thing then?"

Amy frowned. "You think I'm giving up just like that?"

The goth shrugged. "The cops copied my laptop's hard drive before they gave it back to me, so I hope you realize everything we know, they know. For now, at least."

Hunter looked at her. "What does that mean?"

"It means when we get somewhere dry and with a damn power outlet I can get back online and delete it all from their records."

Blanco met Hunter's look of astonishment. "She can do that."

"I guess that's a good thing."

"Hey, hacking's one rung up the ladder from car thief," Quinn said.

"You got me there."

"And as far as I know right now," she said. "We still have not one damn clue about what to do next."

"No," Amy said. "That's the sad but true part – but we're not giving in."

They wandered away from the museum and Hunter slipped his hands into his pockets as he stared up at the giant glass pyramid. Standing there in the morning light with the drizzle slick on his forehead, something changed inside him.

"My God…"

"Max?" Amy asked.

He felt his heart pounding in his chest. "How could I have been so stupid! It's been staring me in the face all along."

"What?"

"The Mozart horn concerto," Hunter said. "It's the last thing Julian said to me when those thugs were dragging him out of the door. He said the next time I listen to the Mozart horn concerto, Köchel 18, I should think of him and the old days. I forgot about it in the excitement of the car chase."

"What the hell does that mean?" Jodie said.

He shrugged. "Don't ask me," he said. "I never listen to classical music and Julian knows that. He must have been telling us something he didn't want them to know, but what the hell is Köchel 18?"

"The Köchel catalogue," Amy said. "Mozart wrote well over six hundred pieces of music so it helps if they're numbered. That's what the Köchel catalogue is. Every Mozart composition has a Köchel number, but they're sometimes abbreviated to K numbers."

"K18?" Hunter said.

Amy frowned. "Which is odd, because none of the horn concertos are K18."

Hunter looked at her. "How do you know all this?"

"Mom was principal violinist for the Boston Philharmonic for many years."

"Like I said," Quinn said. "Blue bloods helping each other up the greasy pole."

"For the record, none of my instructors at the FBI ever knew who I was. My father made damn sure of it. He wanted me to cut my own way through the ice and that's what I did."

"Fine, and this is starting to give me a damn headache," Jodie said. "Think I'll stick to breaking into cars and apartments."

Amy turned to Hunter. "The Mozart horn concerto was K447, not K18."

"I doubt Julian would have made a mistake like that," Hunter said. "He loves classical music. He's a pianist."

Amy pondered for a moment. "Or KV, they're also called KV numbers, making it KV18."

Hunter gawped at her. "KV18?"

"Sure – why?"

Hunter grinned. "KV18 just happens to be the designation of Ramesses X's tomb."

"Keep talking."

"Like your Mozart compositions, there are so many tombs in the Valley of the Kings they're designated numbers."

"The Valley of the Kings?" Jodie said. "What's that?"

"It's a vast necropolis," Hunter said. "A city of the dead, and we'll be dead too if we don't watch out."

"I still don't get the KV thing," Quinn said.

"KV stands for Kings' Valley. KV1 is the tomb of Ramesses VII, for example. It's in the East Valley. KV18 is the tomb of Ramesses X, which was cut for him in the southwest wadi. It was left unfinished and if it's the same as last time I visited, it's still full of debris. The Pharaoh's body wasn't found there, or anywhere else, either. There's nothing there, believe me – it's no more than a narrow entranceway and two narrow passages."

"Epic," Quinn said sarcastically.

"So how does this help us?" Blanco asked.

"Julian said the horn concerto was KV18," Hunter said. "The whole reason the Egyptians chose that location for the necropolis was because of the mountain to the west of it – El-Qurn, it means the Horn in Arabic. Julian was telling us that the real tomb of Ramesses X is to the west of the mountain, on the Horn."

"Whoa," Lewis said. "That's some deductive reasoning right there, Max."

"It sure is," Amy said, beaming.

Hunter grinned. "I know where it is, Amy! I know where Ramesses X is buried… where the tomb is! Where the so-called gift from the gods came from! There's only one part of the mountain that conceals an entrance – a truncated spur on the northern face just above a boulder field. I know it well. We need to get to Egypt in a hurry."

"But Fabius wants to lock us up for car theft," Jodie said, smirking. "We're not allowed to leave the EU."

"Yeah, right," Quinn laughed.

Amy was already on her phone, talking into the tiny speaker. "Get me Director Gates, right now. This is a Code Red emergency."

# CHAPTER THIRTY-SIX

As the plane flew to Luxor, Hunter reflected on how he seemed to spend more time in the air than on the ground these days. Glancing around the corporate jet's small cabin, he saw that Amy and her FBI team looked as tired as he felt. He couldn't blame them. Blanco and Lewis had military experience but the rest were all civilians.

More pressing was the abduction of his mentor. How the old man had thought so fast on his feet and given them the clue about the Valley of the Kings, he didn't know. He stretched his long, aching legs out in front of him and closed his eyes, but then he felt someone crash down in the chair beside him,

"Tell me about Atlantis," Amy said.

Opening his eyes, he turned, holding back a smile. "You're a believer now?"

She shrugged. "I think maybe I might be."

"The first thing to know is that we know almost nothing about the place. Apart from the description Plato left in his *Critias* dialogue we knew no more until I discovered the *Diocles* dialogue in Athens a few months ago. Even then, the new material was scant in its description of Atlantis itself, but it did offer me the vital clue about the three winged angel statues and the possible location of one of them in Nineveh. That was when all of this kicked off with a vengeance."

Her lips broke into a stunning smile. "So you're to blame, huh?"

"Sorry."

"If it was so real, then what the hell happened to the place?"

The question came from Blanco. He had been listening to their conversation from across the cabin while pretending to sleep. Now, he opened his eyes and swung his legs off the long seat and looked at Hunter earnestly.

"Yeah," Jodie said. "What happened to the place? If it was as real as Plato said, it couldn't just disappear."

Hunter leaned around his seat's headrest and saw his young partner in crime trying not to look overly interested in the subject, but staring at him with a question on her face all the same. He hardly knew where to begin.

"There are many theories and they have all been well-documented in literally thousands of publications. If we accept there was once a great civilization called Atlantis and it no longer exists, then clearly there was a catastrophic event which wiped it out. Among current theories are a massive electrical output from the sun, triggering massive flooding, or the perennial favorite, the comet."

"I read about that," Blanco said. "Is it possible a simple comet strike could wipe out an entire island?"

"It didn't have to wipe out all traces of the island of Atlantis itself, only all signs of civilization on it. There are ways that could happen."

"Like what?" Jodie asked.

"Anyone hear of the Younger Dryas?"

Blank faces and silence.

"The Younger Dryas was an event that occurred around twelve thousand years ago, where we had a return to glacial climate conditions following what climatologists call the Late Glacial Interstadial."

Jodie closed her eyes. "Wake me when we get to the interesting part."

Hunter ignored her, knowing she was still listening. "The interstadial was a period of warming after the Last Glacial Maximum, or Ice Age. In other words, after the Ice Age things started to warm up again until the Younger Dryas, when there was very rapid cooling and a strong decline in northern hemisphere temperatures."

"What caused it?" Amy asked.

"There are several theories, but my money's on a comet – or more precisely a series of comets as our planet orbited through the Taurid Meteor Shower, which it does every June and November. During this time, comet strikes increase sharply. There are various hypotheses claiming that twelve thousand years ago this planet flew through the Taurid meteors and got unlucky. Large comets crashed into the northern hemisphere and caused massive flooding which wiped out Atlantis."

"Wait," Jodie said, opening one eye. "You mean we fly through this meteor storm twice a year and its comets could blast us at any time?"

"Yes," he said coolly. "Welcome to the solar system."

"Holy crap."

"Where did they hit specifically?" Lewis asked.

"We know from very recent research that they hit the planet in the north of Greenland and would have caused massive and rapid flooding." Seeing he had their undivided attention, he went on. "As I say, so much data from the Younger Dryas event suggests that there was this period of extreme and rapid cooling directly following the warming that ended the last Ice Age. Tie this up with the new discoveries of massive comet impacts in northern Greenland dating to the exact same period and we have a possible link."

"You really think comets struck Greenland and created a massive flood?" Blanco asked, gripped.

"Yes, I do. Like I said, new research earlier this year revealed a massive comet impact nineteen miles wide under the Hiawatha Glacier, and more recently a second impact site has been discovered around one hundred miles from the first and it's even bigger. These impacts were colossal, easily big enough to melt the ice sheet up there and massively alter the world's climate in the very recent past, in geological terms, at least."

"Wow," Jodie said. "It's getting kind of interesting now."

Hunter smiled. "And best of all, this period dates to around twelve and a half thousand years ago which was nine thousand BC."

Amy whistled. "Exactly the same date Plato puts on the fall of Atlantis."

"That's one hell of a coincidence," said Quinn.

"In my opinion, it's no coincidence," Hunter said. "There's just too much data tying it all together. On top of the famous Plato reference to Atlantis, we now have all this other research cementing it all together, especially the comet strikes on Greenland which caused a colossal flood across North America and Europe, not to mention all the islands in the Atlantic. Throw in the sea-level rise after the end of the Ice Age wiping out anything that survived and we start to understand the fate of Atlantis."

After a long pause, Amy said, "Is this for real?"

"What do you mean?"

"I mean, I know the way academics can get carried away."

"It's real," he said firmly. "The Ice Age meant rising sea levels, but after that we have the Younger Dryas which just had to be caused by the double comet strike in Greenland."

"I want my mommy," Lewis said with a grin.

Hunter smiled. "Like I said, this brought catastrophic and flash flooding across the transatlantic region, and had a knock-on effect even further afield. For example, geological evidence is mounting that the Sphinx is at least ten thousand years old, twice as old as mainstream archaeology allows for, and they date it this way because of the water erosion patterns on its base."

Amy accepted what he was saying, but frowned. "Okay, fine, but while this might give us a plausible reason to believe in Atlantis, none of this gives us any clue about its location. The sort of flooding you're talking about would have wiped out half of the North American continent and much of Europe."

"It did."

"So Atlantis could still be anywhere."

"Not anywhere," Hunter said. "But very definitely somewhere, and Ramasses's lost tomb in Egypt is going to tell us where."

"This is heavy," Jodie said. "I mean, I'm really starting to believe we might find Atlantis."

"Good, because we are," Hunter said. "I've spent my whole life looking for it and now it's within my grasp."

"We land in three hours," Amy said. "Do you think we'll have any problem getting into the site?"

"Not at all," Hunter said. "It's open to the public, but I have a good friend who can help us if there's any problem."

"Who is he?"

"Omar works at the Department of Egyptian Antiquities and curates a good part of the fifty thousand pieces there. I've already sent him a message and asked him to meet us at the site. More than that, I asked him to get digging and try and get us a head start."

"Great," Amy said. "Everyone get some sleep. Remember, the Creed snatched Professor Walters several hours ago and if they got the location of the tomb out of him they'll be ahead of us. Egypt is two hours ahead of France so we're touching down just before nightfall. I'm guessing the Valley of the Kings will be closed, right Max?"

"Five PM closing time, so yeah. We can't go out there at night because it's guarded by the army to protect it from the likes of Brodie McCabe and other artifact thieves. We have to wait till morning, and so will McCabe, for sure."

"So we get one night in the hotel in Luxor," Amy said. "And we leave at daybreak, but we have to be prepared that McCabe and the Creed's disciples could still get there before us."

Hunter turned and looked out of the small window at the stars over the Alps. "Over my dead body."

# CHAPTER THIRTY-SEVEN

Hunter relaxed when they reached the hotel in Luxor. After a shower, he left his room and stepped outside into the hotel courtyard where the scent of jasmine drifted in the warm air. He sat down and took in his new surroundings.

The courtyard was centerd on an ornate tiled fountain, ringed by Madagascan dragon trees and bright pink pentas flowers. The height of the surrounding hotel kept the sun out of the yard until an hour either side of midday, and now the entire area was cooling in the evening shade. With the sound of water trickling out of the fountain, the team took some seats outside the hotel's restaurant and started to unwind.

As they disappeared into their conversations, Amy pulled up a chair next to Hunter and gave him a tired smile. "We made it to Egypt."

"That we did," he said.

"It's starting to feel like we've known each other our whole lives."

"Not to me," he said. "I hardly know anything about you."

"Ask away," she said with an honest smile.

He finished his beer and fixed his eyes on her. "All right. What was that Quinn said back in Paris about you being a New England blue blood?"

Amy looked at his face and saw nothing but honest curiosity. "I don't like talking about it, but since you asked, the Foxes are an old Connecticut family, going right back to the Saybrook Colony. That's all she means."

"Wasn't your father a former Director of the FBI back in the eighties?" Quinn said from behind her menu.

Amy sighed. "Yes, I suppose he was."

"And wasn't your grandfather a senator for Connecticut during World War Two?"

"Uh-huh."

"And your great-grandfather a previous governor of the state?"

"I believe so."

"And didn't President Lincoln once stay at your family home during the Civil War?"

Amy scowled at Quinn. "He might have done."

"Like I said," Quinn grinned. "Blue bloods."

Hunter reflected on what he had just heard. "That's an impressive family background. I'm sure you're very proud."

"It's what it is," Amy said bluntly. "And we have our family problems just like anyone else."

"I bet," Quinn said. "Like whether to use the silver or gold plates on Thanksgiving."

"I'm not going into this all over again with you, Quinn," Amy said. "And I'm not apologizing for an accident of birth."

Hunter said nothing. The atmosphere at the table was cooling faster than the desert air blowing over the courtyard.

"Anyone want a drink?" Blanco said. "I know I'm parched."

Lewis snapped his menu shut. "That sounds like a great idea, Sal old man. I'll come with you and help you bring them back to the table."

Amy watched them leave. "That's my story, but what's yours, Hunter? And I mean the real you," she said, pointing to his heart. "Not the Indiana Jones façade."

"What do you want to know?"

"You can start with what you meant when you started to talk about your mother back in Paris."

Hunter watched Blanco and Lewis return with the drinks and decided to open up. "I was at school when it happened," he said quietly. Just an ordinary day in an ordinary school in West London and then one of the women from the front office interrupted the class and called the teacher out. It was geography, I remember it all so well. Mr Richardson was a good teacher, too. Intelligent and kind. When he walked back into the class, I knew straight away something bad had happened because of the look on his face. When he looked over to my desk and asked to speak to me, I felt my legs turn to jelly. I was only twelve."

Hunter reached over for the beer bottle and emptied it in one long pull. In the respectful silence of the cool courtyard, he wrapped both hands around the bottle and blew out a deep, long breath. "Anyway, he called me out into the hall and the three of us walked back to the office. The old boy put his hand on my shoulder. I knew right there everything was about to change. When we got back to the office there were two coppers there – one man and one woman. They told me Mum was gone and Dad was on his way back from Russia."

"That's rough," Blanco said. "I'm so sorry."

"What happened?" Quinn asked.

Hunter shrugged. "It was what we call a debris avalanche, out at her dig in the Black Desert, in Jordan. She was an archaeologist, see. Just an accident." His voice grew quieter. "No one to blame."

Blanco sensed the pain starting to claw at Hunter and stepped in. "When I was a kid…"

"We know, it was idyllic," Jodie said.

"Most of it, but not all of it. Dad had a dark side."

Amy flicked her eyes over to him. "You never told me that, Sal."

"You mean he hit you?" Jodie asked.

"No, nothing like that. I had a good background. Spanish father, Italian mother. Pops was the best – not the kind of scum that hits kids. If he saw anyone doing that, then book that guy an undertaker, y'know what I'm saying? He fled the Spanish Civil war back in thirty-seven when he was a kid, with his parents. Those people understood what real suffering was."

"I bet," Lewis said.

"But the thing with my mother is that she had brothers. Lots of brothers – she was Italian, y'know? There was Uncle Matteo, Uncle Sergio, Uncle Luigi, Uncle Paolo… all good men, but Uncle Giulio was different. He got mixed up with the mob in Vegas and found himself in a heap of trouble. My old man stepped in and fixed it. He never talked about what he did, but there was talk maybe he killed a guy." Blanco looked sad, almost apologetic for what he had said. "Pops was a good man."

Jodie swept her hair over her ears and flicked some ash off her cigarette tip. "I'm sure he was, Sal. I know that just by knowing you."

He held her hand and squeezed it. Hunter had noticed how close they were before, and the look on their faces right now was more father and daughter than good friends.

The moon reached its zenith above the courtyard and the Englishman sipped his fresh beer, speaking almost without thinking. "Things were different after Mum died. Dad was a diplomat with a serious career. The Foreign and Commonwealth Office moved him around every year or so and I got dragged around behind him. Germany, France, China, Japan, Korea, Brazil… you name it. I never had friends, just people who taught me how to swear in their language for a few months and then I was gone again."

"I'm guessing you went into archaeology because of your mom?" Amy asked.

He nodded. "When I got out of the army I was lost. Following in her footsteps just seemed like the right thing to do. I feel like I'm finishing her legacy, working hard to make sure she didn't do all that work for nothing, plus I love the hell out of it."

She brushed his hand. "I'm pleased it's working out for you, Max."

"That's why I got so annoyed with Brodie when he accused me of copying him. If anything, the bastard got the idea from my mother. Then he used his money and connections to work his way into the best college in the country and set up his own archaeological foundation, including prizes and awards. With each check he wrote he pushed me and my work further into the shade."

"But you won in the end."

"I guess so."

"But only because you worked so damn hard, right?" Jodie asked.

"Nothing wrong with hard work," Hunter said. "I'd go mad without my work. Brodie can buy all the success he likes, but he'll never be a better archaeologist than me, and he wasn't a very good soldier, either."

Blanco laughed and gave him a look of sympathy. "You can't buy class, Max."

The group grew quieter and more solemn. Hunter was again struck by how he had known these people for only a few days and would likely never see them again when the mission to find Atlantis was over. He glanced at Jodie's cigarette jealously but fought back the urge to ask for one. Over ten years without a smoke, he thought. *Don't blow it now.*

The quiet was broken by Amy. "Nothing I ever did was good enough for my mom," she said pensively. "She was the *real* blue blood, was Annabelle Fitch. She never gave me an inch, never cut me any slack. She kept the pressure up all the time – work hard at school, pass your exams, get into Princeton get into the state government. When I followed Dad into the FBI, her head almost popped off like a champagne cork. Even when she finally accepted it, it was get to the top, Amy! Never take your foot off the gas, Amy!"

"I'm starting not to hate my parents so much," Quinn said out of nowhere. Everyone turned to look at the young goth.

"You care to expand on that?" Amy said.

"No. I shouldn't have said anything, so just go back to flaming your own families and leave me out of it."

"C'mon, Quinn," Blanco said. "Everyone's being honest here tonight. Sharing a little piece of their lives with the group. What about you?"

She gave an insolent shrug. "No one knows anything about Ghost."

Jodie sighed and blew out some smoke, fighting the urge not to look too bored. "That's kind of the point Sal just made."

"Besides, you're not Ghost anymore," Amy said. "You're Quinn Mosley, IT consultant. You have a real life with real friends who appreciate you. You're part of the team. You're one of the family, as far as I'm concerned."

"And you're mom?"

"Hey, I'm not old enough to be *your* mom, that's for sure."

"Either way, I don't want to talk about myself."

Amy dropped it and yawned. "That's enough for me. We have to get up at dawn and get out to the desert to find this tomb. I'm going to bed."

"Me too," Lewis said.

Quinn pushed back from the chair. "And me."

Blanco was next to turn in, yawning and getting to his feet at the same time. "Night everyone."

Hunter watched them wander back to their rooms. Only Jodie stayed behind. One of the waiters opened a door and a breeze blew through the bar out into the courtyard, lifting her hair in the moonlight.

"Why did you steal the car?" Hunter asked.

She turned. "Huh?"

"Back in Paris you told me you stole your neighbor's car."

"I never planned it," she said quietly, suddenly lost in thought. "I guess I was just angry with my parents. When my dad walked out, it was like a bomb went off in my life. It left a hole too big to fill."

"I can understand that."

"Yeah." She started fiddling with her coaster. "I'm sorry about what happened to your mom in Jordan."

They shared a long silence, broken only by the sound of the waiter clearing drinks from a nearby table. "At the time," Jodie said at last, "I was angry, like I said, but it wasn't until years later that I realized just how much it damaged me. It *ruined* me, Hunter. I will never forgive him."

"I guess that's your right."

"I was eating ice cream when Mom told me. She bought me ice cream to soften the blow."

"That's rough. I'm sorry."

"It was a long time ago," she said wistfully. "Back then, it wasn't so common for families to break up. I was the only kid at school without a father and some of the other kids gave me hell for it. I felt like shit. It would have been better if he *had* died, at least then I would have gotten some sympathy."

"Don't say that."

She faced him. "What the hell do you know about it, anyway? Don't tell me what to say."

"I'm sorry."

"You just walked into our lives a few days ago, dude. You don't know anything about us. We're not going to connect just like *that*." She snapped her fingers.

"Take it easy, Jodie. I was just trying to help."

She settled down when she saw Blanco step back out of the hotel bar. He walked over to them across the courtyard and gave a warm smile. "Sorry, forgot my glasses. You two crazy kids not in bed yet?"

"We're just trying to connect," Hunter said with a smile at Jodie.

Jodie turned away without a smile and finished her drink. She pushed away from the table, chair legs scraping on the tiles. "And I'm beat."

Hunter watched her walk away into the shadows of the hotel entrance.

Blanco, who had caught the end of their conversation, sat down in her seat and tapped his glasses case on the rim of the table. "Don't take it personally. She didn't give me a smile for about year after I met her."

Hunter nodded. "Sounds like she had a rough time."

"And she's as strong as they come because of it, Max, but that means a hard shell."

He laughed. "I got that, yeah."

"Quinn puts on a show of being tough, but she's just playing. She's an enigma all right, and no one really knows anything too deep about her, but with Jodie it's no act. She got burnt when her dad walked out on her and going to juvie baked the rage into her, hard."

"I can see that."

Blanco got up and slammed a hand down on the Londoner's shoulder. "I love her and she's a great girl, but don't expect miracles, Max. She'll open up to you when she's ready."

"Thanks, Sal."

"No problem, friend."

Hunter waited until he was alone and tipped his head up at the sky. The crescent moon hung there like a model, surrounded by stars. Tomorrow was going to be one of the most important days of his life. He got up from his chair and walked back to his room.

# CHAPTER THIRTY-EIGHT

Next morning, they drove out of the city, crossing the Nile on the Luxor Bridge and following the west bank through the Model Village. Here, the oil police guard at the Qurna checkpoint stopped their car and asked them about their intentions. The West Qurna-1 oilfield operated by ExxonMobil was in the vicinity and anti-terror suspicions were running high.

Turning west and heading out into the desert, they made good time and soon found themselves approaching the border between the Luxor Governate and the New Valley Governate. The desert grew more mountainous as they drove south into the world-famous Valley of the Kings.

"We pull up here," Hunter said, bringing the SUV to a stop. "This is the car park."

"Parking lot," Amy said.

"Car park."

"Hey," Blanco said, pointing through the windshield. "Whatever you call it, at least it's not too far from where the action is, right?"

"That's right," Hunter said. "It's a short walk down that slope and then we're almost where we want to be."

"Almost?" Quinn asked. "I'm not too big on desert sand and dust, so *almost* isn't filling me with confidence."

"Yeah," Jodie said. "I thought the Valley of the Kings was right here?"

"It is," Hunter said. "But we're not going to the Valley of the Kings, are we? Julian's clue told us that the actual tomb of Ramesses X is up on the Horn, not down in the valley. The wadi is made up of two valleys, the West and the East. Most of the tombs are in the East Valley, but the Horn is up there to the west. That's where we're headed, at least it is as soon as Omar gets here."

"Would your friend go in for jaunty linen jackets, bright silk pocket squares and felt fedoras by any chance?" Amy asked.

Hunter's eyes widened. "Where?"

"Check your mirror."

"Omar!" Hunter said, and climbed out of the car into the desert heat.

"Good morning, Dr Hunter, you old horse thief!"

The Egyptian archaeologist waved at them and walked briskly over to their car. He was wearing white chinos and a blue shirt, his face shaded by a broad-rimmed, battered fedora with a small tear in the front of the crown.

"Morning, Omar."

"I couldn't believe it when you called me."

"I couldn't believe what I had to say," he said as a woman walked up behind Omar. "Hey, Jehan. How are you?"

"I'm good, Max. You look well."

"As do you. When are you going to leave this guy and marry me?"

They all a laughed and Omar waved a fly away from his face. "I am a very lucky man, I know. My wife is more beautiful than Nefertiti herself."

"Stop it, Omar," Jehan said, clearly enjoying the compliment.

"I take it the men I told you about aren't on site?" Hunter asked.

Omar shook his head. "Not that I know of."

"Maybe Julian held out."

Amy stepped over to them. "Aren't you going to introduce us? I'm starting to feel like an unwanted cousin."

"My apologies," Hunter said. "This is Dr Omar Salem, and this is his wife, Queen Nefertiti." Another chuckle. "But you can call her Dr Jehan Salem. They are both distinguished archaeologists specialising in Ancient Egypt's Twentieth Dynasty and we're very lucky to have them on board."

"If for no other reason than to organize the paperwork," Omar said with a sly smile. "You owe me, old friend! You will never guess what we found when we started digging at your coordinates this morning."

"In that case you'd better tell me."

"Better that you see for yourselves, and we must hurry. We only have access to this area for today, and after that the authorities will close it off once again. Knowing Egyptian bureaucracy, it might be another three thousand years before they get around to allowing us back in."

Laughing at his own joke, Omar led them out of the beating sun and up the mountain slope toward the shady tomb entrance. Inside, they walked down a shallow gradient, untouched by the countless tourists who visited the valley below every year, until reaching a tunnel carved into the rock on their right. It was a perfect vertical rectangle of smooth limestone, so precise it looked like it had been created with modern stone-cutting equipment.

"This is spectacular," Hunter said, gently rubbing his palm along the stone. "How the hell did they get such a fine finish, Omar?"

The Egyptian shrugged. "When you told us to dig up here, I thought you were insane. Imagine the look on my face when I found this tunnel. And no, I have no theories about why it is so smooth."

"Keep moving, Omar," Hunter said. "I can't wait to see what you found."

"I'll say one thing for him," Jodie said from the back. "He sure starts acting like a little kid when there's an unexplored tomb around."

"Don't we all?" Omar said. "If we really have discovered the tomb of Ramesses X, including possibly the preserved mummy of the pharaoh himself, we have made one of the greatest archaeological and historical discoveries of the century."

"Then let's speed it up," Quinn said. "I've got some serious *Em Em Oh* gaming to get back to when this is over. That's the real world, to me. I'm not really into dirt and dust and gravel and flies and heatstroke and mosquito bites. Call me crazy."

Omar and Jehan looked at her, confused. "Huh?"

"Forget about it," Amy said. "Quinn's world is mostly online."

"That explains the complexion," Hunter muttered. "Shall we go and take a closer look at what lies ahead?"

Amy gave him a sly smile as they followed in the Egyptian's hurried footsteps, down the tunnel and around a ninety-degree bend into another long passageway. As they turned the corner, Omar stopped and pointed at the end of second passage to a solid gold door.

"Holy crap," Jodie said. "That can't be real gold."

Omar burst into a childish chuckle which he struggled to control. "It most certainly is real gold, and by the sound it makes when you knock on it, I would say it is at least two or three inches thick."

Hunter examined the magnificent sight of the giant golden portal. Beside it, a small alcove carved into the limestone hosted a miniature pyramid. He stared at it for a few seconds and made some calculations. "There must be at least fifty square feet of gold in that thing. That's sixty thousand pounds of the stuff."

"At current gold prices," Quinn said, "that makes this the million dollar door."

"I'm more worried about its weight," Hunter said. "If we're right and it really is sixty thousand pounds of gold, then that's around thirty tons. We're not just going to push this thing open and walk inside."

"Probably why they made it of gold," Amy said. "Just another line of defense."

"I agree," Omar said. "But the primary reason must be as a sign of great respect to the pharaoh who was buried behind it."

Hunter dropped to his knees and placed his face in the dirt, looking in the direction of the door.

"What the hell is he doing?" Jodie said.

"He's feeling for a breeze," Omar said. "I already did that, Max, and there is none. The door goes right down to the floor of the passageway and I'm presuming there is nothing but an enclosed tomb behind it."

"Yeah." Hunter clambered back to his feet and dusted his hands off. "I think you're right, but the question is how the hell do we get it open? There's no obvious handle and it's too heavy to push anyway, plus brute force is out of the question. This door is already one of the most precious objects I ever saw in my entire career. I'm not throwing a load of dynamite at it just to see what it's hiding from the world."

"So what do we do?" Blanco asked.

Hunter took a step back and stared at the door.

"Immovable," Amy said.

Omar sighed. "Impassable."

"Impossible, more like," said Quinn.

"You're all wrong," Hunter said. "Someone pass me the winged statue we got in El Salvador."

Blanco pulled it from the bag and handed it to him.

Hunter fitted the complex inverted ziggurat in the base of the statue over the top of the miniature pyramid in the alcove beside the door. A deep clunking noise was followed by a puff of dust belching out into the tunnel from all around the outside of the door. Without comment, Hunter waited as the door slid down into a slot in the floor, slowly revealing a room behind it, dark and cold and untouched for thousands of years.

"What are we waiting for?" Quinn said. "Because right now, this is kind of a waste of my time."

Amy shrugged. "She makes a solid point, Max."

"Youth," Hunter said, shining his flashlight into the chamber, "is wasted on the young. Let's go."

# CHAPTER THIRTY-NINE

Passing the door, he stepped inside the chamber and after sweeping his flashlight over the area directly in front of him, he whistled in disbelief. The flashlight had illuminated the base of a giant golden statue and as he angled the beam up to the top and saw the face of Ramesses X staring back at him, he knew he had found the missing pharaoh.

"We did it," he said, shining the beam around the statue and lighting up an enormous mural behind it. "This is the final tomb and resting place of Ramesses X. I can hardly believe I'm seeing it with my own eyes."

"Me neither," Omar said.

"Where's the sarcophagus?" asked Quinn.

"Must be further in."

"What makes it so special?" Jodie asked.

Hunter was walking around the tomb with his flashlight. "The original tomb of Ramesses X was found not far from here but there was no body in it. The same thing happened with Ramesses II. They buried him here in the Valley of the Kings but later moved his body to the royal cache, also right here in the Theban Necropolis. The only difference is they found Ramesses II and moved everything to the Louvre."

"Like the giant statue?"

"Right. We know a great deal about him for that reason. We can see from his mummified body that Ramesses II clearly had red hair, which means he came from a family with red hair. This was important because in ancient Egypt, red hair was strongly linked to the powerful god Set."

"Who killed Osiris," Omar said.

"Precisely."

"But we know very little about Ramesses X, until now. Check this place out! Treasure, records, funerary objects. There's even an original chariot! It's the jackpot."

"You can say that again! Look at all this stuff," Jodie said in awe as she passed her flashlight over the floor. "I'm talking about gold, silver, diamonds, sapphires, rubies… there's treasure everywhere you look. There must be billions of dollars down here."

"When do we fill our boots?" Quinn said.

"We don't fill our boots," Hunter said, looking disapprovingly at the young gothic upstart. "We're not thieves and smugglers, Quinn. I'm an archaeologist and you're a… whatever it is you do."

"Keep disrespecting me like that and you'll find out."

"Looks like a lot of old pottery is in here too," Amy said, changing the subject. "I'm guessing that has more than historical value, too."

Omar laughed. "You could say that. The 4500 year-old Sekhemka statue sold for twenty-five million dollars to an anonymous Qatari millionaire. It's seventy-five centimetres tall. Just a quick glance tells me most of the treasures in this cache are equally as valuable, if not more so."

With Blanco and Lewis standing watch at the tomb's entrance, Hunter lifted the chariot by the shaft, wheeled it out of the way, and prised the lid off a wooden and copper chest. Inside, he saw flared copper cauldrons and bronze urns, ornate golden holders for plant reed candles, canopic jars and some small paintings, but nothing resembling a map of Atlantis.

"Anyone like to see a genuine *ushabti*?" he said.

Quinn arched a curious eyebrow. "And that is?"

Hunter lifted a small clay statue from the chest. "It's a funerary figurine."

Quinn took the statue and turned it over in her hands. "Looks like a mini-mummy."

"Or as we say in the trade, *mummiform.*"

"No, I'll stick with mini-mummy. Is it expensive?"

"Why, looking to retire in your twenties?"

"Are you kidding me? I could have done that when I hacked the Bank of America."

"It's not particularly expensive, no, but it shouldn't be here so maybe that might up its value to a serious private collector of this sort of thing. They're the ones with all the money, not the museums."

"What do you mean?" Amy asked.

"Ushabtis are usually found in excavations and tombs from the Old Kingdom. Ramesses X is much later than that, by over a thousand years." He was still rummaging around in the chest when he stopped suddenly and gasped.

"What it is?"

"Something's off," he said. "This one has a false bottom."

They heard a clunking sound and then he straightened himself up to his full six-feet-two-inches. "It gives way to a ladder. Looks like we might have found something after all."

"After you," Quinn said.

"I wouldn't have it any other way."

He carefully stepped inside the chest and climbed down the ladder. Shining his flashlight around the cavity at the bottom, he gasped loud enough for all to hear.

"What is it, Max?" Amy asked.

"If I said the gaping jaws of a giant black marble sphinx, would you believe it?"

"Only coming from you."

"Then you're in luck. Want to keep me company?"

*

They gathered around the base of the ladder and took in the sinister sight of a giant sphinx's head with wide-open jaws. Through the mouth was a corridor leading to a dark cache fifty yards beyond.

"It's Akhenaten," Hunter said.

Jehan swept her beam over the smooth marble jaw. "I can confirm that. Very strange."

"For us plebs," Quinn said. "Who was that?"

Hunter said, "Akhenaten was one of the first pharaohs to suggest there might be only one god instead of many. Before his dynasty, there were endless numbers of gods and origin myths, but he began the idea of the one true god. He was so serious about there being only one sun god, he had the names of other gods chiselled off stonework all over Egypt."

"Are we going to see what's inside, or what?" Blanco said.

Hunter was already stepping up over the lower jaw. "Wild horses couldn't stop me."

They walked through the jaws and down the corridor to the cache. The small space was stuffed with treasure piled up around a giant marble sarcophagus, and a single hole was in the floor. "We found him," Hunter said in a whisper.

"Nice," Quinn said.

Ignoring the sarcophagus, Hunter dropped to his belly and shone the flashlight inside the hole. "Hold on a minute, I think I might have found something else."

Lewis peered down over his shoulder. "What's lurking down there in the cobwebs, Doc?"

"Looks like we're getting somewhere." Hunter turned and grinned. "I just found what looks a hell of a lot like a map room. Wait here, I'm going down."

He stuffed the flashlight inside his belt and lowered himself carefully down inside the hole. Holding onto the edges, he extended his arms fully and still had around a foot below him. He dropped to the floor with a gentle thud and kicked up a small cloud of dust.

"It's incredible!" he called up, spellbound in wonder. "You have to see this place, Omar. You too, Jehan."

Sweeping the beam of light from side to side, he took in the breathtaking sight of an intricate model of a city. In the center was a giant pyramid, closer to the one he had seen in El Salvador than the Great Pyramid at Giza and he realized he was looking at an Atlantean city, probably the capital. He felt his heart quicken. Rows of futuristic buildings on neat semi-circular grids of streets reminded him of Amsterdam, and rivers and canals criss-crossed the roads. Behind it on the wall was a line of glyphs similar to those he had seen on the base of the Ramesses statue in Scorpion Ravine.

"Damn it," he said. "Looks like we're going to need Julian to decipher these."

"Then you're in luck!"

His blood turned to ice when he heard the voice. It echoed down the hole and bounced off the rock walls of the underground map room, almost stabbing a hole in his heart.

"Brodie?"

He heard Amy scream.

"That's me, Max. Always late to the party."

"And never welcome."

"Aww, don't be like that old friend. Why not climb up out of that little hidey hole before I put a bullet through your girlfriend's head?"

He heard a scuffle, then a hefty punch and the sound of Blanco gasping for breath. He considered smashing the glyphs at the end of the map room and trampling over the model, but he had no photos of any of it and didn't trust his memory.

Halfway up through the hole, he felt hands grab him by the shoulders and haul him back up into the cache. The disciples who had pulled him out pushed him toward McCabe who was shining a bright light in his face. A badly winded Blanco was on the floor in the corner and the rest of the team were standing against a wall with their hands on their heads, disciples of the Creed pointing guns at them. The winged statue they had found in El Salvador was now in a bag over one of their shoulders.

"You did it again, Max." His dark eyes were shaded by the rim of his favorite pinched-front safari hat. "Selflessly working for the betterment of my career. I don't know how to thank you."

"I suppose a kiss is out of the question?"

McCabe's lip curled, but before he could speak, a woman stepped into the flashlight beam.

"Klara Steiner," Hunter said.

"We meet again, Dr Hunter."

"It was her all along, Max!" Amy said. "She was the one communicating with the Creed from inside the Rorschach Foundation, not Oskar."

"Silence!" Klara yelled, slapping Amy hard across the face.

Enraged by the brutality of the assault, Hunter surged forward to defend her. Steiner snapped her fingers and a man brought him down with a pistol whipping. His face hit the floor and when he opened his eyes he saw two more disciples hauling Julian Walters into the cache. His face was beaten hard, with swollen purple eyes above cheekbones covered in cuts and bruises. When they let go of him, he slumped down into the dust not far from Hunter.

Walters spat out blood and dust. "You always were trouble, Max."

"I'm doing just great, thanks. How are you?"

"Having the time of my life, thanks to you."

"I take it you found something of note down in the hole?" Steiner said.

"Why not slither down and take look?" Hunter said. "A snake could get down there much easier than I did."

She kicked him in the stomach. It was enough to knock the wind from his lungs and make him cough hoarsely into the dust as she strolled around him in a circle. "Pick up Walters and take him down into the map room. He has five minutes to decipher the location of Atlantis, and the weapons arsenal there, or I start shooting his friends, starting with Professor Omar Salem."

# CHAPTER FORTY

Disciples grabbed Hunter, pulled him to his feet and pushed him over to the wall where the rest of the team was standing. Blanco was up on his feet again and looked calm and in control, like Omar and Jehan. So did Amy and Lewis but Quinn and Jodie were scared. He saw it in their eyes. A wave of guilt rippled over him. This was all his fault.

"I'm sorry, guys. I shouldn't have brought Julian in. He was the weak link."

"Relax," Blanco said. "No one's shouldering any blame here."

"That's right," Jodie said. "Except you, Hunter, because this is all your fault."

Hunter looked from Jodie to Blanco. "Is she being serious?"

"It's possible."

"What do you want with Atlantis?" Hunter asked Steiner. "What was that about a weapons arsenal?"

"Nothing to concern you."

Hunter laughed. "You're the sort of person who always concerns me."

"Let it go, Dr Hunter. To say we are powerful would be to risk a considerable understatement. Suffice it to say, the

Magus keeps the leaders of many nations in his pocket, and uses them like loose change. Rubbing you out would be nothing at all."

"The Magus?"

"Our leader," she said. "The leader of the Creed. Anyone steps out of line and he'll pull the plug on the money. He can drain a national economy in a day and ensure no one else ever invests there again."

"Charming."

Steiner spoke to a disciple and ordered him over to the hole in the map room ceiling. When he was there, he got down on his knees and called down to McCabe. "You have two more minutes and then Salem's dead."

"I can't work like this!"

They all heard the desperation in Walters's voice.

"Clock's counting down," the disciple said.

"Maybe…" Walters said.

"What is it?" said McCabe. "You have something?"

"I'm not sure – I need time."

Steiner looked at her watch. "No time. Kill him!"

One of the disciples obeyed without question, firing on Omar and killing him in cold blood. Amy stared with disbelief as the blood-soaked corpse crashed down onto the cache floor. When Jehan saw her dead husband, she cried out in anguish and rushed toward him. "Omar!"

"Get back or I will have you shot!" Steiner's voice was as cold as steel.

Jehan froze on the spot, her chest heaving up and down as she sobbed with grief.

Blanco stepped forward and put his arms around her, wheeling her back toward the main group. "Don't give her any excuse to kill you, Jehan."

"And she'll do it," Hunter said. "Believe me."

"What's happening up there?" Walters said. "Did someone get hurt because of me?"

"Not because of you," Hunter said, looking at Steiner in disgust. "But someone got killed. Omar."

"My God."

"Shut up and keep working!" McCabe screamed.

"Four more minutes and his wife dies," Steiner said. "Hurry up, Professor Walters, because all of this blood is on your hands."

No response, but when they saw Walters's face appear in the hole, crumpled with fear and guilt, they all knew Steiner had what she needed. He had deciphered the glyphs. "I have the information you want. I know where the Gate of the Gods is."

"Good work, Professor," Steiner said. "I do hope you're telling me the truth when you say you have translated the glyphs."

"Yes," he said sullenly.

"Then, come here and tell me," she said. "And only me."

McCabe walked him over to her and the old man whispered in her ear. They all saw the smile on her face.

"Destroy the map room," she said.

Hunter lunged forward but was stopped by a disciple. "No!"

Another disciple dropped a grenade into the map room. A deep thud was followed by a thick column of smoke pouring out of the hole.

Steiner smirked. "Good."

"That was a terrible crime," Hunter said.

"You'll get over it in time."

"Please, don't kill any more of these people." Walters said.

Steiner passed a silent message to McCabe, eye to eye. "Sorry, but no can do."

McCabe drew a gun and fired it through Walters's back. The bullet punched a bloody exit hole the size of a fist in his chest and he collapsed down dead onto the floor, surprised terror etched onto his bloody face.

Quinn screamed, and she and Jodie reached for each other. Powered by an uncontrollable rage, Hunter charged McCabe. He reached him just as his gun exploded with a dazzling flash in the darkness of the cache.

# CHAPTER FORTY-ONE

Smacking McCabe's arm to the side, the bullet went wide and buried itself in the cache wall. Hunter crashed down on top of his old nemesis and belted the gun from his hands.

"You son of a bitch!" he yelled. "I'll kill you for that."

McCabe struggled beneath the more powerful man's weight as Hunter wrapped a hand around his neck and squeezed. "Die, you bastard!"

Another gunshot exploded in the cache. Hunter froze and heard Steiner screaming at him to release McCabe. Surrounded by armed disciples, he leaned in close to his ear and lowered his voice. "You're mine, McCabe. That one was over the line."

Both men got to their feet. McCabe looked panicked, but composed himself enough to power a punch into Hunter's stomach and send him to the deck, doubled over and coughing hard. "No one threatens me, Max. Least of all you."

"Enough," Steiner said. "The Apostle awaits us at Black Rock." She turned to McCabe and threw him back his gun. "Kill them all and meet me on the surface. We're flying immediately. Bring *her*," she pointed at Amy. "We need some insurance."

She walked past Hunter with a face of cold stone, stopping only to blow a mock kiss at him. She vanished into the tunnel, flanked by disciples who were dragging a kicking and screaming Amy Fox out of the cache behind them.

"We'll get you back, Amy," Blanco said. "Count on it."

"I know, Sal..."

"Shut up!"

When their shadows had receded in the tunnel, Hunter looked on his old friend with contempt. "You heard her, Brodie. Kill us all."

Standing between two disciples, McCabe raised his gun and pointed the barrel at Hunter.

"I'm going to enjoy this more than sex."

"But wouldn't you have had to have sex to make that statement?" Jodie said.

They saw his fading smile. "Goodbye, Max Hunter and friends. So near and yet so far."

He pulled the hammer back and Hunter dived behind the sarcophagus. McCabe spun around and tracked him across the cache, firing a sustained burst of rounds at him as he flew through the air. Still using the momentum of the dive, Hunter rolled over to Omar's corpse and pulled back his jacket. As he had expected, his old friend was carrying his usual pocket pistol.

He fired back, urging his friends to take cover while he pinned McCabe and the two disciples down. One of the disciples ran toward the sarcophagus under the cover fire of his two colleagues, but Hunter fired back.

The weapon kicked back in his hands when he unloaded the mag on the approaching men; the army was in his deep past now, but nothing ever rubbed out the feeling of firing a gun. The smell of the smoke, the sound of the spent cases spitting out of the ejector port, the firm *dunk* of the recoil. Bullet weight, caliber, velocity, the thoughts came rushing back to him and then the magazine was empty.

The disciple vaulted over the sarcophagus and chaos exploded in the cache. Blanco and Lewis charged the other disciple and disarmed him, forcing McCabe to take cover behind one of the giant treasure chests and fire on them. They scrambled behind the other end of the sarcophagus and returned fire as Hunter ran hard at the man attacking him.

He tackled him around the waist and forced him to the cache floor before he could pull his weapon. They landed with a heavy thump in a cloud of ancient dust and Hunter got the first strike in, cracking the man's jaw with a feisty jab.

Jodie leapt into the air, not knowing what the hell was going on. Falling out of the leap, she extended her right foot and fired a hook kick into a disciple's chest, blasting him back into the wall. He struck his skull on the smooth carved rock and grunted in pain, tumbling onto his knees, dizzy and disoriented.

Reaching down to his belt, he grabbed at the handle of a spear-point knife and flicked it across the chamber at her. Blanco's reaction was like lightning, tackling Jodie to the ground just as the knife ripped past through the air and smacked against the rock on the other side of the chamber. The disciple leapt to his feet, his boots scuffing on the dusty tiles and made a move toward Blanco and Jodie who were still on the floor on top of each other.

Down in the dirt, Jodie huffed out a rare laugh. "Really, Sal, this is hardly the time."

The Brooklynite had no time to react. Rolling his hefty frame off of her, he found himself on his back as the disciple snatched up the knife and ran toward them with it raised in his clenched fist, blade-down.

Behind them, McCabe screamed and fired his gun as he worked his way around to the cache entrance. Across the other side of the chamber, Hunter landed another punch on the other man's face, striking his head back into the enormous carved flagstones and knocking him out. Rolling off his unconscious body, the Londoner scrambled to his feet but wasn't up for long. Another disciple rushed him from behind and struck him on the side of the head with a swift haymaker.

If Hunter had seen it coming, he would have rolled with it, but it was a surprise attack and it knocked him over like a sack of potatoes. He hit the deck and fought like hell to stay conscious as the man padded over to him and drew a knife from his belt.

"I'm going to make you beg for this to end."

"Stop, please. You sound like my ex."

"I see you cannot even take your own death seriously."

"Y'know, I'm starting to get the impression you don't like me very much."

He heard the sharp report of a gun and blood poured out of the man's mouth. He slumped to the side, freeing Hunter and revealing Blanco standing behind him. He held a smoking gun in his hand. "All good?"

Through the smoke and dust, he looked at the man from Brooklyn. "All good, Sal, and thanks. What's going on?"

"McCabe appears to have slipped out in the chaos," Jodie said.

"But all the disciples who stayed behind are dead," said Lewis.

Blanco looked grim. "And we have to get after Amy in a hurry, Max. Her life is at risk and we have no idea where they're taking her or the location of Atlantis."

"And we have none of the winged statues," Quinn said.

They headed out of the cache and sprinted back along the tunnel, passing through the sphinx's jaws and heading up to the surface. Emerging into a bright, hot day, they scrambled through rubble and scree on the ridge above the newly made entrance on the mountainside, trying to keep as low as possible to stay out of sight.

Blanco spoke first. "Jeeps! Three of them driving east in the valley."

"They're already on their way," Lewis said.

Hunter squinted as he watched the Jeeps traverse a gradient at the base of the Valley of the Queens and head east toward the main road leading through the Valley of the

Kings and then back to Luxor. Instead of turning onto the main road, they pulled up at the side and waited in the sun.

"What are they doing?" Jodie asked.

"Hear it?" Hunter said.

"Hear what?"

"The intoxicating sound of a General Electric CT7 turboshaft."

"Huh?"

"It's an engine," he said. "And it belongs to a Bell Relentless, a medium-lift chopper capable of transporting nineteen passengers."

Blanco cursed and kicked a rock. "And one hostage. We have to save her."

"It's number one on my list, Sal."

"Steiner said they were going to the Black Rock," Lewis said. "That's all we have."

Blanco wiped blood from his lip with the back of his hand and followed the helicopter fly away over the desert to the west. "Wrong. We also have Quinn Mosley."

# CHAPTER FORTY-TWO

The one hour drive to the castle was made in an old-school Mercedes-Benz G-Class SUV, a serious vehicle which combined solid V8 engine power with no-nonsense off-road capabilities. Sal Blanco was at the wheel, driving with the radio tuned to a local station determined not to leave the nineteen-eighties, but he seemed to like it well enough.

Using passwords created by Amy in her undercover roll as Dr Kirsten Anderson, Quinn was able to break into the Rorschach Foundation network. From there she was able to search for references to the new information they had. Black Rock turned out to be the name of a castle in Germany's Black Forest owned by an international shareholder consortium headed by a man named Karl Adler. Quinn's work yielded nothing on Adler or the consortium and the team drew their own conclusions, deciding he must be the notorious Apostle.

Driving southwest toward the castle was quiet and uneventful. Gates had arranged for them to pull into a CIA safehouse in Stuttgart and collect some weapons. Loading bullets into the magazines had concentrated the minds of Hunter, Blanco and Lewis, the three military-trained members of the team. They all knew what was likely if they wanted to rescue Amy and prise the location of Atlantis from Adler and his lieutenants.

Halfway into the ninety-kilometer journey, they started driving up into mountains along roads flanked with rows of endless black pine trees.

"I can see why they call this place the Black Forest," Lewis said, peering into the snowy woods.

"Yup," Quinn muttered. She had been researching the castle on the drive and now she shut up her laptop and dropped it into her bag. "Not much gets by you."

"I think maybe they were leaning more to pragmatism than the romantic when they came up with that one," he said. "What else have you got?"

"I might not be able to find out about the consortium or Herr Adler, but I now know more about Black Rock Castle than anyone else on earth."

Hunter leaned down and put the loaded gun into the bag between his feet, then settled back in his chair. "All right, let me have it."

She explained what she had learned, her voice soft and level against the hum of the new car on the autobahn. Every now and then someone would interrupt with a question and after twenty minutes they knew what she did.

Blanco turned in his seat. "That's what I call a briefing."

Quinn went on. "Anyway, that's the history and even some information about the layout, but unfortunately the place is too old for anything like planning documents or schematics."

"You did your best," Lewis said.

Hunter's eyes were closed and the gentle motion of the car had almost pushed him to sleep, but he had listened attentively to the briefing. "Yeah, good job, Quinn."

Quinn looked genuinely surprised. "Really? I thought it lacked anything of real use."

"No way," Hunter said. "It was useful, especially the images you found. At least we know the best way into the place."

Another silence fell over the car. Hunter thought about how much he had come through in the last few days. His narrow escape in McCabe's desert camp to meeting Amy and Rorschach in Switzerland. The assault on Vazquez's private liner and the discovery of the Cuban's brutal slaying at the hands of the Creed in El Salvador. The death of his mentor in Egypt and Omar's brutal murder. How would poor Jehan ever get over his death? He already felt sick when he thought about it.

And beneath it all, a lethal undertow waiting to destroy them all.

Atlantis.

But they had to get there first, and that meant infiltrating Adler's castle deep in the Black Forest. Maybe, he thought with a shudder, not all of them would make it to the grand prize at the end of the journey.

"Max."

It was Blanco, his voice low and calm.

Hunter's eyes were still closed but he knew what was coming; he felt the car turn a bend and climb a gradient and then come to a stop. "We're here?"

"Yup, we're here."

He opened his eyes. They were parked just off the road inside the forest which surrounded the entire castle at the base of the black rock it was built on. Schloss Schwarzenfels or Black Rock Castle as it was known in English, was the ancestral seat of an ancient imperial German house. The dynasty had controlled the region for centuries and built their first castle on the site over a thousand years ago. The current castle was only two hundred years old – a sprawling Gothic Revival masterpiece adorned with palatial courtyards, formal gardens and its own chapel.

"Willkommen nach Hölle," Quinn said.

Jodie looked at her. "Huh?"

"Welcome to hell," she shrugged. "Just sort of seemed like the appropriate thing to say."

Blanco pointed through the trees. "Is that our way in?"

Quinn shook her head. "That's the *Adlertor*, or the Eagle Gate. It's kind of Adler's front door so not our best choice for a covert ingress. Our way in is just off to the east of it – a small entrance used by the servants in years gone by."

"And probably still today," Lewis said.

They stepped out of the car into a light drizzle and made their way through the trees to a small black wooden gate set into the stones at the base of the castle wall. Blanco wasted no time in hefting a rock and smashing the handle off the gate. After a few moments fiddling around with what was left of the lock, he swung open the door.

Inside, the cobblestone drive up from the southern gate was empty and silent. High on the side of the mountain, even inside the castle walls, the wind was cold and sharp. When it blew, it howled like a ghost through trees lining the side of the drive. "I guess we get walking," Jodie said.

With Hunter in the lead, they started up the slope toward the castle.

# CHAPTER FORTY-THREE

Amy Fox tracked Klara Steiner as she walked across the room and joined Karl Adler by the enormous medieval stone-lined fireplace. A fierce fire was raging in the hearth and smoke twisted up into the chimney above it. On the long oak table, a gold candelabra held three black candles which lit the dank room.

"Who are you people?" Amy asked. "I mean, really."

Adler stirred the fire with a fire-blackened brass poker. When he spoke, his voice was mellow and serene. "The Creed are impossible to describe to an outsider. Let me put it like this. We rose from the ashes of the Illuminati when they were banned over two hundred years ago, and that should tell you a lot about us. We hold the values of that society, but we take it further. We draw our strength from sources you would consider unimaginable."

The fire spat and crackled and wrapped its long flames around the soft white heartwood of a new log. Amy followed Adler as he slumped down into the leather chair beside the giant hearth. Over his shoulder, she saw the sun twinkling on the oxbow lake meandering around the base of the castle.

"Unimaginable?" she said.

He smiled and shook his head. "There is no way you could understand what we do, or why we do it. All you need to know is we have our reasons." His voice lowered to something like a bestial growl. "And we are in total control of this world. No one can change that."

Amy's skin prickled. Something in this man's eyes frightened her more than anything else she had known. Staring into the threatening depths of his dark eyes was an unnerving experience. She stepped over to the chair and sat down beside Klara Steiner. The moment was surreal. Chalky motes drifted in the air, occasionally buffeted by the thermals of the roaring fire.

"Why are you looking for Atlantis, Adler?"

The Apostle selected a cigarette from a silver case and lit it. He crossed his legs and settled back into the old chair's velvety, worn leather. "Because the Magus ordered me too."

"Cute. Why is the Magus looking for Atlantis?"

He paused, staring into the flames. "The Illuminati always knew about Atlantis and its secrets. That knowledge was passed down to them from much older secret societies who in turn were enlightened by even more ancient sources of the truth. It goes right back to a place and time beyond your comprehension."

Amy considered his reply. "If the Creed runs the world, then this means our leaders know about Atlantis."

"And always have done," Adler said. "We have guarded the secret for millennia, keeping this knowledge away from the greedy, grasping hands of humanity. The entire basis of these societies, including the Illuminati and now the Creed, was to protect the knowledge of Atlantis and the mighty secret it holds."

"The mighty secret?"

"Again, beyond your comprehension," he said, drawing on the cigarette. He flicked some of the pale ash into the fire. It missed and drifted down onto the vast stone hearth. "The people of Atlantis were more advanced than you can imagine and knew the secret to human origins. Why do you think one of our most precious symbols is the pyramid? This was chosen to remind us of our beginnings, of where our story began. The pyramids of Egypt and the Americas were built in homage to those of the motherland, of the center of the empire and the cradle of all civilizations on earth – Atlantis!"

Amy looked at him, eyes narrowing. "But you don't know where Atlantis actually is, do you?"

"Unfortunately no," Adler said, frowning. "So ancient is that civilization, and so devastating was its destruction that its location was lost forever. Not even the secret societies were able to pass it down through the ages. The Freemasons searched for it for centuries, then the Illuminati searched for it, and now the Creed. Finally, it is within our grasp."

"All the knowledge and power in the world, except for the location of Atlantis," Amy said with a smile. "Tragic."

"True," Adler said, suddenly animated and jabbing a pale finger in her direction. "But now the tragedy is over. Thanks to the late Julian Walters and the efforts of your team, we now have not only the location of the kingdom of Atlantis, but also the critical components of the fire lance."

Amy's eyes flicked up from the fire and stared at him. "Fire lance?"

"The three winged statues, Special Agent Fox," he said.

Klara Steiner laughed. "You have our guest at a disadvantage."

"Yes, apparently so," Amy said. "You're saying they're *not* statues after all?"

"They're statues all right, but they have another role, another meaning. They are critical to our quest."

"A quest that is nearly over," Klara said.

"Indeed, and nothing can stop us now."

They all heard the sound of distant gunfire at the same time, and Adler turned in his chair to hear better through the window. The sound was not the explosive thunderous fusillade of an army or a police force besieging the castle, but the tinny crackle of sidearms and the occasional sound of people shouting outside the castle.

Adler stared at Klara's drawn face and they each paled.

"Nothing can stop you now," Amy said. "Except my team."

# CHAPTER FORTY-FOUR

Hunter rolled through the gravel and slammed up against the stone wall in the castle courtyard. Changing magazines and reloading the heavy weapon in his hands, memories of past combat flashed before his eyes. Iraq. Afghanistan. Dust and blood. Men blown to pieces by IED and mortar shell.

He wiped the dust from his eyes and watched his small platoon making their way up the slope and into the yard, jumping over a low wall and crashing down beside him. Only minutes earlier, they had been running up a paved walkway from the servants' gate, then a disciple up on one of the turrets had spotted them and opened fire. After that, things had gone downhill fast.

"We can get inside through one of these windows, but we need to make sure the room's clear," he said. "Use one of the grenades from the safehouse, Sal."

Blanco was already ahead of him, gripping an M67 fragmentation grenade with his thick fingers. He pulled the pin and yelled at everyone to cover their heads. Three seconds after the grenade went through the window, a deep explosion blasted a cloud of smoke and dust and detritus over their heads.

"Go!" Hunter yelled.

Blanco was first in, up over the sill and firing into the smoke with his MP7. As Jodie, Lewis and Quinn clambered up inside, more disciples ran up through the grounds and took cover behind a wall on the courtyard's south side. Hunter fired on them, giving valuable cover to his team as they got inside the room.

"Need a hand, Sal!"

The man from Brooklyn said nothing, but Hunter knew his reply when he saw another of the fragmentation grenades sail over his head and crash into the men behind the wall. He buried his head in his crossed arms to avoid the devastation, and to shield his eyes from the terrible vision of so many deaths and injuries.

The grenade exploded hard and close. He felt the thump deep in his chest and heard screams as body parts tumbled back to earth and slapped onto the gravel with a wet smack. All over again he saw visions of war that he had worked so hard so repress, but the sound of Jodie calling out to him brought him back to reality.

"Are you okay, Hunter?"

"I'm all right!" he yelled.

"Then get your ass up here!" she yelled.

A smile broke on his lips. *Maybe Miss Hardass gives a shit after all*, he thought. He reached up to the sill and felt two hands pulling him up. It was Lewis and Jodie. They heaved him inside and he crashed down on a burnt, smoldering rug. Blanco was at the door, firing on more disciples with his MP7. The weapon jerked in the big man's hands, empty shell casings spitting out of the ejector port as he cleared the hallway.

"We're good to go!" he yelled, waving them forward with a soot-smeared paw.

Hunter and the rest of the team followed him through the door and up a grand wooden staircase. Bullets from the fire fight had shredded the intricately carved Baroque newel posts, and a man lay dying on the first landing, his lower right leg almost severed by rounds from the MP7. He moaned as blood pumped from his artery. Hunter hesitated, but Blanco fired another shot into his head and killed him on the spot, pounding past him without even stopping to look.

It shocked Hunter, even with all his combat experience. He knew the Brooklynite was right. You never leave the enemy alive behind you as you advance, and yet this place was a castle, not a theatre of war; the man some sort of acolyte, not a soldier. He remembered what he had learned about Blanco being a former mercenary and had dark thoughts about what else this man had done. Friendly and loyal on the outside, but maybe driven by some darker mechanism deep on the inside.

"Cover!" Lewis called out, spraying lead on disciples further up the staircase. Bullets rained down on them from above in response.

"I see around half a dozen more men!" Blanco yelled, swivelling his MP7 up and firing on them through the gap between the stairs. Rounds raked down the steps, chewing into the wood and pinging off the plaster walls. The team slammed up against the wall out of the line of fire and provided cover for Blanco as he advanced to the next landing.

When he got there, he swivelled around and fired again, emptying his magazine on the men at the top of the stairs. "I see Amy!" he screamed.

"What?" Jodie said. "Where?"

"At the top of the stairs," Blanco called back. "They're dragging her across the landing. We have to get up there! Amy, we're on our way!"

"Let's get up there, then!" Quinn said.

Blanco hesitated. "Wait, they're setting up a damn GPMG on the top landing. There's no way we can get through that."

"And we have more good news," Lewis said. "We have at least twenty armed disciples running up the stairs behind us, Sal!"

"We're trapped!" Quinn said.

Jodie quickly leaned over the bannister and saw the men Lewis had described. There were at least twenty, maybe more, all armed with submachine guns and grenades. "Doesn't look good, Sal! We'll have our hands full trying to stop these guys advancing on our position."

"Then we need to change position," Hunter said. "We go up."

"What about the GPMG?" Jodie asked, eyes desperately searching him for an answer.

"Sal, a grenade please."

Blanco tossed him a grenade from his bag. Hunter caught it, pulled the pin and rolled it down the stairs to the lower landing. "Run!"

He led the team up the stairs to Blanco on the higher landing. As the disciples turned the corner beneath them, the grenade detonated. The explosion blew four of them to pieces and drove the rest back down the stairs to regroup. Hunter wasn't waiting for them to get their act together. He was up on the landing with Blanco. The team stared at him for direction.

"Our only hope is taking out the machinegun nest with a grenade," he said.

Blanco nodded. "Agreed."

"How many grenades left in the bag of tricks?"

"One."

"Excellent," Hunter said. "How's your aim?"

"Better than yours."

"Even better. Listen up everyone. When Sal throws the grenade and hits the two-man crew, we have a window of no more than thirty seconds before they get more men on the gun."

"Maybe the grenade will destroy the gun, too?" Quinn said.

"Or maybe it won't," Hunter said. "And maybe they have another gun. See where I'm going with this?"

She said nothing, giving him a petulant look and rolling her eyes.

"Good," he said. "We have to charge up the last flight of stairs in half a minute, guns blazing. All good?"

Quinn looked horrified. "No, that is *not* all good! This is like the damn Somme or something."

"You'll be fine," Hunter said. "Stay at the back with your shoulder against the wall and keep your head down. Got it?"

"We can't stay here, Quinn," Lewis said. "We're trapped in a pincer movement."

"Ben's right," Jodie said. "We have to go up. Besides, that's where they're keeping Amy."

She nodded. "If you guys all say so."

"Good. Then let's get going." Hunter got into position, ready to lead the charge. "It's grenade time, Sal."

# CHAPTER FORTY-FIVE

Blanco threw the grenade and blasted the machinegun nest into the next world. Hunter screamed the order to advance, raising his gun and charging up the stairs. Three steps up, he opened fire on the sulphur-reeking cloud of ash and smoke and dust. The muzzle strobed orange and white in the foul darkness as he powered forward to the landing, sweeping the barrel from right to left and back again.

The daring gambit had worked. When the smoke cleared, there was no sign of any disciples. The two men working the GPMG were dead, blown to pieces by the grenade's devastating force. Hunter knew they were the enemy, but hated seeing it. This was no movie, no CGI effect. Visions like this stayed in the mind forever.

"What now?" Jodie asked.

"Where did they take Amy, Sal?" Hunter asked.

He pointed to a heavy dark, hardwood door on the left, covered in old carvings of roses and thistles. "In there."

Hunter tried the door. It was locked, and a shoulder barge failed to move it an inch. "We need to blow the lock. Stand by!"

He took a step back from the door and raised the MP7's muzzle, but whey heard the sound of gunfire, it wasn't his.

"The disciples from the lower landing," Jodie said.

Quinn looked scared. "Hurry, Max!"

Hunter fired and ripped the lock to pieces. After that, a second shoulder barge sent the door crashing out of the frame and smashing back into the stone wall inside the room. "Okay, everyone in, now!"

He fired on the disciples sprinting up the top of the stairs, giving Jodie, Lewis and Quinn time to duck inside the room. Blanco fired on the men as they vaulted over the dead machinegun crew. "You too, Sal."

He followed Blanco into the room and slammed the broken door shut. "Great, we have twenty seconds at best – that way!" He nodded at a door on the other side of the room. Blanco tried it, and this time it opened onto another corridor. Gunfire echoed behind them. Its sound inside the castle was raw and terrifying.

"Move!" he yelled.

They forged ahead down the second corridor. It was darker than before. A long antique runner stretched away from them like a red river over the floorboards. Behind them, Hunter saw shadows bobbing up and down on the passageway wall as the disciples barrelled toward them through the room, guns raised. Another sharp report of deafening gunshots boomed in the corridor and now they were close enough to see the enemy's muzzle flashes.

"Another damn door," Blanco said.

It was beside a small lead-lined window looking out onto part of the castle roof. When Hunter peered through it, he saw an executive helicopter ready to take off, blades whirring.

"They're dragging Amy into a chopper."

"Shit."

"Exactly, and the window's too small to go through. Blow the lock, Sal."

Blanco stepped in front of Quinn and Jodie and raised his gun. Quinn fought the urge to turn and flee. She was frightened, but she didn't want the others to know it. Hiding behind the goth makeup and the hood was enough to shield herself from the ordinary experiences of life, but what was happening now wasn't something she could get away from, and it terrified her.

She tightened her hoodie's drawstring and took a step closer to Lewis. "They're almost here, guys. How are we doing?"

Blanco fired on the lock and blasted the door open. At the other end of the corridor, the disciples turned the corner and raised their guns into the aim.

# CHAPTER FORTY-SIX

Hunter was ready for them, and fired on the disciples in a brutal display of ruthless and bloody precision. Quinn screamed and covered her ears as the former Guards officer drilled the men full of holes, blowing their insides all over the white plaster wall behind them.

Even with the gun jerking and rattling in his hands, Hunter felt sick at the devastation he was causing, but he had no choice. The disciples were here to kill him and the rest of the team. It was kill or be killed in the most raw way imaginable. He chose to kill.

Quinn screamed behind him, the black mascara around her young eyes streaking with tears of terror and uncertainty.

"It's over," Jodie said. "At least for now."

"I never saw anything like that in my entire life," the goth said, pointing.

Jodie grabbed the fabric of her hoodie and shook her. "Take it easy, hun."

The young goth raised a trembling, white hand at the dead men sprayed all over the walls. "I…I…"

Hunter saw from her face she had never known war. A good thing, but this was a savage introduction. "It's over," he said quietly. "For now."

Blanco moved through the doorway and stepped out onto the roof. "Let's go! The rotors are almost at take-off velocity."

"I see that bastard McCabe," Hunter said. "And more sodding disciples, including Gaius. I've had enough of this!' He burst through the door and opened fire on the chopper. Disciples instantly took up defensive positions and returned fire, driving them back into the blood-soaked corridor.

After a short exchange of fire, Hunter changed magazines and aimed the MP7's barrel at McCabe, opening fire on his old nemesis just as he hurled himself to the ground and rolled under the chopper. Hunter broke cover and charged, sweeping the muzzle after him and blowing chunks out of the roofing felt.

Chasing him all the way into his cover position, he turned and ran toward the silver metallic Raven sitting on the roof behind him. The light, single-engine aircraft was smaller than the Gazelles and Wildcats and Apaches he was used to flying in the army, but easily big enough to take four people. He guessed those four people were Adler, Klara Steiner, Brodie McCabe and Amy, but they could forget about taking Amy anywhere.

He fired again, clipping the shoulder of the disciple holding Amy. He released her and hit the deck, writhing in agony as blood plumped from his wound. Realizing Amy was free, Adler and Steiner shared a look of terror.

"Gaius!" McCabe yelled. "Get the girl!"

McCabe and the other disciples pinned them down while Gaius ran to Amy. Hunter raised his weapon and fired, killing him with a single shot to the head and dropping him to the roof. Chaos erupted as Blanco broke his cover and charged the helicopter. Adler saw the danger of the moment and ordered their evacuation.

Klara Steiner was in the pilot seat now and lifted the chopper off the roof. Hunter tried to fire on them but it was too late. They dropped below the level of the roof and raced low over the oxbow lake until the aircraft was no more than a tiny black dot on the horizon.

The team rushed to their shocked and confused leader. "Are you all right?" Quinn asked.

"I'm okay!" Amy said. "And I know what Julian told Steiner!"

Hunter searched her face. Had he heard her right? "You know where Atlantis is?"

She nodded. "Greenland."

"Greenland?" Lewis was shocked. "I thought it was going to be an island."

"Greenland is an island, moron," Quinn said.

Lewis sighed. "I know that. I meant I thought it was going to be some sort of undiscovered island."

Hunter had been silent, but now he smiled. "It all makes sense now," he said. "Damn it, I just knew it had to be something like this. Remember what we talked about with the comet strike and the flooding?"

Jodie gasped. "Holy shit – but how is it even possible to have a civilization on Greenland?"

"It was arboreal forest eight hundred-thousand years ago," Lewis said. "So it was habitable once. Depends how far you want to go back."

"I thought it was always icy," Jodie said.

"Yeah, don't strain your head too much," said Quinn, slowly getting over the terror of the fire fight. "But why do you think they called it Greenland and not Snowland?"

"Hey!"

Amy held up her hands to silence everyone. "We can talk about that later. Right now we have to stop Adler from getting there. The statues aren't just statues, but part of some kind of ancient weapon the Creed have known about for centuries – something Adler called a fire lance."

Blanco shared his look of astonishment with the others. "A fire lance? What the hell is that? Max?"

Hunter shouldered the MP7 and wiped sweat from his forehead. "I think I know, but we need to get going in a real hurry. If there's a doomsday weapon lurking in Atlantis, we have to get to it before these psychos."

# CHAPTER FORTY-SEVEN

Hunter studied the topographical glacier maps on Quinn's laptop, turning the three-dimensional image and using the zoom function to close in on the coast. A ferocious Arctic storm was lashing the window of their Reykjavik hotel room and everyone knew Greenland would be even worse.

"How long is this storm in for?" Jodie asked.

Hunter looked through the window and fought off a shudder. When Amy had told them the location of Atlantis, he had felt an electrifying mix of excitement and dread. As an archaeologist, he also had a keen interest in geology, and he knew all about the treacherous coves and fjords of Greenland's eastern coast. More satisfying had been the confirmation that the notorious lost civilization was in Greenland, his leading personal theory for years.

"The latest weather report says three more days," said Amy, staring over Hunter's shoulder at the surging grey ocean out beyond the harbor. "Looks like we're in for a rough ride."

"Maybe we can sit it out?" Quinn asked.

"No way," Amy said. "Adler and Steiner got away from us in Germany and we know they're at least half a day ahead."

Jodie shrugged. "For all we know, they could be waiting for the storm to end, just like we should be doing."

Amy shook her head. "That doesn't sound like the people I talked to at the castle. The Atlantis myth has consumed them for centuries and now we know why – the fire lance."

"I guess," Jodie said reluctantly.

Hunter looked up from the laptop and cast his eyes across to her. "You don't need to guess – you can count on it." He jabbed a thumb over his shoulder at the storm closing in on the harbor. "They're out there right now in the middle of that storm on their way to Greenland and we're the only people who can stop them."

"And how the hell are we going to do that?" Quinn asked. "Swim?"

Amy grinned. "No, I have a good friend who wants to help."

"What can Gates do?" Hunter asked. "Get the US Coast Guard or Navy up here?"

Blanco shook his head. "It would take way too long to get the clearance, plus we don't know which members of the US Government are in the Creed or not."

"Sal's right," Lewis said. "Just too risky, and as a man with a baby on the way, I'm not big on risk right now."

"So, what then?" Jodie asked.

Amy looked at Quinn. "I need your laptop."

"Go ahead."

Amy's face disappeared behind the laptop screen for a few seconds and then she turned the computer around so the team could see a Skype screen and the face of Oskar Rorschach.

"Ahh," Hunter said. "Now it becomes clear."

"It's good to see you again, Dr Anderson," the old Swiss billionaire said with an honest chuckle. "I believe you go by the name Special Agent Amy Fox these days?"

"I'm sorry for deceiving you, Oskar."

He dismissed her apology with a wrinkled hand. "You thought I was in the Creed and you did what you had to do. You have explained everything to my satisfaction. We can move on now, and believe me, no one is keener than I am to bring these people down. I trusted Klara Steiner and she betrayed that trust. Now she must be punished."

"Thank you."

"I must say, I was shocked when you told me in your message about Atlantis being located in Greenland."

Hunter stepped in. "I think it's more a case of Greenland *being* Atlantis, rather than Atlantis being located there."

"But surely Greenland is far too big."

Hunter shook his head. "On the contrary, it fits perfectly. Plato described Atlantis as being greater in size than Libya and Asia, by which he meant Turkey. We know the sizes of all these places now and Libya and Turkey are coming in at around the same size as Greenland today, but they were very different places back when Plato was describing them."

"Like how?" Quinn asked.

"For one thing, much of Asia Minor was under Persian rule, so it's hard to know precisely what Plato meant. Either way, even if we take the area measurements of the countries today, he was about right on the scale. He also described mountains surrounding the main city there, and the presence of lakes and rivers, all of which were abundant on Greenland before the ice sheets."

Silence as the team considered what he had said, then Blanco spoke. "What exactly was it like before the ice sheets?"

Hunter smiled. "Amazing. If there were no ice sheets on Greenland it would be a very different place. Imagine a giant island, roughly the size of Mexico, surrounded by mountains and with a giant lake in the center of it."

"Sounds cool," Jodie said.

Rorschach laughed. "It's cold, if not cool! Now, tell me more about this Adler person."

Amy took over. "Karl Adler is what the Creed calls the Apostle. It's the second highest position in the structure beneath the Magus. We do not know who the Magus is. Klara Steiner is his junior and McCabe and the disciples worked for a man named Gaius, who was killed in Germany."

"Talk about a motley crew."

"You can say that again," she said. "According to my Director, all of them are flying out to Kulusuk Airport on the east coast of Greenland right now. There is a helipad across the bay to the west in Tasiilaq, but we don't think this is their next play. The location on Atlantis they're searching for is a specific city – the capital, we think. It's too far away along the coast to the north for a chopper. The only thing they can do is board a ship in Kulusuk and sail along the coast. This is our chance to overtake them and beat them to the prize."

"But how do we get there?"

Rorschach smiled. "I have a vessel you can use."

Amy looked out of the window at the raging pulse of the sea. "I'm not sure I want to sail on the sea right now."

"But you're not sailing on it," Rorschach said. "You're sailing under it."

Amy was confused. "I don't understand."

"I believe I can offer something that will help you to beat Adler and the rest of the Creed to Atlantis. Some years ago, I commissioned a submersible vessel named the Seawolf. When I say a submersible vessel, I mean a five-hundred foot submersible yacht. She is capable of speeds over eighty-five kilometres per hour, making her the fastest submerged vessel on earth."

Stunned silence.

"I thought you would be impressed," Rorschach continued. "And I hope this gesture allows you to see just how much I want to see Steiner fail. She deceived me for years and now I will do anything to bring her down."

Hunter took in the excited faces of his new friends. "Where's the Seawolf right now?"

"Where it usually is, in Bergen on the Norwegian coast. It can be in Reykjavik in eighteen hours and go onto the Atlantis coordinates in another six."

"That means we'll be there in twenty-four hours," Jodie said.

"It's amazing how some people can do such complex math in their heads," Quinn said.

"When does the Creed get there?" Amy asked.

"It's a four hour flight to Kulusuk," Hunter said. "The location is another two-hundred and fifty kilometres farther up the coast. In the current weather conditions, I would be surprised if they're making anything better than twelve knots per hour. So maybe another twenty hours."

"In other words we're arriving at the same time," Amy said. "How cosy."

"I'm still convinced you can beat them to it," Rorschach said. "The Seawolf can be pushed much harder than we did in her later trials. I'm sure of it, but we must be careful. This is a very dangerous stretch of coast."

"Many of the fjords in Greenland are UNESCO World Heritage Sites," Hunter said. "So I'm more than aware of the local geography. The fjords of eastern Greenland are particularly magnificent in their beauty and isolation, but don't be fooled."

"There is one more thing," Rorschach said. "In your email, Amy, you mentioned something about Adler and the Creed wanting to find Atlantis because of some sort of weapon. What did you mean? Should I be fearful for my crew on board the Seawolf?"

All eyes turned to Hunter. "Amy heard Adler and Steiner talking about the Winged Guardians, which they claimed were not just statues but also part of an ancient weapon they called the fire lance. I don't know exactly what they mean by this, but there was a weapon called a fire lance in China around a thousand years ago."

"Go on."

"It made very rudimentary use of gunpowder to propel a weapon a bit like a spear at the enemy, but by today's standards it would be very weak and ineffectual. I'm not certain what the Creed think they're going to find up there, and we all know the knowledge passed to them by the Illuminati is a closely-guarded secret so from here it's just speculation."

"So, speculate," Quinn said.

"In that case, I would argue that if they're expending this much effort in the search, the weapon they believe they're going to find there is significantly more powerful than the Chinese fire lance. Maybe something more like Archimedes's heat ray."

"The what?"

"It was a fabled weapon that some say had the ability to destroy Roman ships. No one knows even if it was real, but it sounds like it might be in the same ball park as the fire lance."

Rorschach stroked his chin. "And what about my men?"

"They'll be in no more danger than we will," Amy said.

After a long pause to consider, Rorschach nodded once. "Very well. I will approve the Seawolf and send her to sea at once."

A bank of cloud broke and let sunshine spill into the room, momentarily lighting their faces, but it was quickly swallowed back up again, dimming the room and changing the mood from excitement to fear.

Hunter blew out a deep breath and looked at his new friends. "Looks like we're going to find Atlantis at last."

# CHAPTER FORTY-EIGHT

A day later, Amy was standing in the Seawolf's conning tower looking at the northern lights dancing in greens and purples across the twilight sky. Beneath this spectacular light show on the horizon, a rich crimson sunset ribbon divided the earth from the sky. She took a second to marvel at the majesty of the ice cliffs of eastern Greenland rising above the sea in the distance.

They had surfaced in the Denmark Strait a few miles from their destination on Greenland's rugged east coast and she felt excited, frightened and exhausted all at the same time. Flying in and out of so many countries and dodging death at every turn had taken its heavy toll.

She took a deep breath, enjoying the cold, fresh Arctic air after so much heat and dust and humidity. It reminded her of when her dad used to take her and her brother ice-fishing out in the Connecticut woods every winter. Those innocent days were a long way back now, yet at the time they seemed to last forever. If she closed her eyes, she could smell the woodsmoke drifting from the chimney of their little cabin by the lake.

The Seawolf rolled on a wave and listed to starboard for a few moments before righting itself. The sound of the icy water splashing on the gunmetal grey hull brought her back to the moment and the hell she was enduring to find the greatest discovery on earth. A discovery, it seemed, some very powerful people were determined to keep from her. But she was still alive, even after so many attempts to take her life over the last few hours.

She believed Gates's decision not to inform his superiors in the FBI was risky, but the right thing to do. The original Illuminati had grown so large and infiltrated so many governments and organizations in eighteenth century Bavaria that it had to be banned. There was no way to tell how deep the Creed went, but as Hunter liked to say, discretion was the better part of valor.

And with Gates's old Strike Team on board alongside Rorschach's crew, they had a fighting chance. If her director said he trusted those men, then that was enough for her. They were all former SEALS who had sworn to protect the United States. Maybe they were past their prime and a few pounds over their fighting weight, but better that than mix with traitors and get killed by them at the final hurdle.

With the Strike Team on their side, and Rorschach's generous decision to loan them the Seawolf, maybe they had what it took to find the Atlantean capital and defend it from Adler's insane new world order. Or maybe not. She worried about what the hell they were going to find over there in those ice-encrusted, snow-whipped granite cliffs just coming into view on the western horizon.

Hunter climbed up out of the hatch and joined her at the front of the conning tower. "I'd stay up here if I were you. Gates's Strike Team just ordered the bean stew and Captain Evans says it's not serious enough to break out the gas masks."

"Eww, thanks for telling me that."

He looked up at the sky and smiled. "The lights are amazing."

"There's that smile again."

"What smile?"

"The one that makes me feel safe and nervous at the same time."

"I'm not sure if that's a compliment or not."

She turned around and leaned on the cold metal rail, facing into the center of the small tower and toward him, the sea at her back. "Mostly a compliment. It's just that whenever I see you smile like that, it usually means something crazy is about to happen in my life."

"A seasoned adventurer like you?" he said.

She hesitated.

"What?" he asked.

"There's something you need to know about us. We're not quite the adventurers I made us out to be. We work for the FBI, true. We chase down stolen artifacts, true. We've even brought several smugglers to justice, true. But the rest of the truth is a little different. This is the biggest mission we've ever done, and by far the most dangerous. None of us has ever risked our lives like this before."

"Sal and Ben were in the military."

"Yeah, and that's true, too. They're very brave men with a lot of combat experience, but I'm talking about now, in this team. We're not like you, leading some crazy Indiana Jones lifestyle. We're very... bureaucratic."

"I'm sure you'll be just fine. Look at what you did in Cuba and El Salvador or Egypt. Hell, look at what you all did in Germany!"

She looked down at the metal floor. "I just hope we don't let you down."

"Are you crazy? These have been the best few days of my life! And I'm no bloody Indiana Jones, Amy. I'm just an archaeologist doing what most people would consider dry, boring academic work."

"Yeah, right. You were on the cover of the New York Times after your discovery of Nefertiti's tomb. Stop being so modest."

"Well..."

"Wait, look!"

He followed her hand to an alcove above a large fjord. Wispy parings of pale blue smoke circled up from a freshly blown hole in the rock. "Looks like they beat us to it."

Captain Evans climbed up and joined them. "All good up here?"

"Not really," Amy said.

Evans looked at the cliffs. "I see what you mean. A large transport helicopter on the top of the cliff just above the coordinates... not good."

Hunter walked over to Evans "Looks like an AW101," he muttered. "Capable of carrying around thirty seriously armed troops."

"Then they outgun us," Evans said. "In terms of a landing party, we have the six men on the Strike Force, plus you, Sal Blanco and Ben Lewis makes nine men with military experience. I recommend we wait until we can be sure they have no backup."

"What about your crew?" Hunter asked. "Any landlubbers?"

Evans sucked his teeth. "Mr Rorschach was very clear about my duty to defend the Seawolf at all costs. I can't let it fall into enemy hands and that means leaving a substantial force on board while you go ahead to Atlantis. I can spare no more than four, but they're all good men with combat experience. There's Borten, Norwegian army; Blocher, Swiss Air Force militia; Salter, a former Royal Marine commando and Alvarado who was on the US Navy's SWCC Special Boat Team."

"I understand you need to defend the Seawolf, but you must be able to spare more than four men, Captain! We're looking down the barrels of at least thirty men and if they're anything like the other disciples we've fought, they're going to be highly-trained, well-armed and bloody lethal. Can't you take the Seawolf out to sea and dive?"

Evans shook his head. "There is no way I'm prepared to leave any of my crew, or you, up here while we go out to sea and submerge the boat. You've seen the geography of this part of the coast! Adler's team had to fly in on a transport chopper and abseil down into the cave because there's no other way in. That means there's no way *out* either. If something goes wrong and you need to pull out, the Seawolf is going to be sitting in the inlet waiting for you all."

Hunter nodded reluctantly. "You're the captain of this boat, Evans, and that means you're making the call."

"I'm not doing it any other way, Hunter. I hope you can see why."

Hunter backed down. "I understand, Captain."

"In that case, Lieutenant Borten and his men will prepare you for the swim to the coast." He raised his hand and pointed at the rugged cliffs. "Because somewhere behind those rocks is Atlantis and you have to get there first."

# CHAPTER FORTY-NINE

Karl Adler watched with an increasing sense of apprehension as McCabe directed the disciples into the tunnel. The prospect of discovering the unimaginable treasures of Atlantis was now more real than ever. "Our destiny awaits us, Klara."

She reached out and touched his arm lovingly. "I know how long you have waited for this day, Teacher. The Magus will be very proud."

Ahead of them, the Creed disciples had uncovered the old Nazi submarine pen where the German sailors had found the first Winged Guardian during their wartime excavations. As they dug and hacked their way through tons of ice and rubble, more of the earlier expedition began to reveal itself.

Old Kriegsmarine equipment was lying around in the tunnel's mouth. Tarpaulin Zeltbahns were draped over coconut canteens and aluminum cups. A ski cap had been slung over the handle of an ice pick still sticking out of the cave wall. Shovels leaned up against the ice walls, exactly where sailors had propped them nearly eighty years earlier.

Adler surveyed the abandoned field equipment with unveiled delight. "After a lifetime of hunting, I have found it at last. This is the exact location where Lieutenant-

Commander Reinhard Schultze found the Acassuso Idol. The Map Room in Ramesses's Royal Cache has led us directly to our destiny, my darling. The path to Atlantis is before us at last."

The disciples were at the end of the ice passage now. Those at the end hacked with the picks and shovels while a team working behind them shovelled the ice into barrows and ran them back to the entrance where they dumped it into the inlet. Then, they broke through the ice and one of the disciples screamed. "We're in!"

*

Hunter watched Borten and his men lower their swimmer delivery vehicles into the water and slide down after them. He and Amy's team, all in wetsuits to keep out the cold, watched what they did and copied them. He was impressed when he saw Quinn slip down into the icy water. They had told her she could stay on board the Seawolf but she had stepped up to the plate and demanded to join them.

With everyone in the water off the portside of the submarine, Borten led the way, gripping hold of the grab handles at the back of his SDV and allowing the motorized propulsion vehicle to pull him toward the coast. Hunter followed the Norwegian commando's lead and drove his SDV toward Greenland. The rest of the team followed in his wake.

Halfway along, Hunter caught glimpses of the coast through his mask. Cold saltwater lashed at him as the SDV ploughed forward, but every second he was one step closer to fulfilling his lifelong dream of discovering Atlantis.

*

"The Gate of the Gods," Adler said. "I always knew one day I would walk through it."

He leaned forward through the ice hole like a dumbstruck child, staring up at the colossal stone archway stretching over his head. It seemed to reach almost to the very top of the ice cave, held in place by two gargantuan stone piers.

"They're carved into the bedrock," Steiner said.

"They'd have to be," McCabe said. "Looking at the size of this archway, I'd say each one of these piers is supporting thousands of tons of granite, not to mention the tremendous pressure that must be being exerted on those voussoir stones at the very top."

"It's a miracle of engineering," Steiner said, staring up at the arch with wonder sparkling in her cold blue eyes. "Surpassing anything done by the ancient Egyptians. It's exactly what we knew it would be – the greatest ancient construction anywhere on earth. The true home of the gods. The Magus will be overjoyed."

"Not if we let this slip from our grasp," Adler said impatiently. Turning to the disciples, he raised his voice to an angry growl. "Hurry up and clear the last of this ice away so we can get through the gate!"

*

On the shore inside the ice cave, Hunter unzipped his waterproof kitbag and changed into the Arctic warfare gear they had stowed back on the Seawolf. Guns, knives and even a small Ruger pistol in an ankle holster – he was ready for action. Beside him, the Strike Team and Borten and his men were already waiting, guns in their hands and breath pluming from their nostrils in thick smoky columns.

Hunter pulled down the front of his balaclava to speak. "We all owe Oskar Rorschach a cold beer. If it weren't for the Seawolf we'd be abseiling down those sodding cliffs by now just like Adler. Bollocks to that."

"It's bad enough they beat us to it," Amy said. "I guess we should have taken the idea of them flying through the storm in a chopper and abseiling out of it a bit more seriously. They're crazier than we thought."

"Crazy they might be," Borten said. "But they're also ahead of us, and judging by these tracks, our guess about his manpower was about right. It looks like a herd of cattle has trampled into the cave system at the bottom of this slope."

Hunter agreed, but there was no turning back now. They made their way down the icy slope, knowing that an attack could come at any moment. The Apostle was down here somewhere with Steiner and McCabe and an army of disciples, all searching for the fire lance.

Deeper inside the strange subterranean network of tunnels and caverns, they began to see evidence of the lost civilization all around them. Abandoned like the Nazi relics nearer to the entrance, they found broken pottery and weapons partially sticking out of the ice. The Apostle's army had also left its own mark – cigarette butts and empty drink containers – strewn along the floor of the tunnel like trash.

"Judging by the cigarettes we can't be far behind them," Hunter said. "This one here still has ash on the tip."

They marched on with their boots crunching on the ice. Breath plumed in the freezing air and noses grew numb. Anticipation was building fast, and when they turned a bend in the tunnel and found the hole the disciples has smashed in the ice wall, they were all stunned into silence.

They stepped through and moved forward until they were standing on a ledge overlooking a frozen city. A broad river, frozen solid for millennia cut the great metropolis in two sections joined by a colossal stone archway. High above it all, a sky of dark black ice hung ominously above them like the vaulted ceiling of a magnificent medieval church.

"Bloody hell!" Hunter gasped. "The Gate of the Gods… we found it."

"Look at all this ice," Lewis said. "That flood theory might just hold water."

Hunter turned and looked at him. "I'll forget you said that."

Amy looked up at the ice-sky. "I don't get why the ice sheet didn't just crush the entire city. What kept the city inside this giant cavern? Why wasn't it swallowed up by the ice sheet, Max?"

"I don't know, but I'm going to find out. C'mon – and keep your flashlights down. We don't want to alert the Creed."

Flanked by the soldiers, they followed a crumbling rock path twisting down from the ledge and reached the city's street level. Walking farther along the street, the darkness gradually revealed more detail all around them.

"It looks like there are constellations in the ice above," Amy said. "Something's sparkling."

Hunter looked up and squinted. "It's not stars sparkling, but ice melting. That explains why this place never got crushed by the ice sheet. Something down here is melting the ice and keeping it off the city."

"The fire lance?" Blanco said.

Hunter's heart quickened with fear. "That's what we're here to find out."

At the end of the street, they turned and found they were looking down on a lower section of the city, in a valley where the river turned into a vast frozen lake. Beside it, they saw something else that left them breathless.

"My God!" Amy stared up at the pyramid. "Is that thing bigger than the Great Pyramid of Giza?"

"It looks like it," Hunter said. "And by a large margin as well. I've never seen anything like it before in all my life."

Quinn raised her flashlight beam, but Hunter grabbed her wrist and pushed it back down. "Are you insane?"

"Sorry."

"Adler and his men are around here somewhere!"

"I said I'm sorry!"

"I think maybe we got away with it," Amy said. "If they…"

Hunter hushed her. "Get down!"

They crouched, and the English archaeologist glanced across to their right along a street which ran along the edge of the rise just above the valley. When he saw the first disciple he thought this eyes were playing tricks on him. He moved like a lizard, vaulting out of the darkness and swinging his gun up into the aim. Behind him, he saw at least six more armed men and was quickly dissuaded he wasn't going crazy.

"Looks like the main group is in the wrong part of the city," he said.

"Here they come!" said Lewis.

"Take cover!" Hunter called out. "They've seen us!"

"No!" Borten screamed. "You must get to the fire lance. We'll cover you!"

"And we'll back them up," said the leader of the Strike Team.

Hunter made the decision to head down into the pyramid; Borten's men and Gates's Strike Team would work better without having to look after them as well. He gripped his gun and looked at the others. "Ready?"

A round of anxious nods.
"Then let's get into that pyramid."

# CHAPTER FIFTY

With Borten and his men covering them, Hunter led the team down the slope toward the bottom of the giant pyramid. They reached a bricked-up entrance in the vast stone base and took cover behind a row of polar bear statues. They drew their weapons and a moment of eerie, absolute silence filled the vast underground city.

"The calm before the storm," Amy said. "I don't like this at all."

The silence ended when they heard Borten ordering his men to pull back to another position closer to the pyramid. Seconds later, another violent barrage of gunfire opened up in the tunnel at the top of the slope. The muzzle flashes of Borten's small team lit the icy-blue darkness like fireworks, but they all knew what the retreat meant.

Looking ahead, they saw Borten ordering his men into a new defensive position.

"I don't see the Strike Force," Blanco said.

Amy scanned the top of the slope. "Me neither."

Then, they heard Borten's voice crackling over the radio. "Strike Force terminated by the enemy. Get into the pyramid. Not sure how long we can hold them."

"They killed the Strike Team?" Blanco said, bringing the heel of his gloved hand down on the pyramid's base with a hefty smack. "Those men gave their lives for us! I'm not going to let these freaks get away with their murder."

"Take it easy, Sal," Jodie said. "Remember what you always tell me – don't get mad, get even."

"But I *am* mad about it. They cut them to ribbons like they were wild dogs!"

"Adler's not playing around," Hunter said. "This isn't just his life's work, but the culmination of hundreds of years of searching, first by the Illuminati and then the Creed. This is the endgame and he's not going to pull any punches."

"That feeling when the word *psycho* just isn't enough," Quinn said drily.

A tense silence hovered over the team as they stood alone at the base of the Great Pyramid of Atlantis. Up at the crest of the gradient, Borten and his team were unleashing hell on Adler's army of disciples, but there were just too many of them. Slowly, the warriors of the Magus's Creed were overwhelming Captain's Evans's tiny force.

"Not sure we're getting out of this alive," Lewis said.

Hunter had enough combat experience to know that you always felt camaraderie strongest at the bleakest times. When hope was almost gone and the end loomed over you like a monster bearing its teeth at you, only then could true friendship be known. He felt that now. But who were these people standing alongside him in this frozen, lost city, ready to face death with him?

Ben Lewis.

Jodie Priest.

Quinn Mosley.

Sal Blanco.

Amy Fox.

From the looks on their faces, he knew they all felt the same sense of belonging together, and just as the darkest moment comes right before dawn, now Borten and his men were finally pinning the disciples down. They had their chance and Hunter seized it.

"We need to blow a hole in this thing," he said.

Blanco already had the explosives in his hand and was packing them around the bricked-up entrance. When he detonated them, they blasted a massive hole in the side of the pyramid.

The freshly blown hole created a vacuum and a gust of icy wind raced across the city, blowing the fireball over the disciples' position. Dozens caught in the explosion were killed instantly, and tumbled down from their positions, cartwheeling to the icy temple floor like dolls.

Quinn looked down and saw one of them dead, crashed on the floor at the bottom of the slope with a broken neck. The look of horror on his face would haunt her for the rest of her life. She took a step back away from the ridge and moved closer to Blanco. "That's not nice."

"In this life, you get what you pay for," he said. "And it looks like there are no exceptions, not even for the Apostle's army of devotees."

"Hurry!" Hunter said. "We have to get inside."

Making their way inside the Great Pyramid, they all felt a strangely warm current of air washing over them.

"How come I feel warm air?" Jodie asked. "We're in Greenland."

"And what's that glowing up ahead?" Quinn asked.

"I don't know, but keep going," Amy said. "This, I have to see."

With the sound of submachine guns and grenades behind them, Hunter led the team down the passageway until they reached a large altar room filled with statues, each one recognizable as a god from various cultures through world history.

"Holy crap," Jodie said, brushing the stone thigh of Zeus. "Your insane theories were right after all, Hunter."

"I knew they would be," he said, marvelling at the ornate masonry all around them. "But that's eclipsed now. We're here to find the fire lance."

Blanco pointed to an area behind the shrine. "In that case, shouldn't we follow the glow?"

They walked slowly around the towering stone altar and were shocked into silence by what they saw. Nestled on top of a concave marble dais was a perfect sphere glowing with a rich amber light. They felt its warmth and when they moved closer it seemed to get hotter.

"What the hell is that thing?" Amy said.

Hunter dropped to his knees.

"What are you doing?" Jodie said. "Worshipping it?"

He turned and looked up at her. "Are you crazy? I'm trying to translate these glyphs."

She looked closer and saw dozens of small hieroglyphics carved into the floor where they were standing. Hunter was running his hand over them and muttering to himself.

"Some of these glyphs are an equivalent of binary code," he said, shocked. "This civilization was incredibly advanced." After a few tense seconds, he passed his hand over his forehead and sighed.

"Oh no…"

"What is it?" Amy said.

"I was wrong about the comet."

"What do you mean?" Blanco said, nervously looking over his shoulder at the entrance.

"I mean it was no comet that wiped out Atlantis, and we're in much deeper shit that we thought."

The realization struck them at the same time, but Amy spoke first. "My God… it was no comet that destroyed Atlantis, but the fire lance!"

Hunter nodded. "Uh-huh – it was their own technology."

"Are you sure you're translating these hieroglyphics correctly?" Lewis asked.

Hunter stared at the vast wall of hieroglyphics in disbelief. Nothing in his years of experience could have prepared him for what had just confronted him. "Dead sure. They vary slightly in form from the Egyptian glyphs I'm more used to, but they're fundamentally the same, plus with the stuff I worked out from Julian's recent translations, there's no doubt."

"Great," Quinn said.

Hunter said, "Whoever wrote these glyphs was making sure the madness that overtook their culture was never forgotten. They were leaving a warning to future generations not to make the same mistakes they made. This sphere is part of the fire lance, part of the monster that destroyed their world."

"Isn't there any mention of the comet strikes at all?" Lewis asked. "After all, we know they hit Greenland."

Hunter took a step back and swept his eyes across the long lines of carved glyphs one more time, line by line, until he reached the bottom again. "Here, they describe something like the wrath of the gods, a fire raining down from the black vault of heaven. This is undoubtedly the night sky. It says the gods hit them three times and brought a great flood over their lands, but they survived. Yet more evidence of the so-called flood myth!"

"So they survived the comet impacts," Blanco said.

Hunter traced his finger along the white granite. "And according to this, they developed the fire lance weapon to try and defend themselves from future strikes. I think that's how you'd translate this glyph – fire lance."

Quinn leaned in closer. "That glyph right there looks a lot like the statues we found."

Hunter looked at her, wide-eyed with uncertainty, and angled his beam across to where she was pointing with her gloved hand. "Bloody hell, she's right. I don't like this."

Amy shared an anxious glance with Blanco. "And what don't you like it about it?"

"I might be wrong, but remember how we commented that the statues were an odd shape, the way they curved outwards with their arms outstretched and their wings spread out behind them like angels in flight?"

"Sure, it was only a few days ago," Quinn said. "We're not goldfish."

"Ignore it," Jodie said. "And please tell us what the hell is going on. I'm starting to get a bad feeling about this."

"That makes two of us," Hunter said. "I think Quinn is right and that this glyph portrays the statues."

"So what's the problem?" Lewis said.

"The problem is that this glyph is a picture of the fire lance."

Amy gasped. "Then Adler and Steiner were telling the truth – the statues really are part of the fire lance."

Hunter nodded solemnly. "Yes, I think the statues we've been hunting for are actually a part of the weapon that destroyed Atlantis. They called them the Winged Guardians because they were supposed to protect the civilization from another strike from the Taurid Meteor Shower. Instead, they wiped themselves out with their new weapon."

"You think right, Dr Hunter."

He spun around and saw Adler. He was standing in the entrance with Klara Steiner and Brodie McCabe. Several disciples were moving into view behind them, cut and bruised and wounded but armed and strong enough to fight.

"Where's Borten?" Hunter yelled.

"With the rest of his men," Steiner called back. "Dead."

"You bastards."

"Your security guards turned out to be no impediment to my plans at all." Adler laughed. "Crixus! Gannicus! Take them prisoner. Castus and Oenomaus will come with me and secure the statues to the sphere. We will bring the fire lance to life after being dormant for millennia!"

"You can't activate it, Adler!" Amy said. "Don't you understand? The Atlanteans created a weapon so powerful they destroyed their own civilization with it!"

"And the Magus will destroy Western civilization with it. Now, drop your weapons and raise your hands."

# CHAPTER FIFTY-ONE

Amy stared at the Apostle with a burning contempt in her eyes that Hunter never thought was possible. "You can't be serious, Adler! Don't you realize what happened here? If you try and use that thing you could wipe out millions of people."

"Millions?" Adler repeated. "There's no need to be so pessimistic. This has the potential to reap a much higher harvest than millions of human dead. If we activate it in the right place, we should be able to create the same climate havoc that annihilated Atlantis in the first place. The conductivity of the orichalcum in the statues is unlike anything else on earth."

"You mean you knew about this all along?"

The Apostle laughed. "The destruction of Atlantis by the fire lance is written in the Creed's Holy Scriptures. It is to us, as your Bible is to you. The consummation by fire of this cradle of humanity is an important part of our origin story."

"Sounds like a laugh a minute," Hunter said.

"You wouldn't be laughing if you knew what that origin story was." The Apostle sneered at him and turned to watch his men, now loading the sphere into a metal trunk beside the three winged statues. They secured the lid and waited for the next command.

"Why don't you enlighten us?" Jodie said. "Instead of just waving your junk in our faces."

The Apostle looked at her with derision. "You're too small to receive enlightenment."

Hunter had been watching the disciples move the sphere. They looked nervous but in control, and when the Apostle told them to take it back to the entrance cave by the inlet and secure it to the transport chopper's lashing chain, he knew this was their last chance.

"You must feel pretty pleased with yourself," he told the Apostle. "To succeed where so many of your forebears failed. To find the fire lance, the weapon that the Atlanteans destroyed themselves with. That brought their civilization to its knees."

"What I feel is irrelevant," he said. "I serve the cause of an ancient society, the ancient Egyptian and Greek Mysteries, the Freemasons, the Illuminati and now the mighty Creed. That is what I am; a humble servant to the cause of something much greater than I. The Atlantis Covenant is a sacred agreement made by all members of the Creed to safeguard this knowledge, the inherent truth about mankind's origin, the existence of this very place. It is the fulcrum of our civilization and I am the servant of this cause."

"And here I was thinking you were something special," Hunter said with a dismissive shrug. "I thought you were the man, but you're nothing, are you? Who's pulling your strings, Adler? Who is the Magus?"

Quinn took a step closer to Blanco. "What's he doing?"

"Get ready," Blanco whispered. "He's trying to get him to lose his cool."

"I'm saying he's nothing but a marionette," Hunter said, catching Amy's eye.

"I am no one's puppet!" he said. "I am the Apostle. I hold knowledge handed down direct from Akhenaten! If anything, I am more powerful than even he! Do you hear that, Akhenaten?"

"I've hear of speaking truth to power but this is ridiculous," Hunter said.

"Silence! How *dare* you speak to me in this way. You will drop to your knees and beg me to make your death swift! Bring him to me!"

Disciples marched forward, but it was too late. Amy knew what he was doing, and now she slipped out of McCabe's arms and jerked her elbow into his face, pulping his already smashed nose across his face. He teetered back on the ice and brought his hands up to his re-broken nose just as the disciples flanking the Apostle drew their weapons and fired on Hunter's team.

"Take cover!" Hunter yelled, reaching down for his ankle holster. He drew the Ruger and fired on the Apostle three times, striking him in the chest and throat and spraying a cloud of blood out over the ice wall behind him.

Chaos erupted, and Crixus turned his gun on Hunter. The Londoner dived for the protection of one of the pyramid's enormous ice-caked cornerstones. The rest of the team scattered in all directions, ducking down behind rocks and walls and anywhere else they could find to shield themselves from the barrage of bullets.

Crixus had seen Hunter take cover behind the cornerstone and chased him all the way with his gun, splintering the ice in his wake as he dived for cover. Hunter landed face-down, spinning around on the slippery ice and firing on his pursuer. The bullets buried into Crixus's stomach and chest and sent him straight down to the icy floor.

Hunter peered over the cornerstone and saw a fire fight had exploded across the pyramid's plaza. Blanco was firing on Gannicus and Lewis was brawling with Castus. It looked like Jodie had killed Oenomaus and Amy was firing on Steiner and McCabe as they tried to push the wheeled trunk up the slope toward the tunnel. Steiner saw Quinn tucked down in the shadows of one of the statues in the plaza, and stopped pushing the chest.

"What are you doing?" McCabe asked.

"I can't let her live!"

Steiner slipped her MP5 off her shoulder and aimed it at Quinn, but Hunter was ahead of her, with the Ruger already raised into the aim. He squeezed the trigger and the bullet ripped right through her throat, blasting half of it to pieces and spraying blood and tissue all over the ice behind her.

When she fell, she hit the ice slope like a dead deer and rolled all the way back down to the bottom, the look of surprised terror still etched on her still, white face.

McCabe saw what had happened and bolted, screaming at the disciples to cover him as he sprinted up the slope toward the tunnel. Hunter fired on him, his rounds drilling into the ice a few inches behind his nemesis as he scrambled up the slope and slipped around the corner, leaving nothing but a shadow receding on the wall.

"Damn it," Hunter said, jumping when he registered the report of a gunshot across the plaza. He turned to see Lewis walking back over to him. Castus was dead, as was Gannicus. Blanco and the former US Marine had easily overcome the two men and the rest of the stray disciples. Now, the team gathered around the metal trunk containing the sphere. Chests rising and falling, adrenaline pumping through their veins.

"We did it," Jodie said.

"So much blood…" Quinn's young voice was a hoarse, terrified whisper. "All this death."

"It's over." Amy put her arm around her shoulder. "You did great."

Blanco and Lewis were walking cautiously around the plaza, making sure the disciples were all dead. Jodie was sitting on one of the cornerstones, staring at the trunk with a strange, unfocussed look in her eyes. For a long time, no one said anything.

The low amber glow seeping through the trunk's hinges focused their concentration too much. No one knew what the sphere was, or what it meant. No one had ever seen anything like it. They knew that when it was combined with the winged statues it formed some sort of weapon the Apostle had called the fire lance. They knew it had destroyed Atlantis, and for now that was enough.

A radio crackled, making everyone start. It was Amy's. She reached down to her belt and raised the microphone to her mouth. "Go ahead."

"This is Evans," he said. "Was the mission target achieved?"

The cold static hiss of the radio echoed eerily across the plaza at the base of the Great Pyramid, high in the Arctic. Amy looked over at Adler and Steiner, both dead, and then to the strange glowing trunk. "Yes," she said, collapsing down on the cornerstone beside Jodie and lowering her head. "Mission target achieved. We're on our way back to you."

# CHAPTER FIFTY-TWO

An ordinary office in Washington DC one week later. Neutral-shade wool carpet, cream walls and vinyl-faced ceiling tiles. Long laminate conference table and a dead projection screen on the far wall. James Gates pushed opened the door and led the rest of the team into the warm room, taking up position at the head of the table.

"Welcome to HARPA's first briefing."

"HARPA?" Blanco asked.

Amy smiled. Hunter saw she already knew what it meant. Just her and the Director, though. They were close.

Gates said, "The Heritage, Artifacts and Relics Protection Agency. It's a new department I've been tasked with directing, formed out of the ashes of our previous incarnation. We work for the government but at the same time we don't, if you catch my drift. Think of us as kind of like privateers. Amy is my 2IC and if the rest of you want a job then I guess you're in, too."

"Seems fair enough," Jodie said.

"Quinn?" Amy asked.

She shrugged. "I have nothing else in my calendar for this year, so fine. Count me in."

"Ben?" Gates asked.

"You know I'm in."

"Great, and how's Megan?"

"Baby's due in two weeks, sir."

Gates's face broke into a reluctant smile. "Good luck with that."

"What about Hunter?" Jodie asked.

Hunter was surprised she had asked.

"Dr Hunter is not on the team," Gates said, turning to the Englishman. "If you want to join, then you can make a formal application and I'll consider it."

"Thanks, but I'm happy where I am."

"That's your decision."

Hunter thought he saw a flash of disappointment on Amy's face, but the moment was already past. Gates had moved on. "First, you did a good job on the Atlantis mission. The fire lance's component parts, both the sphere and the winged statues have been catalogued and removed to a secure location for analysis."

"When will we be briefed about what they find?" Amy asked.

"If and when my superiors tell me, I'll tell you. Suffice it to say, if this weapon is anything to go by, parts of the Atlantean civilization were much further ahead than our current technology. This could present big problems for the world if the wrong people get hold of it. That is why we will be sending a covert military team to the site to secure it."

"It needs to be studied by archaeologists," Hunter said. "There's a hell of a lot to learn about Atlantean culture and technology over the coming months and years and we need to start right now. It should be a UNESCO site."

"I'm not able to discuss it further, Dr Hunter," Gates said, ending the debate. They all saw his face change.

"What is it, Jim?" Amy asked.

"There's just more one thing I have to tell you. After your successful storming of the Black Rock Castle in Germany, the authorities moved in and took the place over. They treated it as a crime scene and they found something alarming in the dungeon."

"What did they find?" Amy asked.

Gates brushed his jaw with his knuckles, nervous and stalling for time. Unsure what to say. "They found human bones in some kind of animal pit. They were broken and smashed and looked like they had been gnawed."

"My God," Blanco said. "What are we talking about here – a bear, a wolf?"

Gates shook his head. "It doesn't look like it, no. They also found tooth and claw marks in the pit, none of which resemble any animal we know of. Whatever killed the people in there was considerably larger than a grizzly bear and stronger than a Siberian tiger."

Amy was stunned. "I'm sorry, but I don't understand what you're saying, Jim."

He looked at her, an old friend with no more answers. "The authorities were looking into it, and then they were ordered to stop and the castle was made off-limits by the very top of the German government. It looks like the Creed shut down the investigation. We don't know what was in that dungeon, but it's gone now."

"What the hell did those sick bastards do down there?" Jodie asked.

"You know what I know," Gates said.

"And the Magus?" Hunter asked, his voice loud in the stunned silence.

He shrugged. "No sign of the Magus, either."

Another long, tense silence as they thought about what he had just said. When he spoke, his voice seemed frailer. "Moving on, it looks like we've had another alert." He pushed a button on the desk and a plasma screen slowly descended from the ceiling. "And this one's promising to be even more significant than the mission you just closed."

Jodie kicked back in her chair and stared up at the screen. Beside her, Lewis was already taking out his phone ready to take notes. Blanco was slipping on his glasses. When he snapped the case shut, Quinn jumped. "Must you make so much noise?"

Jodie sniffed and cracked open a can of Coke. "Must you whine so much?"

She shared a high five with Blanco and they laughed, but the room grew deathly silent when they saw Gates's first slide.

"Am I seeing what I think I'm seeing?" Hunter said.

"Yes, and I don't need to tell you anything you see in here is highly classified."

"Just as well," Quinn mumbled. "Because that shit right there's going to scare the hell out of millions of people. Stock up on toilet paper, right?"

"Thanks for your contribution, Agent Mosley."

"More than welcome, chief."

Hunter was rubbing his temples. "I know I'm not on the team, but is this for real?"

"It's for real, Dr Hunter," Gates said. "I only ever do real."

"Yeah, I'm starting to get that."

*

Later that afternoon, Hunter wandered out onto the balcony of Amy's Georgetown apartment. Like most buildings in the nation's capital, its height was governed by a legal restriction put in place in 1910, designed to preserve the city's unique layout.

Still shocked by what he had seen earlier back in HARPA headquarters, Hunter sipped from a cold bottle of beer and watched the sun sink down in the southwest. As its fading rays shone on the copper-blue surface of the Potomac, a cool breeze blew up off the street and rippled softly through the potted ferns and boxwoods on the balcony.

Amy joined him, setting her phone down on the iron balcony table by the sliding doors.

"That was Sal."

"Yeah?"

"He's taking the others out for pizza. He raves about this new place on Pennsylvania Avenue."

"Sounds good."

"I think so. Even Quinn's looking forward to it, apparently. You want to go?"

He shrugged. "Hey, it's your apartment, your town and your country and that puts me well and truly in your hands."

"I'm paying."

He smiled. "I don't care what they say about you, Amy. I think you're all right."

She gave him a play slap and laughed.

"What?"

"You've been in my hands since the day we met, Max."

"Maybe," he said. "And I can take some handling, I know."

"Tell me about it. It feels like a hell of a lot longer ago than one week that we met."

Hunter sipped his drink and leaned on the balcony. He was relaxing for the first time since Juliette had told him to fly out to Rorschach's private complex in the Swiss Alps, and it felt good. Realizing how easy it felt to be in her company, he turned and gave her a cautious smile.

"We got the *when* sorted out, but I still need to clarify the *where*."

"Sorry?"

"Where did we meet?" Hunter said.

She leaned on the balcony beside him and gave him a confused look. "I'm not following you."

"Did we meet in Switzerland or Cuba?" he asked.

"I met you in Switzerland," she said without hesitation.

"But I met Dr Kirsten Anderson in Switzerland," he said. "I never met Special Agent Amy Fox until she introduced herself to me on a plane in Cuban airspace."

She smiled sweetly. "O, what a tangled web we weave when we first practise to deceive."

"Ah, I know this one – Shakespeare!"

"Sorry, but wrong. Walter Scott."

"Damn, they really need to widen the syllabus at Sandhurst. But seriously – where did we meet, Switzerland or Cuba?"

"You choose." She leaned forward and gave him a quick kiss on the cheek. "But whichever one you pick, I'm just glad we met at all."

"Me too."

After a long pause, she sighed. "And?"

"And what?"

"What's it to be? Are you joining the team and coming with HARPA on Jim's next mission, or do I have to find another archaeologist as stupid as you?"

"And as brave," he said. "I'm stupid *and* brave, and I still don't know what Amy stands for."

A long silence. "It stands for Amadea," she said reluctantly. "Dad was a big fan of Mozart, so after realizing there was no female version of Wolfgang, he had the idea of using the female form of Amadeus…Yeah, I know."

"It's better than Maximilian."

She looked up at him, glad the moment of revealing her name was over. "That's what Max is short for? I presumed Maxwell."

"Everyone does."

"Any reason?"

"Not that she ever told me, but knowing Mum, it was after some old king somewhere."

"I like it. And by the way, I'm still waiting for an answer to my question. Are you joining HARPA or not?"

Hunter took a long, slow sip of the beer and looked out across the twilight at the rushing river. "I think you already know the answer to that." Raising his bottle to her, he grinned mischievously. "Here's to HARPA."

"To HARPA," she said, and they chinked their bottles and toasted the new team as the sun slid down into the water. "Something tells me the time of our lives has only just begun."

# AUTHOR'S NOTE

The next release will likely be *The Doomsday Cipher* (Avalon Adventure 3), and this is slated for February 2020. Following that, Joe Hawke is scheduled to return in March 2020 in his fifteenth adventure, *Shadow of the Apocalypse.* This novel will bring to a dramatic close the current arc in the Joe Hawke world and launch them on another epic adventure with some great new ideas I can't wait to share with you.

This brand new series starring the Hunter crew was a lot of fun to write, especially getting to know some fresh and very different characters. I hope it will be able to deliver some first-class archaeological and historical action stories to run alongside my other series. Certainly, there are one or two surprises regarding the Hunter Files that should provide some excellent adventure for us all in the near future, so stay tuned!

If you enjoyed the first Hunter File and want to see more, as with any of my other books, please take a few seconds to leave a short review. They are the lifeblood of indie authors and if you want to support me and my writing, and see more of it, then please smash that review out!

# ABOUT THE AUTHOR

Rob Jones has published twenty-one Kindle bestsellers, including the Joe Hawke series, the Avalon Adventures, the Cairo Sloane series, the Raiders series and the Harry Bane Thriller series. He has also recently published *The Fifth Grave*, a romantic suspense thriller starring DCI Tom Jacob, set in England's beautiful Wiltshire Downs. *The Atlantis Covenant* is the first novel in The Hunter Files, a brand-new series of fast-paced archaeological adventure thrillers.

If you would like to stay up to date with new releases and other information from Rob Jones, visit his website at robjonesnovels.com

Printed in Great Britain
by Amazon

45609940R00232